She's With Me

She's With Me

JESSICA CUNSOLO

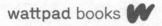

wattpad books

wattpad books **W**

Copyright © 2020 Jessica Cunsolo. All rights reserved.

Published in Canada by Wattpad Books, a division of Wattpad Corp.
36 Wellington Street E., Toronto ON, M5E 1C7

www.wattpad.com

First Wattpad Books edition: January 2020

ISBN: 978-1-98936-502-1 (Softcover edition)
ISBN: 978-1-98936-503-8 (E-book edition)

Library and Archives Canada Cataloguing in Publication information
is available upon request.

Printed and bound in Canada.

1 3 5 7 9 10 8 6 4 2
Cover design by Sayre Street Books
Images © wundervisuals on iStock

I'd like to dedicate this story to you, my readers.

To all my fans, friends, and Violets: this story is for you.

1

I've always suffered from this horribly disadvantageous condition—it's called being directionally challenged. It's self-diagnosed of course, but I'm almost positive it's an actual thing, so it's not really my fault that I'm having trouble navigating this maze known as King City High School.

The warning bell rings and animal-like students scramble from their assembled groups and lockers and head to class. Shit. I'm going to be late and I still have no idea where my first class is. It doesn't help that I can only walk so fast since I hurt myself a few weeks back, and that injury is still healing.

When I got here this morning, the curt secretary sent me off with no more than a map and dismissive "Good luck." Starting a new school a month and a half into first semester is hard enough—having my face planted in a map would just scream *New girl, eat me alive!*, not to mention trash my plan to get through senior year without drawing too much attention to myself. Not that I'd be able to read the map anyway. As I said: directionally challenged.

Pulling out my schedule again, I see that the name printed at the top reads *Amelia Collins*. It's a pretty name this time, but it'll still take some getting used to.

I reread the room number that I've already committed to memory, as if reading it again might magically transport me to it. Glancing at my brand new cell phone, I huff out an aggravated breath as I realize I only have five minutes to get to class before I'm late.

"Screw it," I mutter as I rush aimlessly down the hall while searching my shoulder bag for the school map—I really hate being late.

Not really paying attention to where I'm going, I'm blindsided by a group of giant walking trees slash teenage boys. They're talking and joking among themselves—walking through the halls as if they own the whole school. Without slowing down, I hug close to one wall, and reach into my bag to grab my map. Instantly, I'm thrown back as I collide with an outcrop of bricks, stopping just short of falling on my butt. Who designs a stupid wall to stick out like that?

My belongings have poured out everywhere, and I grab them hastily before quickly turning around, only to come face to face with something both hard and human, if the colorful curses are any indication. My stuff crashes onto the floor again as the pain in my ribs intensifies.

Great. Just freaking great.

"Are you blind? Can't you see I was walking here?" a voice growls.

My eyes meet the agitated gray ones of the most breathtakingly gorgeous guy I have ever seen. He's a member of the walking trees I saw before—tall with broad shoulders, a scowl plastered on his face.

His attitude sucks. He was equally at fault, if not more, since

2

the skyscrapers had to walk in a horizontal line in the hall, but I seriously don't want to draw any more attention to myself.

"I am so sorry." I apologize as we bend down to retrieve our belongings.

"Is your brain not able to communicate to your legs where you can and can't walk? If you didn't notice, there was someone in front of you, which means you move out of their way," he shoots back as he stands up with his binder.

A small crowd is gathered around us, clearly interested in seeing the poor girl stupid enough to incur the wrath of this intolerant jerk.

Think first, Amelia. Don't say something stupid. You're supposed to keep your head down and get through the year unnoticed.

"Sorry. I'm new and really don't know where I'm going." I stand up with my now-collected belongings and push my strawberry blond hair out of my face. "You wouldn't happen to know where room 341 is, would you?"

"You're new, not blind. Don't use excuses to cover up your stupidity. Get out of my sight while I'm still being nice," he scoffs, and runs a hand through his blond hair.

This is him being nice? Bemused faces of the other walking trees and the larger assembling crowd surround me, and I'm doing the exact opposite of blending in. Not wanting to stand out any more, I contain my anger and don't even glance at him as I stride by.

"Oh look, she does have some good ideas in that otherwise useless brain of hers," I hear him say to his friends, like being a jerk is part of his genetic build.

That's it. I turn and walk back to him, looking straight up and into his gray eyes with my narrowed hazel ones.

"Oh, I guess her brain is a hundred percent useless after all," he says to his friends.

He bends down to match my full height, three inches taller than usual thanks to my gorgeous tan wedges, and looks me straight in the eyes, talking as though he was speaking to a toddler.

"Do you need me to draw you a map of how to get the *fuck* out of my face?" he slowly asks, putting emphasis on the curse.

"No, thank you," I say evenly and calmly. "But I can draw you a map, so when I tell you to go to hell, you'll know exactly where to go."

Everyone standing in the now-crowded hall takes an audible inhale and stops breathing as they absorb the scene. By the looks of this stunned blond asshole and his friends, it seems like no one has ever said anything that daring to him before.

He gets up really close to my face and growls, "Now you listen to me, you little—"

"No, you listen to me asshole," I say calmly. "First of all, get out of my face, your breath stinks from all the crap that spews out of your mouth. Second, your dick belongs to your body, not in your personality,"—I push him out of my personal space— "so I suggest you pull your head out of your ass and realize that you're not the only person in the damn school. Maybe if you and your walking skyscrapers didn't bulldoze down the hall in a straight line people wouldn't have to dive out of your path to avoid destruction. I'm sorry if someone pissed in your Froot Loops this morning, but please do us all a favor and check your issues at the door. Finding a hobby or going to group therapy could really help you with your social problems. So thanks for the friendly welcome to your school, but I'd like to get to class now."

The hallway is hushed still and quiet. Blondie looks completely stupefied.

His friends are laughing—like, out-of-breath-gasping-for-air cackling. These other mountains are all just as breathtakingly gorgeous as asshole number one. The late bell rings. Great. I'm late for class.

Confident that my point was made and this jerk face was properly put in his place, I spin on my heel so my hair hits him on the shoulder and walk through the parting crowd, leaving him steaming.

"Oh my God, she so told you, Aiden! That was *hilarious!*" one of his gorgeous friends says through bursts of laughter.

So, the jerk's name is Aiden. It's a shame really that such a pretty name and face is wasted on such an ugly personality. So much for going unnoticed; I have a feeling everyone is going to have something to say about me after this. Well, at least I look cute in my skirt and heels.

Now that the entertainment is over, the crowd departs. As I strut down the hallway and turn a corner, I realize that I still have no idea where the hell I'm going. Taking a minute to collect myself, I check to see if maybe there's someone left who might know where to find my classroom.

Anxious at the best of times, hearing rather large and determined footsteps stomping behind me catches me off guard, and then I'm suddenly turned around and hoisted up and over Aiden's shoulder. With my face planted firmly against his back, my butt in the air over his shoulder, and my bag hooked through his arm, he takes off down the hallway.

"What the hell are you doing? Put me down right now!" I yell.

Aiden's stride doesn't slow, and he chuckles beneath me, the bastard. I strain my neck to see the bemused faces of two of the three gorgeous tree friends who were with him in the hall.

"Can't you two talk some sense into him?!"

"Sorry, babe," the one with short brown hair and chocolate-colored eyes yells back at me with a grin of thorough amusement. "Skyscrapers aren't much for talking."

I can't help but see that Aiden really does have a very nice back. His muscles are noticeable under his tight, but not too tight, plain black T-shirt. We round a corner and I'm met by the curious gazes of some people still in the halls—they clearly have no desire to help me either.

Pain shoots through the left side of my chest. Shit. Running into the wall, followed by the very muscular Aiden hoisting me up, coupled with this uncomfortable position is not good. The pain spreads. I have to get down before I make things worse.

"Listen, bud. I'm sorry about what I said before," I lie. "But kidnapping people is not the way to deal with your problems."

He adjusts my body, causing a burst of pain in my ribs. Without even slowing his pace, he runs up a flight of stairs. Man, this guy is like the Energizer Bunny, not even tiring once. I'm having trouble breathing. "Please," I gasp. "Put me down and we can talk this out."

He ignores me and continues his unwavering stride.

"Can you just let me go gentl—"

Aiden abruptly stops moving and deposits me on the floor.

I look up at him, the wind knocked out of me. The left side of my ribs are on fire—yup, I hurt them again.

"Room 341," he says, dropping my bag beside me and turning to leave the now-deserted hallway.

Dazed, I try to get up but pain shoots up my left side, forcing me back down to the floor. This isn't going to end well. Determined not to lie on this gross floor a second longer, I try again, but the pain spreads through my chest. Sprawled on the floor, I'm incapable of moving. Damn it. Looks like this isn't going to be my first day after all.

I've hurt my ribs three times now, which is less than ideal. Reaching into my bag beside me, I fish around for my phone and pull it out. My mom ignores my first call. Typical. The second time she answers on the third ring. "Hello? Haile—I mean Amelia?"

"Hey. I think I hurt my ribs again. I'm going to drive myself to the hospital. I'm only letting you know so you don't freak out and think the worst when the school calls saying I didn't show up for class even though I was here today," I say from my position on the floor.

She sighs as if she's wondering how I managed to screw up on my first day of school. "How did that happen? You need to be more careful. He's still out there and this isn't ove—"

"I know. It doesn't matter. I'm just letting you know." Even talking hurts. "I'll call you when I get the—" My voice cuts off when the pain becomes too much.

"Amelia? You can't drive yourself." I try to ignore the hint of annoyance creeping into her tone. "I'll come pick you up from school—I'll be there soon. In the meantime, try not to draw even more attention to yourself."

"Okay, I'll meet you in the parking lot."

Hanging up the phone, I shove it back into my bag. Staring up at the ceiling, I think of the most logical way of getting up.

"Okay, Amelia. You have three broken and two bruised ribs healing—you got through it the first time, you can do it again." I psych myself up.

Bending my legs at the knees, I pull off my heels and shove them into my bag. Before I can change my mind, I quickly roll from my right side onto my stomach, careful to avoid making my left side touch anything.

With my arm through the strap of my shoulder bag so I can avoid having to bend down and get it later, I place my arms near my head in push-up position and use my knees at the same time. Getting my feet underneath me, I stand up carefully and lean against the lockers.

"Great, you're up. Now you have to find the damn exit from this maze-school," I say to myself.

I'm trying to get my bearings when my eyes lock with a pair of familiar chocolate-brown ones. Shit. How long has he been here? Aiden's brown-haired friend who remembered my skyscraper line is standing beside an open locker, staring at me. The dirty blond-haired member of the walking trees is beside him, eyes wide and unblinking. Swallowing my pride and refusing to show weakness, I break my gaze and walk in the opposite direction.

"The exit's the other way." A hesitant voice calls from behind me—it's the dirty blond.

Damn broken internal compass.

"How much did you see?" I ask as I make my way toward them.

"Well, pretty much everything since Aiden turned and left you," he answers hesitantly.

Great, so all of it.

"And it didn't occur to either of you to *help the girl lying on the floor in pain*?"

That snaps them out of their stupor. The brown-eyed one quickly closes his locker, and they rush toward me.

"I don't need your help now!" I exclaim, wincing from the pain and causing them to freeze in their tracks.

"Are you sure you don't need our help?" asks the brown-haired one with a smirk.

Cocky bastard, way to kick a girl while she's down. It didn't help that they both look like male models, and now I look like I was dragged through a restaurant's dumpster. I'm about to tell him where to go, but my breathing starts to get worse, and I realize I still didn't even know how to get to the parking lot to meet my mom.

I take a deep breath. "Can you point the way to the parking lot, please?"

"We'll help you there," says the blond.

"Shouldn't you be in class?"

"Nah," he says. "We're in this class with you. It's the most boring thing ever, and this is much more interesting."

"Glad my misery can break up the dull monotony of your day," I say dryly.

"Damn, I didn't mean it like that," he says sheepishly, moving to my left to put my arm over his shoulder as the brunet does the same on my right side.

"*Ow!*" I exclaim to blondie as the pain pulses through my side. "That's the side that hurts, just leave it."

"Shit, sorry," he says as we make our way down the hall painfully slowly, blondie in front and my right arm around the brown-haired model, who is helping me walk.

"Screw this," the guy my arm is slung over mutters. He stops walking and scoops me up bridal style into his tanned, muscled arms, and starts walking again.

"Noah, get her bag and open the doors for us," he says, clearly tired of our slow descent.

Grateful for not being on my feet anymore, I hold my tongue uncharacteristically, too tired and in too much pain to argue. We get to a pair of heavy-looking doors that lead outside to the parking lot. Noah holds them open as we walk through, and I shield my eyes from the sudden blinding sunlight as I look for my mom.

"You can put me down now; my mother should be here soon." He sets me on my feet but keeps an arm around me, making no move to leave. "You don't have to wait with me."

"We can't leave you standing here alone, right?" Noah says, taking a seat on the concrete steps and looking at his friend, who nods in agreement.

"Aren't you guys going to get in trouble for ditching school?" I ask curiously.

"Nah. I'm Mason, by the way." He smiles and helps me sit down on the step. "And you've met Noah. You are?"

"Amelia," I reply.

The ache in my chest hasn't let up, and although I don't want to admit it, I'm kind of glad they're keeping me company.

"You know," Noah starts hesitantly, glancing at me with pale-green eyes, "Aiden's really not a bad guy. He didn't know he'd hurt you."

"If he knew you were healing from broken ribs already, he wouldn't have picked you up. It's just guys fooling around, you know? He'd never intentionally hurt anyone, especially not someone smaller than him."

I really wish they hadn't heard me talking to myself in the hall.

"He seemed perfectly fine tearing an innocent girl to shreds verbally. And from what I can tell, it seems like it's not the first time," I reply.

"He doesn't do it often—he's easily aggravated and having

a rough time right now. Plus, he was in a really bad mood this morning, so naturally he snapped at the first thing that gave him a reason—you," Noah says, as if this is a perfectly acceptable excuse.

"Besides, you handled yourself amazingly. Watching you tell him off was by far the best thing I've ever seen." Mason smiles.

"Really?" I ask cautiously.

"Seriously. The drawing him a map to hell? Priceless! And did you see his face when you told him how to fix his problems?" Noah laughs.

"My personal favorite part was when she told him where his dick belongs." Mason winks at me.

"You guys aren't mad at me for what I said?"

"What? The comment about how we're walking skyscrapers that bulldoze down the halls and destroy everything in our path?" Noah asks with a cute smirk.

"Something like that," I murmur.

"Nah, it was funny, plus totally worth seeing someone other than us rip on Aiden. Especially a teensy little girl like you," Mason replies with a chuckle.

"I was getting sick of listening to his bullshit," I say.

"He isn't a bad guy, really." Noah chuckles. "And he'd feel horrible if he knew he's the reason you're going to the hospital right now."

"It's not his fault, I'm not mad at him. Annoyed by his attitude, sure, but I get that he didn't mean to hurt me," I confess. "If my ribs were normal, I would've just gotten up, gone to class, and called him a slew of bad words the next time I saw him in the hall.

"Plus, I'd rather this stay between us," I tell the two gorgeous boys beside me. "No one needs to know about my injuries, okay?"

The boys share a look, and Noah studies me. "How did you break, what was it, three ribs? And bruise another three?"

"Broke three, bruised two," I say, purposely not answering his question.

"Right, so how'd it happen? The classic singing in the shower and then slipping?" Mason jokes.

Memories of that dreadful night make me shiver, and I think about the dead, brown eyes that still haunt me—he's the reason I had to move states, *again*.

"No, honestly, I'm just accident-prone," I say, trying to get them to drop it.

"That must have been a pretty bad klutz moment," Noah chuckles.

My mom pulls up in front of us, sparing me from having to respond. The disapproving look on her face makes me immediately tense. Crap, I should've fought harder to make these boys go to class. I'm going to get a lecture from my mother now. All five foot four of her gets out of the car, and she lifts her sunglasses to the top of her head, pushing back her shoulder-length brown hair as she glares at Mason and Noah. "Thanks for helping her, boys, but I can take it from here. Get back to class."

They look at each other hesitantly, but I reassure them that I'm fine, and thank them for keeping me company.

"Really, Amelia?" my mom says as she tears out of the school parking lot, her fingers tight on the steering wheel.

"It's not what it looks like."

"It better not be. Do you really want to move again?"

I grind my teeth to stop myself from shouting at her. I know. I know all of this. I don't need her to remind me.

"No."

"Then remember what you promised. No boyfriends. No social media. No teams or clubs. You're allowed to go to the gym and practice your jujitsu. I can't stop you from making friends, but you need to be responsible."

We're silent for the rest of the ride to the hospital. I *know* what needs to be done. I have to keep my head down, at all costs.

2

Two weeks and a whole lot of painkillers later, I find myself back in the crowded halls of King City High School.

With basically nothing to do while I recovered from my newly bruised ribs, I made a point to decode the school map that, to me, seemed to be written in hieroglyphics. With freshly found confidence about where I'm going, I strut through the halls like I own them. I toss my loosely curled strawberry blond hair over my shoulder so that I'd look super hot if this were being filmed in slow motion.

As I'm walking down the hall, I feel a lot of eyes on me. I'd like to think it's because of my cute outfit, but deep down, I know it's not.

My fellow students are either looking at me because (1) technically, even though it's mid-October, I'm still the new girl, and seeing as I didn't even make it to my first class on my first day, many of these people still haven't seen me, or (2) the less likely reason, and I'm praying it's not this one, is because they're still talking about my Aiden incident. But in a school this big, I'm sure more interesting things are bound to have happened these past two weeks.

I make it to room 341 and take a seat near the middle of the history classroom. There are a couple of other people here, but most students are still loitering in the halls, savoring their last few precious moments of freedom before suffering through mass education.

I pull my notebook out of my bag and occupy myself with dating the top of the page. I try to underline it in red pen but the ink doesn't come out. Stupid pen. Doesn't even work when I scribble on the side of the page. I'm so immersed in trying to get the pen to write that I'm taken off guard when a pair of hands slides over my eyes. Everything goes black for a moment.

It all happens so quickly, and I react automatically. My hands grab the wrists connected to the hands covering my face. Yanking them with a twist, I apply pressure, knowing that I could snap them if I twisted a little bit more. Jumping up out of my seat, I turn around and stand to face my assailant.

"*Ow, ow, ow, ow.*" Familiar chocolate-brown eyes. I quickly release his hands.

"Damn woman, no need to go all *Karate Kid* on me," Mason says while rubbing his wrists.

"Sorry!" I tell him, embarrassed. "Next time don't sneak up on a girl."

Luckily the bell hasn't rung yet, so only a few people are giving me curious glances; most of the kids in class are totally preoccupied with their phones anyway.

"You seriously have an iron grip. That's so weird because you have such cute, teensy, little hands," he teases, clearly being a good sport about it all.

I don't really know much about Mason, but the kid's kind of starting to grow on me. If only he wasn't BFFs with jerk-face Aiden; I would've considered being friends with him. The bell rings, and instead of replying I stick my tongue out at him and turn around to sit back down in my seat.

"You could do *way* better," a voice to my immediate left says.

A really pretty girl is sitting in the desk next to mine, giving me a disappointed look with her bright-blue eyes.

"Excuse me?" I ask, confused.

"Oh, I don't mean anything by it," she says, pushing curly, shoulder-length brown hair with caramel highlights over her shoulder. "Someone who's as pretty and with as good fashion sense as you could do better than stooping as low as *that* player."

Mason's at the back of the room talking to Noah and some other boys. Almost every girl in the room (excluding the girl beside me) is gazing lovingly in their direction, seemingly in a trance.

"Oh, well, thanks. But me and Mason? *Ew*, like never. I don't want anything to do with him and his jerk-face friends, especially that Aiden asshole."

She looks at me and her blue eyes light up with recognition. "Oh my God! *You're* the girl who told off Aiden a couple of weeks ago! I knew there was a reason I liked you when I first saw you, other than your cute shoes."

"You saw?"

"I didn't have too! *Everyone* was talking about it. What happened? Rumors were going around that you dropped out of school and moved to Antarctica out of fear he'd retaliate."

"Please, I'm not scared of that asshole. Annoyed? Yes. Aggravated? Definitely. But scared? Never," I reply.

"I think we'll be great friends." She smiles at me. "I'm Charlotte, by the way, and no, you may not call me Charlie. Char? Yes. But I am not a man and therefore do not call me Charlie."

"Amelia." I laugh.

"Let me see your schedule. Maybe we'll have some other classes together!" She squeals. "We have chemistry together third period and then we can go to lunch!"

"Sounds good." Genuinely smiling for the first time in a long time, I push down the echo of my mom's voice reminding me that I'm not supposed to be making friends.

A man in his early forties walks in and sets his briefcase down on the teacher's desk, and we can't chat anymore as class begins. After first period and promising a very energetic Charlotte that I'd sit with her in chemistry, I find myself sitting near the front of my second-period class: calculus.

I'm so excited! I'm going to have so much fun in this class! Sarcasm. That was sarcasm.

Just as the bell rings the asshole himself waltzes in, talking to a boy with dark-brown-almost-black hair—the fourth walking-tree BFF.

Neither Aiden nor his friend see me, and they take seats near the back on the opposite side of the class. Sliding farther down in my seat, I pray that I get through my allotted torture without him noticing me.

Class goes by without any problems, answering all my prayers. Wanting to get out of here, like, ten minutes ago, I quickly shove everything back into my bag, but I'm in such a rush that my notebook falls to the floor.

"Shit," I say under my breath.

Just as I'm about to grab it, a large hand gets to it first. I stand up and come face to chest with the breathtakingly handsome Aiden, who is holding my notebook in his hands. This moment is so cliché I'm tempted to roll my eyes.

His gray eyes are indecipherable, and I take my notebook from him without breaking eye contact and without resistance on his part. I stand there, looking into his eyes with my own questioning ones, and then turn around and walk out the door and toward third-period chemistry.

That was weird. And what's he doing in calculus anyway? Isn't it, like, illegal to be gorgeous, physically fit, *and* smart if you have a horrible personality? Wow, I want to speak to whoever decides who gets what genes—this is seriously unfair.

I get to chemistry early and see Charlotte sitting at a desk made for two people near the middle of the classroom. She enthusiastically waves me over, so I take a seat next to her.

"How was calculus?" she asks, as if she already knows how much I adore the subject.

"Oh, you know calculus, it's always fun! But Aiden and his friend are in my class." I try not to sound bitter.

Her eyes widen. "Did he say something? Do something? And wait, which friend?"

"Well, it wasn't Mason or Noah, because I know them. This one was tall, muscular, and pretty handsome, I have to admit." What I don't tell her is that he's not as cute as Aiden. What? I've got eyes! I can't help what they're attracted to! "He's kind of pale, dark-brown hair, almost black," I continue.

"That was Julian," she informs me. "Look, let me tell you how things are around here."

She lowers her voice, even though barely anyone is in class yet. "So, there's the group of guys: Aiden, Mason, Noah, and Julian, and yeah, they're, like, really close, BFFs. They are notorious for their cocky, egotistical attitudes. Everyone loves them. Guys who don't wish they were them want to be friends with them, and don't even get me started on the girls."

"They're players?"

"Please," she scoffs. "They don't keep girls around long enough to be considered players. Noah and Mason can get whatever girl they want, but they've never been in an actual relationship. All the girls basically pine after Aiden, but he barely gives them the time of day. He kind of had a thing with the Queen Bee of the school, Kaitlyn Anderson, for a while, but I'm pretty sure he's done with her. She's a major bitch, so I'm surprised he kept her around for as long as he did."

"Huh. I just keep finding more and more reasons to like these guys."

Charlotte just laughs, but I'm still curious.

"What about Julian? The one I saw with Aiden in my calc class?" I ask.

"He used to be as bad as Noah and Mason, but I think he changed his ways. He's been with the same girl, Annalisa, for about four months now, and they seem to be going pretty strong," she answers.

"What's your problem with them?" I ask.

"What do you mean?"

"You're the only girl besides me not drooling over them."

"I don't doubt their gorgeousness. The one thing they actually have going for them is their looks, and even I can't deny it."

"Talking about me again, Charlie?" says a good-looking guy with inviting brown eyes who just walked into class and heard the last part of our conversation. He takes a seat in the shared desk behind us.

"Get over yourself, Chase. This is Amelia, by the way. Amelia, this humble jerk is Chase." She introduces us, scowling at his use of her unpreferred nickname. "She's the one who told off Aiden a couple of weeks ago."

His eyes widen as he takes me in, then he laughs. "I so wish I was there."

"You're friends with them?"

"Against his better judgment," Charlotte cuts in.

"Come on, Charlie, you know I'll always love you more." He ruffles her hair and shoots her an innocent smile.

"Come on! Not the hair!" She scowls at him.

✄

After chemistry, Charlotte excitedly pulls me through the halls toward the cafeteria, talking animatedly about everything and anything. As we walk inside, we spot Aiden and his friends immediately. They're sitting at a table with some girls.

"See that blond girl practically sitting on Aiden's lap? That's Kaitlyn Anderson. She's the one I was telling you about before—the queen bitch around here because she's gorgeous, scary, and her mom's the principal. She can sometimes be found at their table with them," she tells me.

"Even though none of the guys like her—they more just put up with her," adds Chase, coming up behind us.

"*Anyway*," Charlotte says, clearly annoyed at being interrupted in the middle of her explanation. "She's desperately in love with Aiden, extremely possessive of him—"

"Even though he's told her to eff off more times than he can remember. She just follows him around and brushes off his insults. She has it in her head that they'd make the perfect couple, and is now trying everything to make that fantasy a reality," Chase cuts in, and Charlotte glares at him.

"What?" He winks. "I'm friends with the guy—I'm just helping put the whole explanation into perspective!"

"Right. As I was saying. She's a bitch. Kaitlyn and her second-in-command Makayla Thomas, and their Barbie-wannabe followers are ruthless. Just try to interact with them as little as possible."

Kaitlyn's holding court at Aiden's table, talking to some other girls. From what I can see, she's the classic queen bitch cliché from every teen movie in existence. She knows she's hot and she works it, although she'd be a lot prettier without the entitled look plastered on her face.

"I think I could take her," I say, following Charlotte to an empty lunch table. Charlotte and Chase laugh, telling me that they don't doubt it.

"You gonna eat with us today, Charlie?" Chase nods in the direction of Aiden and friends' table.

Charlotte makes a face like he just asked her to eat a millipede. "Nope. You go have fun, though. And don't call me Charlie."

Chase hesitates but doesn't fight her, telling us he'll see us later before heading over to sit with his friends.

As we eat, we talk about teachers and movies and makeup and almost everything.

Suddenly, Charlotte stops midsentence and looks directly behind me. It's Aiden. He's walking right up to our table, looking gorgeous as usual. His T-shirt stretches across his broad chest, accenting it and slightly outlining the abs I'm positive are hidden underneath it. As he gets closer, his eyes lock on me for some reason.

He stops, looks down at me, and says, "Amelia."

I'm slightly ashamed to admit that my heart flutters a little when he says my name. Why does he have to be so damn perfect?

"Hey, Charlotte." Aiden glances at Charlotte and she greets him in return. Aiden looks back at me. "I need to talk to you, Amelia."

All sets of eyes in the cafeteria are on us. Either Aiden doesn't feel it or he doesn't care, because he's just calmly standing there waiting for my reply.

"Oh, so we're ready to be civil today?" I say it without thinking; it just comes out.

"Already starting with the attitude?"

"Says the guy who snaps at a girl when *he* walks into *her*."

"Look, it won't take long. Please."

Interested in what he has to say, and since he seems like he isn't planning on murdering me, I decide to hear him out.

I glance back at Charlotte. "You okay if I go?"

She nods and smiles, so I shove my lunch back into my bag and stand up. Aiden turns around and walks out of the cafeteria, assuming I'm behind him. It takes every instinct in me not to bolt out of the cafeteria, but I follow him out.

I find him leaning on the wall outside the caf with his arms crossed. "Mason told me what happened."

"Okay? And?" Mason and his big mouth—his promise not to tell anyone obviously excluded his best friend.

"You're back at school, so I'm guessing you survived."

"I'm fine. Thanks for the heartwarming concern."

"You really should watch where you're going in the hallway, especially if you're going to walk that fast with delicate ribs."

"Was this the reason you wanted to talk to me? To lecture

me on my walking speed? Because I've been looking forward to lunch all day, and now you're ruining it with your lack of a point."

If he called me out here expecting me to apologize for what I said to him in the hallway that day, he has another thing coming. There is no way in hell I'll apologize—in my opinion, he needed to hear what I said to him.

"Why do you have to make everything so hard and complicated?"

"No, seriously—there's, like, seven minutes left of lunch and I'm still hungry, so . . ."

"I didn't know that I'd hurt you. That wasn't my intention," he says hurriedly, looking uncomfortable.

Oh. My. God. Is Aiden feeling bad about my ribs? Is this his lame attempt at an apology?

"You were fine with very rudely telling me off when *you're* the one who ran into *me*. Words can hurt, too, you know."

"What I'm trying to say is that I didn't mean to send you to the hospital," he says, growing visibly more frustrated. "Plus, the shit you said to me was ten times worse than what I said to you."

"Aw, that's the nicest thing you've ever said to me," I say in an exaggerated love-struck voice, putting my right hand over my heart.

He sucks at this whole apology thing. So far he's said nothing that didn't make me want to punch him in the face for being so aggravating.

"Are you ever not a bitch? I'm trying to apologize here, but you're making it extremely difficult."

"Are you ever not an asshole? And that is probably the worst apology I've ever heard. It doesn't even deserve to be in the category of an apology. It was more of a subtle insult with some underlying tones of very scarce concern."

"There you are, babe!"

Kaitlyn.

She walks past me to stand extremely close to Aiden, then turns and narrows her eyes at me. "You left *me* to talk to *her*?"

Technically, we haven't even really met yet, and I already know I hate Kaitlyn. Up close I can see she has a little stud nose piercing and icy blue eyes.

"I told you not to call me babe. We're *not together*. Where I go is none of your damn business," says Aiden, clearly annoyed.

"You could do better things with your time than talk to this outcast. Why don't we ditch fourth and go to your house for something much more worthwhile." She trails her hand down his chest.

"Never gonna happen. Seriously, Kaitlyn, give it up. I'm tired of this shit." He pushes her off of him.

This no longer concerns me, which gives me an out to head to my locker, figuring there's no point in going back into the cafeteria since lunch is almost over. Turning the corner, I hear someone jogging to catch up with me. Aiden's suddenly blocking my path, and he's managed to get rid of Kaitlyn.

"Look, I just wanted to make sure you were okay."

"I'm fine. And I'm sure Mason or Noah told you that I don't blame you, so you can sleep soundly tonight knowing that they weren't lying. You didn't know my ribs were healing, but do everyone a favor and refrain from kidnapping and throwing girls over your shoulder in the future."

I step around him and continue along my course.

Everything about Aiden is aggravating. His stupid body, his stupid face, his stupid eyes, his stupid personality, even the way he runs his hand through his hair is stupid. It really angers me that I could easily replace four of those five *stupids* with *perfects*—his personality really is a waste.

After getting my books for English, and with five minutes until the bell rings, I head to the other side of the school for my next class.

"He's *way* out of your league you know."

Kaitlyn. Again.

She's with that other girl—I think it's Melissa or Marcella or something—and her group of followers surrounds them. Somehow they even managed to surround me, leaving me no other choice than to endure this crazed confrontation.

"Excuse me?"

"Makayla, do you think she's deaf?" Kaitlyn looks at her black-haired second-in-command, who gives me the up and down.

"SHE SAID HE'S WAY OUT OF—"

"I'm not deaf, no need to shout in my ear," I snap.

"Good, then you'll hear me when I tell you to stay away from Aiden. He's mine. Always has been, always will be," Kaitlyn says.

Wow, is Kaitlyn ever delusional.

"Did you hear the same thing I did two minutes ago? I distinctly remember Aiden telling you to get lost."

"He'll be mine. Everyone knows we're practically together. I'm warning you—stay the hell out of my way or else we'll have a problem."

Good grief, I don't even want Aiden. He's a jerk—a hot one, but after a while, we'd eventually have to talk. And while my body is attracted to him, every time he opens his mouth, my brain gets mad.

"I don't have time for this." I try to get around Kaitlyn and her drones but they block my path, clearly not done with me.

"If I throw a stick, will you go chase it?" I huff out, getting tired of this.

"Bitch, I'm trying to be nice and give you a heads-up. If you don't stay away from my man, shit will go down, and you'll want to crawl back into that hole you climbed out of." Kaitlyn narrows her eyes at me.

"Don't worry about me, worry about your eyebrows," I say.

She gasps and her hands fly to her face. There wasn't anything wrong with her eyebrows, but I knew that would get her. Shoving my way through the group, I see Mason leaning against a locker on the other side of them, looking amused. He steps in beside me, matching my strides.

"You're full of surprises, koala."

I look at him, confused. "Did you just call me a koala bear?"

"Koalas are not bears, they're marsupials, but yeah, it's fitting. You look all cute and innocent, but once you're aggravated, you turn all vicious—just like a koala."

"I don't know if that's meant to be a compliment or not," I say.

"It could be." He winks. "That's the second time I've seen you in a confrontation with a notoriously vicious person, and you came out on top both times. I was going to intervene this time, but it was damn entertaining. And it's obvious you didn't need my help."

It's easy to see why Mason's such a heartbreaker. I could see myself doing something stupid, like falling in love with him, if I wasn't as smart as I am. Or if I wasn't dead set on not getting into any trouble.

"I'm glad I amuse you, and thanks for *not* telling Aiden about what happened, like you promised."

"Sarcasm is the lowest form of wit," he jokes.

"If I didn't use sarcasm I'd have to flat out tell someone they're an idiot, which is considered rude, and I was raised much better than that." I return his smirk with one of my own.

Mason laughs at me and we stop at a split in the hallway, facing each other. "Always have an answer, don't you?"

"The smart girls always do." I wink at him and turn down the left corridor, silently praying he'll turn right, because that was a damn good last word, and it'd be awkward if he ended up having to come the same way. He turns right, and I mentally high-five myself.

I get to my class and see Chase sitting on top of a desk with his back to me, talking enthusiastically to a bunch of guys. Not wanting to awkwardly cling to Chase, I walk to the middle of the room and sit down at an empty conjoined desk. While I'm pulling out my notebook, the chair directly beside me is pulled out, and a girl with long dark-brown-almost-black hair sits down beside me.

"Hey, you must be Amelia, right? I'm Annalisa, but call me Anna." Her dark-red lips part in a smile.

"That's me. Let me guess, you're wondering how I insulted Aiden and lived to tell the tale?"

"Aiden might be an ass sometimes," she says, laughing, "but honestly, he's one of the best people I know."

"You're friends with him?"

"I'm dating his best friend, Julian. Aiden's really not bad—he's kind of fun to be around once he opens up. He's amazing to the people he cares about, but he definitely knows how to be scary," she finishes.

"I'm not scared of him."

She laughs again. "I know, I got there in time to hear you tell him off—I was laughing so hard! The guys always rip on each other, but it was fun seeing someone else do it, especially someone so innocent looking!"

"Mason and Noah said almost the same thing."

"They're really laid back—they found it hilarious—but you know, boys and their pride. That's why Aiden reacted like that. He feels really bad about what happened though. He never said it out loud, but if you're close to him, you could tell that it bothered him."

"He apologized to me today . . . sort of."

"He *what*?!" she chokes out. "Tell me what happened!"

I told her what Aiden said in the hall, omitting any parts relating to Kaitlyn.

"Wow, he must really like you. Or at least care."

"I should feel honored," I reply sarcastically, feeling momentarily confused.

After the teacher walks in, the class starts and Annalisa and I have to stop talking. But after class we realize we both have a spare period, so we go to the empty cafeteria to sit and talk.

Despite Annalisa being close with that group of boys, I find myself actually liking her. I'm surprised because I didn't picture one of those guys with someone like her. When Charlotte told me about Julian's girlfriend, I pictured him with someone more Kaitlyn-like.

Annalisa has blue streaks in her dark hair and her fair skin and bright-blue eyes are accented by her dark-red lipstick. She is slightly more on the goth side, but not so much that she seems unapproachable. Despite not knowing Julian, I was proud of him for settling down with someone different from the obvious popular girls in school.

But is she friends with Kaitlyn? They were both eating at

Aiden's table. Julian is friends with Aiden and would therefore sit at that table. And Annalisa is dating Julian, so she, too, would sit at that table—with Kaitlyn and friends. I have the worst luck. I actually make some cool friends and one of them is friends with Kaitlyn and her bitches. As much as I like Annalisa, I don't think I can be friends with her if she's friends with those mean girls.

"What's wrong?"

I decide to just ask her and find out. "How do you feel about Kaitlyn?"

"You mean Satan reincarnated? She's actually quite pleasant to be around . . . when she isn't talking. And isn't looking at you. And is in a different room, in a different state, in a different country. With no cell service or Wi-Fi. So if all these conditions are met, then sure, she's cool."

I laugh. "What about if she's in the same room as you, or at the same table?"

"You mean if I had to actually interact with her? Ew. Can't stand her. She knows it too—knows everyone in my group of friends hates her. She's just so in love with Aiden she still tries to find ways to hang out with us."

"Anna, I think we'll get along great."

I'm actually really glad we're becoming friends. But why would someone as cool as she is be dating one of the Boys, as I've dubbed them in my mind? Maybe Julian isn't all that bad, since Annalisa doesn't seem like the type to put up with bullshit. Julian is the only member of the group whom I haven't met yet, and seeing as everyone except Aiden is cool, maybe my first interaction with a member of the Boys just happened to be with the one asshole of the group.

Annalisa and I trade numbers after spare period ends and promise to sit together again tomorrow during English.

I feel a tinge of guilt sweep over me. I'm not supposed to be making friends. I'm supposed to keep to myself and just get through school. But can I really just ignore people? Especially ones I get along with so well? It's human nature to crave interaction with others, right? Plus, it's not like I'm going around putting up flyers that say "Please be my friend! Here's my phone number, let's hang out!" It's just a couple of people; I can handle it. For the risk that every new friend I make brings, I'll be equally as vigilant about keeping my secrets. I can do it.

3

I walk into sixth and last period still thinking about the Boys, even though I wish I wasn't. I stand at the front of the room awkwardly looking for somewhere to sit in the room full of conjoined desks, when suddenly all the breath is sucked from my lungs. There's only one seat left unoccupied in the room—right beside the one and only grouchy pants himself: Aiden.

Checking the room once again, in case my eyes are playing tricks on me, I realize I have no other choice but to sit right beside Aiden. I feel someone glaring a hole into my skull, and turn to notice Kaitlyn sitting on the other side of the room with Makayla. Great, she's in this class too.

Aiden's talking to the two people sitting at the desk behind him—Mason and Noah. At least they'll make this experience less awkward. It can't be that bad now that Aiden (sort of) apologized for being an asshole. Maybe we can count this as a starting over of sorts. As I reach him, I've made up my mind to be friendly, but not so sweet that he thinks I want to be friends—like the respectful kind of approachable that you automatically switch on whenever your mom introduces you to her co-workers.

When I get to the desk, all three boys look up at me, two of the three breaking into big grins.

"Hey," I say with a small smile. "Is someone sitting here?" I indicate the empty seat beside him.

He looks at me, seemingly having some kind of internal struggle.

"No," he answers finally, and moves his bag from the chair beside him to the floor, to make room for me.

"*Amelia!*" Noah enthusiastically greets me. "I've missed you! How was your first day?"

"Noah, I saw you, like, four and a half hours ago."

I get the sense that Noah's the type of person you just can't help smiling around. He's like a cute, innocent little brother, except not so innocent, considering he's probably slept with more girls than I can count on two hands.

"So! That doesn't mean—"

"Okay, class, today you're working on pages 57–68."

Noah is interrupted by a very disinterested looking teacher. I turn back to the board and take my book out.

"Take notes and answer the questions on pages 69–70. Do it in pairs, individually, or in groups, I really don't care."

I sigh inwardly as the teacher goes back to his desk and opens his laptop. Clearly this is one of those classes where you have to teach yourself everything.

"K-bear, be my partner?"

I turn, realizing Mason is addressing me. "K-bear?"

"Short for koala."

"I thought koalas weren't bears?"

"They're not, but it's much cuter if I call you k-bear than k-marsupial."

I hate myself for blushing. "Why don't you just call me Amelia?"

"Because everyone calls you Amelia—it wouldn't be our thing."

My blush deepens. Are we having a moment? I think we're having a moment. Beside me, Aiden's rolling his eyes. What's his problem? Wait, why do I care?

Focusing on Mason again, I look into his eyes and take in how rich and chocolaty his eye color is. He is quite the charmer—I see how girls fall for him so easily. He really does—

"Hey, no fair!" I'm torn from my dreamy stare and brought back to earth by the sound of Noah's voice, and turn to look at him.

"I want to have a thing with Amelia! Amelia, why don't we have a thing?"

I shrug and offer him a small smile. "Wrong place, wrong time I guess."

"Starting now, I am making it my life's goal to find a thing for us!" Noah declares.

Our laughter is cut off by a very irritable Aiden. "God, why don't you guys get a room. I'm trying to learn about human society and your pathetic flirting is making it really hard for me to concentrate."

I guess he's back to being an ass.

"He's just jealous he doesn't have a thing with Amelia like we do," Noah stage-whispers to Mason.

"*I am not jealous!*" Aiden roars, causing the whole class and, surprisingly, even the oblivious teacher to look up at us.

"Care to enlighten us as to what it is that you are not jealous of, Mr. Parker?" He addresses Aiden.

Aiden's eyes narrow to slits. I can almost feel him trying to hold back an offensive response that would surely get him sent to the principal's office.

Mason seems to pick up that vibe as well and jumps in before Aiden can get himself in trouble. "We were just saying that Aiden is jealous of us since we got the answer to a question that he didn't, but don't worry, we'll explain it to him."

The teacher, seemingly bored of the topic already, takes this as an appropriate response and goes back to his laptop.

"What the hell, man?!" Aiden turns his deadly glare to his best friend.

"Dude, Mason saved your ass. You can't get suspended again, and we all saw it coming if he didn't jump in," Noah points out.

"You could've at least thought of a better excuse. One that's more believable. We all know I'm way smarter than you kids."

"Are not! I can out-sociology your ass any day! This isn't math," replies Noah.

"Noah, you get lost tying your shoes," Mason points out.

"What's that got to do with anything?!"

"Are one of you geniuses going to help me with question two or am I on my own?" I decide it's time to intervene in their display of male bravado. God, boys are so competitive over such trivial things. Aiden mutters something under his breath as he turns back to his textbook.

"Screw that. Let's talk about Halloween!" Mason says, completely abandoning their little dispute.

"What about Halloween?" I ask, fully turning my chair around to face them.

Noah looks at me like I just asked him where babies come from. "It's this Friday."

"And?"

"Do you have plans?" Mason asks.

I honestly didn't really think about this Halloween. I used to love getting dressed up and going out with friends. I remember loving putting on makeup and dressing up as anything I wanted, and the best part was that no one could judge because the crazier the outfit, the better. Halloween was the one day you could be anything you wanted.

One year, my best friend and I went as a pair of giant pink fuzzy dice, like the stereotypical kind that would hang from a muscle car's rearview mirror. We even had a fake giant rearview mirror with thin cardboard strips imitating string that attached us. We laughed all day as we kept bumping into everything.

But ever since that horrible, life-altering event I endured, and everything that followed, I can't stand Halloween. It's turned into a day when kids glorify murderers and serial killers, where the gorier and more horrifying the costume, the better. When kids take joy in being able to scare the crap out of one another. Now, ever since *that day*, I just can't go through Halloween without thinking of *him*.

"Probably just going to watch a movie at home or catch up on some homework," I say honestly.

"No you're *not*," Noah states.

"I'm not?"

"Nope, because you're coming to Noah's party." Mason smiles at me triumphantly.

Me. Going to Noah's house. Surrounded by drunk teenagers. On Halloween. "I don't think that's a good idea."

"You're coming, k-bear. No way to get around it."

"No, seriously, guys. I can't."

"We're not taking no for an answer," Noah states.

"You probably won't even notice if I'm there or not!"

"Amelia, seriously. You're coming. It's for your own good." Mason stands his ground.

"Who will give the children candy?" I say.

Noah shrugs. "Obesity in youth is a growing problem."

"Aiden, tell them I'm not coming," I say, hoping he'll back me up since he probably doesn't want me there anyway.

Aiden looks up from his book at me, then looks behind him at Noah and Mason.

He shrugs. "It's Noah's house." Then he turns back to his textbook.

The one time I depend on Aiden's hatred for me he doesn't come through . . .

"You can bring Charlotte! Chase invited her anyway, but you guys can come together!" Mason pushes.

"Yeah, Chase will be there!" Noah adds.

"I don't know," Maybe if I can convince Charlotte to come with me, it won't be so bad.

"Amelia, if you don't come, I'll follow you around making obnoxious siren noises all day at the top of my lungs. And believe me, I'm incredibly annoying and I know how to make quite the scene," Noah says with a spark of mischief in his eyes.

"He wouldn't actually do that would he?" I look at Mason for confirmation, but he just smiles triumphantly.

I look back at Noah as he takes an audible inhale of breath before: "WEE OU WEE OU BEEP BEE—"

"Okay, okay! Stop! You win—I'll come!"

A few students look over at us quizzically before returning to their work, and the teacher gives us a disapproving glare. I wait a minute before I turn back to the boys.

Noah and Mason high-five in victory and grin from ear to ear. "Being the most annoying person in the room never fails."

"I don't know what's worse: the fact that you have no shame or the fact that it doesn't seem like it's the first time you've done that in order to coerce your friend," I say to Noah.

"Hey, no pain, no gain." He winks.

4

Today is Friday. Meaning it's been almost a full week since I made my return to school. Also meaning it's Halloween, and Noah's party. It wasn't as hard to persuade Charlotte to come to the party as I thought it would be. With Chase and I both pestering her, she gave in pretty quickly.

My phone chimes and I read a text from Charlotte: *Be there in 5 :)*

I take a calming breath and try to push my mom's words out of my head. When I told her what I was up to tonight, she did not take it well.

You promised, Amelia, she lectured. *You're not supposed to be out partying and drawing attention to yourself.*

It's just one night, Mom. I'll be on my best behavior.

She shook her head, not believing me. *Fine, go, but this is a bad idea. You need to be more responsible. People around you get hurt, and it'll be your fault if they do.*

Pushing her warning out of my mind, I grab a small purse to put my keys, gum, and phone in, then run downstairs.

At 9:34 p.m. Chase's car pulls into the driveway. My mom is at work, so I send her a quick text, knowing she probably won't even respond until later. She's a flight attendant, so not answering is nothing new. Tonight she's on a long haul to from Seattle to Australia, so I won't see her for a couple of days.

Here, now, in King City, I'm going to do things differently. I may have already screwed up my plan to keep my head down all year, but I am going to have friends. I want to have friends. I want to live through a normal school year. I want to finish my senior year at one school and one school only—King City High.

I lock the door and head toward the car, where Charlotte is getting out of the front seat so we can admire each other's costumes.

"You look hot!" she says with a smile.

I'm dressed as a '20s flapper, in a black dress and dangling beaded necklaces.

"You too!" I smile back at her.

Charlotte's dressed as a Pink Lady from the movie *Grease*. The look is complete with her curly, mocha-colored hair tied in a high ponytail and a small black scarf tied around her neck.

"Um, hello?" Chase interrupts us as he walks around the front of the car from the driver's side. "Why has no one commented on my hotness?"

Chase is wearing black cargo pants, a tight navy-blue T-shirt, and a black hat with the word *SWAT* on it in white block letters.

"Very creative, Chase." I roll my eyes as we all get into the car.

"Yeah, never seen that one before," Charlotte adds sarcastically.

"What? Like a Pink Lady and a flapper are any more creative," he replies as he pulls out of my driveway. "Besides, I figured almost every other girl is going to be dressed as an army/SWAT team girl, a nerd, some superhero, Thing One and Thing Two, or a Minion. So I figured if I dressed to match one of them it'd be easier to get laid. I took my chances with the SWAT team."

Charlotte looks back at me from the front seat and we share an eye roll.

"Very strategic, Chase."

Missing Charlotte's sarcasm, he smiles and continues driving.

"Are you drinking tonight, Chase?" I ask. "If you're drinking, I do not want you to drive us home."

"Duh, it's no fun being the only sober person at a party."

"But alcohol makes you do stupid things, Chase. Remember last Christmas when you tried to do a backflip from the roof into Mason's pool?" Charlotte points out.

"Hey, in alcohol's defense, I've done some pretty stupid shit sober as well."

"Can't argue with that," Charlotte mumbles.

I feel anxiety bubble up in my chest. "Come on, guys. If Chase is drinking, how are we getting home?"

Charlotte looks back at me. "Chase is crashing at Noah's with the other guys. My brother is going to pick us up when I call him."

I breathe out a sigh of relief, and Charlotte and I go back to talking about our costumes.

About ten minutes later, we pull onto Noah's street. His house is easily identifiable from the teenagers loitering around the front, and the loud music pouring out of the open door. There are a lot of people here already. It's almost ten—clearly this is the time when most people show up.

Chase parks the car a couple of houses away on the street, and for late October, it's not that cold out. Walking up the driveway and saying a quick hello to the few people outside, we head up to the open front door and walk into the awaiting Halloween-themed pit of drunken, hormonal teenagers and the imminent promise of making bad decisions.

The music is a lot louder inside, and I start moving my hips a little in automatic response. As we follow Chase through the house, we see that he was right about what girls would be wearing. The crowded house is full of Thing Ones and Thing Twos, army and SWAT team girls, devils, angels, and lots and lots of cats.

Many of the guys aren't dressed up, and those who are, are wearing creepy masks, or are dressed in last-minute costumes like doctors, and there are lots of Federal Boobie Inspectors. *Ew.*

"Booze!" Chase exclaims when we enter the crowded kitchen, and makes his way over to the counter stocked with different types of alcohol.

"Don't overdo it this time!" Charlotte chases after him, leaving me standing awkwardly in the doorway.

I'm not quite ready to drink just yet; maybe I'll have a shot after I check out Noah's house, looking for exits and familiar faces. The house is big, but not so huge you'd get lost in it. For my own sanity, knowing the fastest way to get out of here in case something happens or *someone* shows up is a good thing.

With all the teenagers packed into the dimly lit house, it makes it hard to really appreciate the beauty of Noah's home. It's modern, and each room is painted white.

There are fewer kids downstairs in the basement, and the music isn't so loud that you have to yell. A lot of rooms are closed off, but the large open area includes a bar filled with more alcohol, couches, and a pool table, which is what Mason is leaning against, holding a pool stick in his hand.

I take a second to check him out, and all I can think is *damn*. He's wearing an olive-green tank top, silver dog tags around his neck, combat jeans in army print, and black combat boots. He's finished the look with a strip of black cloth tied around his forehead and two black lines drawn under his eyes, across his cheeks. Overall, he looks hot.

Mason says something to the guys he's playing pool with, gives his stick to another guy, and walks over to me with a smile.

"Hey, k-bear! You look good." He leans in and gives me a tight hug, causing me to blush.

"Thanks, you too," I say as we pull away. "I really like your jeans."

"Yes, my chromosomes have combined nicely." He runs a hand through his hair seductively, striking a model pose.

I laugh. "I meant your pants, not your DNA. But sure, that too."

"*Amelia!*" I turn just in time for Noah to run up and pull me into his arms.

I pull back a little "Ow, Noah. Watch the ribs—they're still sensitive."

"Oh man, I'm sorry. It seems like forever ago that you hurt them again, but it's only been a few weeks. Still, that costume suits you. You look great!"

"It's okay, and I know." I flirt with a wink, causing both boys to chuckle.

Noah's wearing jeans and a white T-shirt, and has a black envelope attached to his shirt.

"What are you supposed to be?"

Noah looks down at his shirt and smiles at me. "Isn't it obvious? I'm blackmail. Get it? Blackmail?"

"That's extremely fitting," I tease. "Seeing how you blackmailed me into coming to this party."

"Hey! Maybe blackmail can be our thing!" He smiles triumphantly.

"Maybe we should keep looking for a thing."

Annalisa waves from across the room, and we all walk toward her. She's with Julian at the bar. I give them both hugs and we all start talking.

Annalisa and Julian are adorable in their Barbie and Ken costumes. Annalisa looks extremely different, having swapped out her normal black, slightly goth clothes and heavy dark makeup for a bright-pink dress, light makeup, and even a blond wig—I almost didn't recognize her.

Noah pours ten shots and we take two each, downing them quickly. I slam my second shot glass down and scrunch up my face—the first ones always taste the worst. As Noah starts pouring us another round, a boy with dark hair I vaguely recognize comes up to him and says something. It must be important because Noah's normally carefree expression turns deadly serious. He gives Mason and Julian a stern look with knowing eyes, and they both seem to tense up slightly.

Mason sighs and downs his shot, then turns to face me. "Sorry k-bear, gotta handle something."

He turns and follows Noah and the other guy up the stairs. Julian gives Annalisa a quick kiss on the temple, then follows Mason, leaving the two of us alone at the bar.

"What's going on?" I ask Annalisa.

"It's either something with Aiden, party crashers, a fight, or maybe all three." She sighs.

"Will they be okay?" I suddenly realize I'm a bit nervous for the Boys; well, the ones I like, anyway.

"Yeah, they'll be fine. Shit like this always happens when one of them throws a party." Annalisa and I down our third shot, and some other girls come up to the bar and start talking to her.

"Anna, I'm going to see if I can find Char; I'll see you later." I turn and head back up to the main floor where the music is much louder. The house has grown even more packed with people I don't recognize, presumably from school.

I check my phone and see a text from my mom: *Just got off my flight. Be careful tonight. Try not to attract any attention. I'll try to call you later when we're at the hotel.*

"Love you, too, Mom," I mumble to myself as a rough hand closes hard around my arm.

My heart automatically goes into overdrive as my brain realizes that someone is stopping me from walking. I turn around to face a broad chest, and tilt my head up to look into the dark eyes of a boy I definitely know doesn't go to King City High.

He's rugged and huge, like a linebacker, and is holding a beer in the hand that isn't holding my arm. He creeps me out. I don't get a good vibe from this guy at all, and the fact that he's still holding me in place is making my panic worse.

He pulls me close and gives me what I'm sure he thinks is a charming smile. "Hey, sexy, what's your name?"

"Not interested." I twist my arm out of his grip, then turn around.

He grabs my arm again, rougher this time. "Did it hurt when you fell from heaven?"

"No, because I dug my way up from hell," I say.

He blinks at me.

I blink back at him.

Then he breaks into a grin. "Feisty. I like it."

He pulls me closer to him, setting his beer down and wrapping his now-free arm around my waist, grabbing my butt. Oh no. No, no, no. I do not like this *at all*. Bringing my arms up, I push at his chest.

"Sorry, I have a boyfriend," I lie, trying to calm my racing heart and keep my panic at bay. "A big one, and he's waiting for me, so I really have to go."

He now has both hands on my butt, and crushes me against him. "Oh come on. Live a little. I'm sure your boyfriend knows it's a crime to keep someone like you all to himself. He won't mind sharing."

I'm having trouble breathing. He's holding me so tightly against him, his hands groping me, and—

His gross, slimy lips are *on me*. I turn my head quickly, my skull hitting his face. Taking advantage of catching him off guard, I shove him, getting enough room between us to allow me to drive my knee up into his groin.

He reacts and bends down clutching himself in obvious pain, but I'm still pissed. I knee him in his stomach, and when he bends down even lower, he gives me access to his back. I bring my arms up and interlock my fingers, then drive my straight elbows into his back, causing him to tumble to the floor.

"No means no, asshat!"

I drag my arm across my lips to wipe away the memory of his kiss, and then look for Mason or Noah to kick this piece of trash out. But two other linebackers standing with their arms crossed block my escape path. Looking up at their pissed off faces, I see that they don't go to my school, either, and they are as huge and intimidating as asshat number one on the floor.

The one on the left grabs me, forcing me back toward the guy I just escaped from. The other guy follows him, blocking us from view. The asshat stands up, looking seriously pissed off.

"You gonna let this bitch get away with that, Dave?"

"I'll show you what happens to rude bitches," Dave snarls.

He lifts his arm and backhands me across the cheek, and I end up leaning against the wall for support. My rising heartbeat rings loudly in my ears, and the panic claws at me, up my stomach and into my throat, almost suffocating me. His hand closes tightly around my throat, but almost as quickly as I feel it, the pressure is lifted, and I hear a body hitting the floor—hard.

With my hand on my throbbing cheek, I force air into my lungs to calm my racing heart. I move my hair out of my face so I can see what's going on.

Dave's lying bloody on the floor, and his two friends are fighting a guy whose back is to me. One of Dave's friends joins him on the floor, groaning in pain, and as the other guy is tackled by my defender, I see his face.

Aiden.

My eyes widen as if to make sure they aren't playing tricks on me.

Yup, my defender is Aiden, and he looks *murderous*. I can practically feel the anger radiating off him in waves.

Someone cuts the music and the crowd thins quickly while those who are left watch Aiden beat the shit out of these guys. He and Dave's friend circle each other, the other guy already dripping blood from his nose. Aiden's opponent suddenly relaxes his tense pose and smiles slightly, looking over Aiden's shoulder with a victorious look in his eyes. Four boys advance on Aiden from behind.

"Aiden!" I yell.

But I'm too late. All four boys charge at Aiden at the same time, tackling him to the ground. My heart stops. The edges of my vision tinge black as Aiden disappears under the pile of boys.

Determined to help Aiden, since the wimps we go to school with are clearly more intent on watching the action unfold, I rush up to the nearest guy and swing my arm out, expecting to hit flesh, but a blur of olive green tackles him to the ground.

Mason punches the guy in the face as Julian pulls a guy off Aiden, who was doing fairly well for taking on four guys—he managed to break someone's nose, forcing him to run out of the room.

Noah comes out of nowhere and pushes me behind him. "Amelia, get out of here, there are a lot more crashers from Commack Silver High on their way, and they're dying for a fight."

He joins in just as more guys from Commack Silver do as well. Aiden, Mason, Noah, and Julian are now facing two of the blindsiders and the eight newcomers, and I notice Chase has just entered out of nowhere and joined Aiden's side in the face-off.

Noah told me to leave, but I'm glued to the spot. My legs will not move. I can't remember how to do anything but stand in one spot and stare at the unfolding scene.

It's ten against five. Oh my God.

The other partygoers look more shocked and scared than I do, so my hopes of someone else jumping in are dashed.

I'm moving before my brain realizes what I'm doing, as if my reasoning has shut off and given over to instinct. All I can think is: *It's uneven, someone has to help. Someone has to do something. It's uneven.*

Just as one of the guys is about to lunge at Noah, I jump in front of him and take a swing at his face, my attack taking him off guard and knocking him to the floor. He looks up at me in shock and rage, and all nine standing C. S. guys shift their attention to me with venomous glares.

Then all hell really breaks loose.

Aiden reaches me first, grabbing me and throwing me behind him, taking a protective stance. The remaining guys all pounce at him, and our friends jump in to help Aiden defend me, their grunts and swears chilling me to the bone.

Aiden fights one guy, all while never moving from in front of me.

It happens before I can warn anyone. Another guy from C. S. High grabs an empty beer bottle and swings it with all his might right on Noah's head. The sound of glass shattering is like a bullet to my pounding heart, and I watch in horror as Noah collapses to the floor. There's blood coming from the gash in Noah's head, and it's seeping onto the floor.

The sudden realization of how serious this situation is must have hit everyone at the same time Noah hit the floor. Girls scream and cry, and I vaguely realize one of the voices is my own.

Aiden pounces on the guy who attacked Noah, beating him mercilessly. The remaining boys from Commack Silver High try to scatter, grabbing the injured guys and running from the house as quickly as they can carry them. Racing to Aiden, who's still punching the attacker on the floor, I yell, "Aiden! Aiden, *stop*! Please!"

He stills and looks at me with raging eyes, breathing heavy.

"We need to help Noah," I plead.

He looks at the guy on the floor, and comes down from his blind rage, getting off of him.

He grabs my upper arms and shakes me. "How stupid are you? Why would you jump in the middle of that? You could've gotten hurt!"

"Aiden! I'm okay—we need to help Noah."

Anna's already sitting with Noah, trying to stop the bleeding with a shirt. Some guys are helping escort the bottle attacker Aiden knocked out from the house.

Mason's on the phone with someone while pacing in frustration—something about an ambulance. Kneeling beside Aiden on the floor, I notice the gash on Noah's head is bigger than it originally seemed, and there is some glass sticking out.

Someone hands me a towel and I pass it to Anna, who discards the shirt and presses the clean towel against Noah's head, being careful to avoid messing with the glass. I hear all the boys around me swearing. Chase says something to Mason about calling Noah's parents. Charlotte is crying beside me, staring at the blood on the floor.

Poor, sweet, Noah. Why him? He's the nicest, goofiest, easiest guy to get along with. And now he's on the floor, unconscious and bleeding.

Damn it, where is this ambulance?

I stay on the floor with Noah and gently run my hand over his forehead, scared to do anything because of the glass lodged in his bleeding gash. Mason is still frantically speaking into the phone, talking to Noah's parents from the sound of it. Chase is consoling a crying Charlotte, and Julian is running around gathering more towels.

And Aiden—he's standing near the door that he just opened for the ambulance, taking in the scene with a blank, impassive face. But I notice the undeniable rage he's managing to control. The anger is in his eyes—they look deadly and murderous, ready to take on and destroy anything that stands in his way.

Noah's secured on the stretcher, and an oxygen mask is fixed over his mouth. Since only one person is allowed to ride in the ambulance with him, Mason follows him in without hesitation.

With the ambulance gone, the adrenaline slowly drains from the room. We turn to look at one another, and at the mess in Noah's house, amplified from the fight. Blood, broken glass, and furniture are everywhere, mixed with scattered cups and bottles.

Chase is the first to speak, unwrapping his arms from around Charlotte and intertwining his fingers with hers. "I called us a taxi. I'm going to take Charlotte home, then sleep these drinks off before going to the hospital to see Noah." He looks at me. "Amelia?"

I shake my head, indicating that they should go without me. Charlotte gives me a tight hug, then goes outside with Chase.

"There's no way I can sit around and wait for Mason to call," a now slightly calmer Annalisa says.

"There's no point in us all going to the hospital; you need some sleep. We all need some sleep. Mason said he'd call the second they know anything about Noah," Julian says, trying to reason with her.

"There's no way in hell I'll be able to sleep. If I can't be useful and help Noah at the hospital, I'll at least make myself useful and start cleaning his house."

Before anyone can protest, Annalisa disappears into the

kitchen. Julian sighs and follows her, and we hear them picking up bottles.

This leaves just me and Aiden in the room, and I still haven't moved from the spot where Noah was on the floor.

Aiden sighs and walks over to me. "Come on, I'm driving you home."

I hesitate, and he stiffens. "I think my saving your ass tonight shows that I'm not going to hurt you. And I haven't had anything to drink, if that's what you're worried about."

"Sav—saving my ass?! I was handling it just fine before you jumped in and caused the whole damn football team to get involved."

"Handling it just fine?! You were being *strangled*. A simple 'Thanks, Aiden' would suffice. Now let's go."

He hoists me to my feet and leads me toward his car.

"Did you not see me take out Dave the first time? I could've handled it!"

The guilt and worry over Noah sit in the pit of my stomach. I know Aiden probably did save my ass, but I can't accept that. If I can't even handle some high school boys without Aiden's help, how am I going to handle it when *he* comes for me?

Aiden doesn't reply and instead guides me into the passenger seat. When he sits in the driver's seat and turns the car on, he looks at me. "Address?"

I recite it, then realize something and get mad. "Why don't you take me to the hospital instead of home? I can't go home—I need to see if Noah is okay."

Where's my phone? I need to—I don't know—find out if someone knows something already. I pat my pockets and search my purse. Damn it. I usually keep my phone in my hand instead of in my purse and I must've lost it without realizing during the fight.

Aiden's grip on the steering wheel tightens, and he continues to drive toward my house; the opposite direction of the hospital.

"*Aiden!* Take me to the hospital! I want to see Noah!"

"Did it ever occur to you that maybe he won't want to see you?" he explodes.

"Wha—"

"Seriously, you've done enough tonight."

"But I don't—"

"It's your fault he's in the hospital! The whole fight started because you got mixed up with the Silvers. We didn't think there would be a problem tonight since Ryan wasn't even here, but a fight started anyway! Because of you! I mean, do you go looking for trouble? Because ever since we've met you, you've done nothing but attract it. After this, you'll be lucky if Noah ever hears your name without flinching, never mind wanting to see you."

I start crying, never thinking to ask about this Ryan. Aiden's right; of course he's right. That whole fight wouldn't have happened if I hadn't gone to that stupid party. And Noah would be at home, partying it up with everyone right now instead of at the hospital.

"They all probably hate you now, since it's your fault we might never see Noah again," he says calmly, his words shooting the second bullet of the night straight through my heart.

5

The tears that started in Aiden's car didn't stop all night. I couldn't get his words out of my head.

It's now two o'clock on Saturday afternoon, and I have no idea what's going on with Noah. I don't have my phone, and even if I did, I'm too much of a coward to call anyone, and I'm too scared to tell my mom I lost it. Then I'd have to explain what happened and she definitely would not be happy about that.

Every time someone gets close to me, they get hurt. This is why I'm supposed to keep my head down, but no, instead I gave into the need for friends.

God, if my mom finds out about Noah, she's going to freak and I'll get one hell of an I-told-you-so lecture. *See, I warned you! You shouldn't be involved with these people, Amelia. You need to keep your distance or they'll end up hurt. He's not even here and one of your friends is in the hospital! Haven't you learned your lesson yet? The people around you get hurt.*

I laugh humorlessly. She wouldn't even be wrong. My last

best friend was clocked over the head with a gun. And that's not something you easily forget.

Moping in bed, like I've been doing all day with the guilt eating me alive, I've debated about going to visit Noah or not a half dozen times. At the top of the cons list is what worries me the most: finding out Noah hates me. Right now, by not visiting, I can prolong finding out and can live in denial a little while longer. He's such a fun, goofy guy. Hurting him is like kicking a puppy, and I can't face the fact that hate would fill his light-green eyes when they looked at me.

When the doorbell rings, I barely get it open before Charlotte pushes it open the rest of the way and walks in like she's lived here forever.

"Why haven't you answered your phone? And why does it look like you haven't moved from bed since yesterday?"

"I lost it," I say, leading her into the house. "And because I haven't."

"Why?" Charlotte sits down on the couch opposite me and crosses her legs.

"It's my fault Noah's in the hospital."

"*What?* No, it's not, Ameli—"

"Yes. It is."

"No, seriously, it's not. You didn't do anything. Tha—"

"If I had just handled things with Dave differently, or not punched that guy when he lunged at Noah, or not gone at all; if I had done *anything* differently, things would have turned out differently."

"Stop interrupting me!" Charlotte looks at me sternly. "You're new, so let me explain how things around here work. The K. C. High boys and C. S. High boys have never gotten along. Since ever. They've been fighting since freshman year. Whether you went to Noah's party or not, a fight would've broken out. The Silvers use any excuse they can to fight Aiden and them—it all goes back to some rivalry between Ryan and Aiden. The Silvers would have crashed Noah's party and fought with them no matter what. You just happened to be the thing that they decided to start the fight over this time. Shit happens. But it's not your fault."

She takes a breath, and I sit there staring at her, trying to process. There's that name again: Ryan.

"People who saw told me what happened between you and that guy, Dave?" she continues. "You don't need to talk about it if you don't want to, but I know he slapped you and started choking you before Aiden pulled him off. That was not your fault, you understand me? No victim blaming here. The Silvers are assholes who go looking for trouble." She finishes her rant and gets up from the couch. "Now, get your sorry ass up, go shower, and get dressed. Noah's awake and we're going to visit him."

I look at her with wide eyes, and slowly get up from the couch. Crossing to her, I throw my arms around her, and she easily hugs me back.

"Thanks," I say.

"What are friends for? No moping on my watch! Now hurry up before visiting hours are over."

On our way to the hospital, I realize something and look at Charlotte. "I thought you hated the Boys?"

"They're not that bad," she mumbles, not taking her eyes off the road.

"Yeah, they're starting to grow on me too."

"I guess in his own way, Aiden's not that bad either," she admits.

I gasp theatrically. "What? Has the alcohol from Friday permanently damaged your brain?! Should you be driving? This is not good—the delusional should not be operating heavy machinery!"

"Shut up." She laughs. "For real, though, he pulled that first guy off you. He beat up, like, six guys by himself to protect you. When they all lunged at you, he pulled you *behind* him. I'm just saying I don't hate the fact that Aiden was at the party. Not that I want to invite him to my house for a sleepover-slash-movie marathon."

At the hospital, I hesitate by Noah's door, nervous to go in. Charlotte assured me that Noah wouldn't hate me, but I'm still worried. Taking a deep breath, I walk into the room behind Charlotte.

"Charlotte! Amelia!" Noah's happy expression reassures me, and I exhale the breath I hadn't realized I've been holding. He's sitting up in bed wearing comfy-looking sweats.

Despite being in the hospital, he still looks cute, his dimples never disappearing beneath the slight bruise on his cheek.

"Hey, Noah." We smile at him. "How are you feeling?"

"Better now that you're here." He winks at us.

"I'm glad to know this isn't a setback for your flirty attitude," I laugh as Charlotte and I sit beside his bed. "For real though, how are you?"

"I'm fine. I have a slight concussion and needed some stitches, but I'm feeling good. Really. I don't even need to be here anymore, but we're waiting for some test results. I should be discharged soon."

"I'm so glad you're okay," I say.

"Why didn't you come to visit me earlier?" Noah asks.

"I—I was scared."

"Scared of what?" he asks.

"She was scared you'd be mad at her," Charlotte explains. "She thought it was her fault you're here and that you'd hate her."

Noah looks at me, looks at Charlotte, then looks back at me, and bursts out laughing. "What? I'd never hate you, Amelia! And this isn't your fault. It isn't anyone's fault. The Silvers hate our guts and are always starting fights."

Charlotte gives me a look, as if to say *Told you so.*

"So you don't hate me?" I ask in a small voice.

"Never! I'm glad you're not hurt, or any more hurt since the rest of us jumped in." Noah says, indicating the forming bruise on my cheek. "Where did you get the idea that I'd be mad at you anyway?"

"Aiden—" I look down at the floor, ashamed of myself for being so easily convinced by him.

"Aiden's just really protective of the people he cares about." Noah sighs. "He didn't mean it."

Letting the subject drop, the three of us talk and laugh until Aiden walks into the room.

"What are you doing here?" His eyes narrow at the sight of me.

"I came to see my friend," I say confidently, done moping around and blaming myself.

"Seriously, Aiden. Don't be all hostile right now. I'm happy she's here," Noah says.

Aiden glares at me, and then tosses Noah a fast-food bag before taking the seat on the other side of the room.

"You have just made me the happiest man in the world!" Noah exclaims and digs into his burger.

Aiden rolls his eyes, but I don't miss the small smile he's trying to keep from forming.

Mason walks in slurping from a fast-food cup. "K-bear!" He hugs me and Charlotte, and sits down next to Aiden.

"Hey, that reminds me!" Noah announces and looks at me. "Maybe hospital trips can be our thing? You were here last time, and now me."

Out of the corner of my eye I see Aiden tense up.

"Maybe we should keep looking?" I say and everyone laughs, releasing any tension in the room.

✗

Later that night, I'm sitting at home making some dinner in my empty house.

My mother's been so distant ever since that *incident* last year. She grows even more distant every time it happens. I know deep down she's tired of how we've been forced to live because of me. She's moved from mainly flying domestic and being home more regularly to doing more overseas and long-haul flights. She's avoiding me, avoiding this life, avoiding the reasons why we had to move three times in the last year.

As I'm doing the dishes, the doorbell rings and I tense. It's almost ten on a Saturday night; who'd be coming here?

He wouldn't be ringing the doorbell if he found you, I reason with myself. Despite knowing this, I grab a metal baseball bat from the closet beside the front door.

Opening the door slowly and peeking out, I breathe a sigh of relief as the crisp autumn air greets me. Aiden's standing there, his flat-black Dodge Challenger sitting in the driveway. He's looking at me with a questioning expression, eyeing the baseball bat in my hand. I quickly lean it against the wall behind the door, out of his inquisitive gaze.

He raises his eyebrow. "Really? A baseball bat?"

"It's a bad neighborhood," I lie, mentally slapping myself for such a stupid excuse.

He looks around at my very suburban block at the two-story houses with beautifully landscaped lawns and expensive cars sitting in the driveways.

He looks back at me and smirks. "Yeah, you could probably get allergies from all the flowers."

"What are you doing here?"

He holds a white phone out to me and I take it. "You found my phone?"

"Yeah, when I went back to Noah's Friday night."

"Why didn't you give this to me earlier? Or at the hospital today?"

"I have more important things to do. Plus, I wasn't going back downstairs to my car to get it."

"Oh."

"I noticed you only had one contact in your phone that wasn't Charlotte, Annalisa, Chase, Mason, or Noah. And that was your mom."

"You went through my phone?" I ask, getting mad. Why didn't I set up my password?

"Yes," he deadpans, not even looking guilty about it. "I thought you moved around a lot, so wouldn't you have other contacts in there? All the people you've met from other schools?"

"I don't believe in long-distance relationships," I lie.

"I also noticed you don't have any apps, photos, notes, or music."

"It's a new phone," I lie again, gritting my teeth. "If you're done interrogating me, I have dishes to wash." I try to close the door.

"Wait," he says, and I stop. "Friday night, I got mad at you—"

"I know. It's okay. I know we were all worried about Noah, and angry about the situation, and you needed someone to blame. The way you reacted wasn't nice, but I guess we all react in our own different ways."

"I shouldn't have blamed you," he says, looking slightly awkward and uncomfortable.

"Is that an apology I hear?" I smile slightly.

"Don't get used to it. It won't happen again."

Aiden is walking off the porch and onto the first step when I call his name. He turns back around, looking at me expectantly.

"Thanks for saving my ass . . . with Dave, I mean," I say, and hold up the phone that he returned to me. "And for bringing me my phone."

I know I said I didn't need to thank him last night, and that I was handling it just fine, but even I can't pull off a lie that big. Bring trained in jujitsu helped me escape Dave, but I wasn't strong enough to take on four giant, hostile boys.

"I got there in time to see you knock that first guy to the floor," he says. "I wasn't going to step in because you handled it just fine, but when I saw the others, I had to get involved," he admits in a quiet voice.

"I'm glad you did," I say.

He looks like he's about to continue down the rest of the steps, but says instead, "How did you learn to fight like that?"

"Basic self-defense classes," I say, our moment of honesty replaced by my lies again. "Good night, and thanks again."

I lean against the closed door and let out a breath when I hear his car rev and drive off.

Back in the kitchen, I open the contacts app on my phone to text Charlotte to say that I got my phone back, and freeze when I notice the new contact entry. At the top of my contact list, since it's in alphabetical order, is Aiden's name and number.

6

Monday morning the students are alive and buzzing about Noah's party.

I'm sick of hearing about the fight. I'm sure if Noah was here he'd lap up the attention, wearing his signature goofy but charming smile. He'd probably even find a way to convince people that he meant to get a concussion so he could get out of his calculus test.

Which is today. And I am absolutely unprepared.

When it comes to calculus, I already need all the help I can get, but this weekend, with all the drama that happened, I didn't have it in me to study. Now, sitting in my seat before the bell rings, I'm frantically flipping through the pages of my notebook, as if I can absorb all the information by glancing at it quickly. But really, I'm just flipping through pages.

Three minutes before the bell. Shove as much information into your brain as you can before class starts, Amelia. Never mind that it's gibberish. Why wasn't I blessed with a photographic memory?

Still, even if I had memorized all this information, I wouldn't have the slightest clue what to do with it.

"I'm guessing you're ready to ace this test."

Aiden's deep voice makes me jump.

"Clearly," I say. "Can't you tell by the frantic page flipping, sweaty palms, doodle examining, super planning, and erratic heartbeat that I'm confident in my ability to pass this test?"

He laughs and sits down behind me, while I return to my frantic page flipping as the bell rings. Somehow, my scattered mind seems to register that this is the first time Aiden initiated a conversation that wasn't unfriendly (sort of). It's also the first time he smiled at me (sort of), and the first time I heard him chuckle. I push those thoughts to the back of my mind. *School comes first, think about boys later.*

The teacher stands up. "Put away your books; I'm passing out the tests."

Shit.

Fifty minutes, a freshly chewed through pencil and some unshed tears later, I hand in my partially blank test. Aiden's right behind me, ready to hand in his, which is filled with his confident, bold handwriting, and not a single question skipped over. His answers look similar to the gibberish I was scanning through before the test.

Thinking about it now, Aiden didn't even look worried when he walked in. Cool as a cucumber. I swear, if he's hot and smart, I'm sending a very strongly worded email to whoever distributes this shit.

I grab my phone from the pile of phones in a basket near the door. Aiden and I walk out at the same time, and I can't help but glare at him. Stupid Aiden and his stupid smarts and his stupid looks, he's just soo—

"Stupid?"

I startle and look up at Aiden, who's finished my thoughts for me. The corner of his mouth is tilted up in a smirk as we fall into step beside each other.

"Did I say that out loud?" My face heats up.

"Mumbled. But I still caught it."

"I'm guessing you got an A?"

He shrugs in response.

"Yeah, me too. Amelia Collins? More like Amelia *Calculus* because I just love it so much."

He smirks one more time before walking down a different corridor without so much as a good-bye. Weird. I get to chemistry and sit beside Charlotte, who's talking to Chase sitting behind her.

"How was the calculus test? I have it fifth period," asks Chase.

"Oh, just peachy. I'm thinking of majoring in calculus in university because I just love it so much."

"Whoa, I didn't order a basket of sarcasm with a side of sass. Did you, Charlie?"

Charlotte glares at him. "Damn it, Chase. How many times do I have to tell you? Call me Char or Charlotte or don't call me anything all!"

"Whoa." Chase's eyes widen. "Maybe I did order the sarcasm and sass, with extra snarkiness on top."

The three of us walk to the cafeteria together after class, and I run right into Annalisa.

"Hey!" she says to all of us. "This is perfect. You just made hunting you down so much easier."

She grabs my wrist and drags me toward her table, but not before I grab Charlotte. If I'm going down, she's going down with me. When we get to the table, Annalisa shoves me down in a seat and sits in front of me. Charlotte's on my right and Chase settles in on hers. Julian's already there.

"Hey, why weren't you in calculus second period?" I ask Julian when I remember that he has calculus class with me and Aiden.

"Skipped," he confessed. "How was it by the wa—"

"*Don't!*" interrupts Chase, causing us all to look at him. "It's a touchy subject."

I scoff and pull out my Nutella sandwich, carefully unwrapping the plastic wrap. I've been looking forward to this chocolate hazelnut goodness all day—it was the only thing that kept me from breaking down during calculus. Who doesn't like Nutella? Do they put drugs in that spread? Because I am seriously hooked on it. While I'm savoring this godlike sandwich, Aiden and Mason arrive at the table. Mason plops down in the seat on my left, and Aiden sits on his left, beside Annalisa.

"What's a touchy subject?" Mason inquires.

Julian starts, "Amelia and calcu—"

"Don't!" yells Chase.

"It's fine, Chase. Everything is good as long as I have my Nutel—" I gasp and almost choke on air.

Mason has just reached out his hand, snatched up the other half of my Nutella sandwich, and *shoved it in his mouth*.

"You—I—but—Nutella?" I stutter, unable to even comprehend such a heinous act.

Mason carries on as if he didn't just steal the one thing bringing me joy, finishing the sandwich half in two bites. "Oh, the calculus test? Yeah, I have that fifth period, totally didn't study. Wow, Amelia, that was a good sandwich."

"But—but—Nutella?"

"Use your big girl words, Amelia." Aiden smirks.

Oh, so today he's deciding to be sociable? Of course. He can't resist commenting on my personal torment.

Mason holds up his hands. "Whoa, retract the claws, k-bear, I didn't know your sandwich was sacred. I'll take you out for ice cream today after school to make up for it. My treat. They have a Nutella flavor!"

Stupid boys.

"If they don't have Nutella flavor, you're dead."

If it was possible for someone to look relieved and worried at the same time, that would be Mason's facial expression. Grabbing my wallet, I get in line to buy something else to eat since I only got half a sandwich.

Mason comes with me to keep me company. "Are you sure you don't want my sandwich?"

I give him an incredulous look. You couldn't pay me enough to eat his sorry excuse of a lunch. I mean, really? Ketchup hastily slapped between two pieces of toast? I almost don't blame him for stealing half of my mouthwatering Nutella sandwich.

"What? I was in a rush and no one went grocery shopping lately," he defends his sandwich.

I order chicken fingers from the hot table and move over to the cash register. Mason offers to pay but I shoo him away.

We walk back to the table and when I try to sit down in my seat, someone roughly bumps into me from the side, sitting down instead and causing me to stumble. My innocent chicken fingers go sprawling to the floor. The. Hell? I tear my gaze from my lunch on the floor to my now occupied seat. Sitting where I previously was between Mason and Charlotte is a platinum blond-haired, blue-eyed girl from hell.

Kaitlyn looks at Charlotte sitting beside her and sneers. "Who invited the trash to sit with us?"

Everyone but Aiden wears a shocked expression. His face is blank, clear of emotion. I look from Kaitlyn, who pulls out her lemon water like it's just any other day, to my tender chicken fingers on the ground, and back. Charlotte frowns at the trash comment and glances at me. She's slowly standing when Chase grabs her wrist and forces her to stay put.

"What do you think you're doing?" he growls at Kaitlyn.

"I'm enjoying my lunch period with my friends," she says, as if it's the most obvious answer in the world.

"What the hell? We're not your—" Mason is cut off when Kaitlyn spots her second-in-command, Makayla, and shouts at her from across the cafeteria. "Over here, Kay!"

Stupidly, I'm still standing there trying to comprehend what's going on. Did she actually just steal my seat *as* I was sitting down, make me *drop* my chicken fingers, and then not even acknowledge me?

Makayla arrives at the table and Kaitlyn glances back at Charlotte. "Ugh, you're still here? I thought you knew that peasants don't sit with royalty. Move, peasant."

Unlike Charlotte, Annalisa lives for confrontation. Aiden is about to open his mouth when Annalisa beats him to it.

"Okay, I think we've had enough of this," Annalisa snaps. She narrows her eyes at Kaitlyn. "I get that you feel like you have some sort of claim on Aiden since you screwed him that one time—"

Aiden interrupts her with a growl, but she turns her burning gaze to him. "Oh, *now* you talk? Shut up, Aiden." She looks back at Kaitlyn without missing a beat and continues. "As I was saying, you think you belong here. You don't. Get over it. We don't need your attitude and quite frankly, I think we're all sick of hearing your grating voice all the time. Aiden's made it more than clear that he wants nothing to do with you. So run along to your little cult followers and *stay the hell away from us*."

"Shut up, Annalisa." Makayla defends Kaitlyn like a loyal dog.

Kaitlyn's calculating eyes narrow at Annalisa across the table from her. "Stay away from you? I don't want to be anywhere near *you*. Why *are* you even here? In fact, why do you even bother coming to school at all? Everyone knows you'll just end up like your pathetic moth—"

She's cut off as Annalisa suddenly pounces across the table, trying to get a hold of Kaitlyn, who shrieks. But Julian catches Annalisa around her waist before she reaches the other girl.

"Julian! Let me go! I have to kill her!" Annalisa struggles to get free of Julian's iron grip. "If you love me you'll let me claw her face off!"

Charlotte jumped up when Annalisa did and is now standing beside me. Mason, Chase, and Aiden are also all standing up, wearing matching enraged expressions. Kaitlyn clutches Makayla beside Charlotte and me while Annalisa still struggles to get at her.

"You're crazy!" Kaitlyn shouts.

If there is anyone in the cafeteria who wasn't already watching us, they most definitely are now. Aiden steps right in front of Kaitlyn, scowling down at her and blocking her view of Anna.

"Leave. Right now. I don't want to see your face ever again. I've told you countless times before, but I guess I need to say it S-L-O-W-E-R. Me, plus you, equals *never* going to happen. It was a one-time thing. I don't make the same mistake twice."

How is Kaitlyn still standing there? Actually, she's moved even closer to him. Aiden's hostile facial expression and voice full of clear animosity would've made anyone else shrivel up into a puddle on the floor. I was honestly a little intimidated, but she's taking it all in stride.

"Oh darling, you're just a little confused."

Aiden looks down at the hand that Kaitlyn places on his chest, and his eyes darken.

"Okaaayyy." Pushing Kaitlyn's hand off Aiden, I slide between the two of them. I'm getting nervous from all the attention we're receiving, and it's already a miracle a teacher hasn't booked us yet. I didn't want to push our luck.

"Kaitlyn, we've all come to an agreement. Collect your shit and leave. Now." Turning to the rest of the room, I call, "Show's over people! Get back to your lunch."

"She said the show's over!" Aiden announces, and everyone scrambles back to what they were doing before, conversations starting back up around us.

Grabbing Kaitlyn's purse, I throw her fancy reusable water bottle into it, and then shove it into her chest. "Go."

She swipes the purse from me like I've infected it and holds it to her chest. "Who do you think you are?" she demands.

"I'm the extremely pissed and hungry girl whose food you threw all over the ground. Now leave so I can peacefully enjoy the rest of my lunch period."

Finally, I'm back in my seat. Charlotte slowly sits back down beside me, and Chase does the same, but Mason and Aiden remain standing with their arms crossed, looking at Kaitlyn and Makayla. Annalisa and Julian aren't at the table anymore. He probably took her to calm her down before she ripped Kaitlyn's trachea from her throat. Something Kaitlyn said *really* triggered her.

"You're picking this whore over me?" Kaitlyn accuses Aiden.

Before he can respond, she leans down and hisses in my ear, "Aiden's mine. I told you to stay away from him. This is your last warning."

"Do I look like I give a shit?" I nonchalantly take out my phone, pretending to look at some texts.

The so-called Queen Bee can't handle being ignored and not getting the last word in. "I'm talking to you!"

Ignoring her, I message Annalisa to see if she's okay. Maybe if I keep pretending Kaitlyn's not there, she'll go away.

She snarls. "Stay away from—what are you doing?"

The snarky reply is on my lips before I can stop myself. "Checking my calendar. Nope. Looks like I won't be giving a shit tomorrow either."

"Kaitlyn, let's just go. Matt's waiting for me anyway." Makayla tries to reason with Kaitlyn.

Finally, a sensible suggestion.

"You've been warned," Kaitlyn states as she finally leaves with Makayla.

I mutter under my breath, and in my state of annoyance, unconsciously reach beside me to Mason's abandoned unwrapped sandwich and take a bite. I realize what I just did as a foul taste overwhelms my taste buds. I spit it out and glare at the innocent sandwich. Distantly, over the sound of my growling stomach, I can almost hear what's left of Kaitlyn's minimal composure shattering.

7

Today is quickly turning into one of the worst days of my life. To top everything off, I just got my period. Getting my period isn't what makes this day suck (although it certainly doesn't make it better)—it's that I don't have any tampons. I usually keep some in my bag for times like these, but yesterday when I was in the washroom, a random girl asked me if I had any so I gave her my last one. It honestly doesn't matter who the girl is or how you feel about her. If she needs a tampon, you give her a tampon.

I'm about to text Charlotte, but then I remember that she has the calculus test this period with Chase, so her phone is in the basket at the front of the room. Annalisa's phone is off, but she's long gone from school by now, judging by what happened at lunch. I don't have any other girl's number, and it's not like I can ask one of the Boys. Since I'm in the middle of my spare period, no one else is in the bathroom to ask for help.

Making a quick run to the convenience store down the road, I buy the only box they have in stock—a giant, hulking package of fifty—and make it back to school and out of the bathroom just as the bell rings.

I hate being late, but since starting here, it seems like it's an everyday occurrence. Abandoning going to my locker, I shove the open box of tampons into my shoulder bag and head to sociology class—the one I share with Mason, Noah, and Aiden. Oh, and Kaitlyn and Makayla.

I get there before the bell and sit down beside Mason. Aiden sits behind us, an empty chair beside him where Noah would be.

"I miss him." I look longingly at the empty chair.

"Class is definitely going to be less enjoyable without being able to laugh at his stupid comments," Mason agrees.

"I'll text him to come get ice cream with us after school today."

Mason shakes his head at me. "The kid's at home with a concussion."

"A *mild* concussion," I correct him. "He won't pass up an opportunity for free ice cream."

"Especially if Mason's paying," Aiden adds.

Aiden's being weird today. Contributing to normal conversations? He could barely even look at me without a scowl on his face last week. He even smirked at me today. Multiple times! Maybe I'm wearing down his gruff exterior and he's starting to like me, or at least feel more comfortable around me. It's just a theory.

Mason mumbles about us being lucky he doesn't back out of promises when Kaitlyn walks by, glaring at me the whole time. She sends Aiden a wink, but other than that, she doesn't cause any trouble. Near the end of class, Mr. Rogers calls me up to the front to collect my homework from last week.

I place my bag on my desk and head to the front to grab my paper. On my way back, just before I get to my desk, one of Kaitlyn's friend's shoots her leg out into my path. I narrowly dodge her leg, and look back at her with a triumphant smile. Ha! Take that!

But my victory is short lived—as soon as I look back at her, I slam right into my desk. My open bag goes flying to the floor, and I steady myself, narrowly avoiding tumbling over the desk.

The whole class is looking at me, some with stunned faces, and some trying not to laugh. I hear a gasp and suddenly some giggles. Soon most of the class is trying to hide their amusement or looking embarrassed for me.

I'm confused. What's embarrassing about stumbling? I do it all the time. Mason's quietly chuckling, and even Aiden's usually stormy gray eyes are light with amusement.

Kaitlyn shouts, "God, Amelia, do you need any more tampons?"

Oh.

My open bag is sprawled out on the floor, and laying a few feet away from it, clear for everyone to see, is the open tampon box that puked out forty-nine tampons, scattered everywhere.

Totally the worst day ever.

✶

Twenty-four hours later, my bad luck's continuing. I'm late getting to school because of traffic and the majority of the parking spaces are all filled up.

"Yes! You're all mine, baby," I say to the open spot in a prime location right near the front door. But when I'm about to pull in, a blur of bright red speeds past me, cutting me off. Slamming the breaks, my seat belt locks, preventing my head from going through the windshield.

"What the actual hell?!"

A cherry-colored convertible Porsche just parked in *my* spot. The owner gets out, and all my questions are answered. Kaitlyn throws her hair over her shoulder and wiggles her fingers at me in a taunting wave. Her malicious eyes shine with victory as she slams the driver's-side door, struts up the stairs, and goes through the front doors.

Seriously? Is this her following through with her promise of tormenting me for not staying away from Aiden?

Please, bitch. You're going to have to try harder than that.

✖

Turns out, she did try harder than that; a little too hard if you ask me.

After having to park a good five-minute walk from the front door, I meet Charlotte at her locker and tell her what happened with Kaitlyn as we head over to my locker together.

Charlotte scoffs, "She loves that car. I swear, she treats it better than she treats people. Ever since her dad bought her that Porsche, she drives around like she owns this town."

There's a huge crowd of students in the hall where my locker is, all gawking at something.

"What's going on?" Charlotte asks as we shove our way through the sea of students. She gasps. Tampons—taped by their strings—hang down, covering the front of my floor-to-ceiling locker. There are so many of them that the metal of my locker isn't even visible. Some are still in the little plastic applicator, but the majority are bare, a lot are red with—

"Is that blood?" Charlotte breathes, looking a little sick.

"That's disgusting. That better be paint," I reply.

On the wall directly above my locker is a sign that reads: AMELIA COLLINS'S TAMPON DRIVE, with an arrow pointing down.

"Who would do—Kaitlyn?" Charlotte suspects.

"That'd be my first guess."

As if just saying her name summons her, Kaitlyn appears from the crowd, the rest of her friends right behind her. People move back a little to give us some more room.

Kaitlyn gives me a triumphant smirk. "What do you think of our generosity, Amelia?"

I'm stunned. She didn't even bother denying the fact that she orchestrated this whole thing. She just got here, so she must have gotten her friends to come early and do it. She's *proud* of it. She wants everyone to know what she's capable of, and publicly humiliating me is her proof.

"Your generosity?" I'm bewildered.

"After yesterday, we realized just how many tampons you need. So, being the kindhearted people we are, we decided to help you out." She turns to the crowd of students and announces, "Students of King City High! Let's show that there's no limit to our generosity! If you have a tampon, step forward and contribute to our tampon drive for Amelia Collins. It doesn't even need to be new!"

I might throw up. Before anyone can react, a loud, furious voice booms from the crowd, "If anyone even thinks about doing that, I'll beat you so hard the doctor who delivered you will feel it!"

The startled crowd parts for the source of the voice, and Aiden steps toward me, looking ferocious. His deadly gray eyes meet my slightly traumatized hazel ones, and they seem to darken even more. Noah and Mason step from the crowd, both looking hostile as they scan the scene before them.

Aiden turns his murderous gaze to the crowd. "Get to class, *now!*"

Everyone scatters like someone detonated a bomb, and soon me, Aiden, Charlotte, Mason, Noah, and Kaitlyn and her friends are the only ones in the hall.

Kaitlyn pouts. "Aiden! Way to ruin the fun."

"You have a problem, Kaitlyn." Mason stands beside me and wraps an arm around my waist, hauling me close to show his support.

"I did warn you," Kaitlyn asserts, looking at her nails like this is just any other day and she didn't just humiliate me in front of the entire school. "I guess this warning extends to you now, too, Charlotte."

Noah steps in front of Charlotte, as if he can protect her from Kaitlyn's venomous gaze.

"I can't believe you went to all this effort just to make a point," I hiss.

"I take a stand for what I believe in. Plus, I promised I'd make your life a living hell, and I'm good at doing that. I *never* back down from my word."

"Well, I'm even better at keeping mine." Aiden steps in front of me and Mason, power and dominance radiating from him. "Go near Amelia *or* Charlotte again, and you'll have me to deal with. And you definitely won't enjoy that, I *promise* you."

Something in Aiden's threatening tone must register with Kaitlyn and her girls because their eyes widen. I guess his ruthless reputation filled in the unsaid threats, and Kaitlyn's girls start leaving. Kaitlyn gives me one last hate-filled glare before turning with Makayla and heading out of sight.

Mason brings his hand to my cheek, turning me to look directly into his chocolate-brown eyes.

"Are you okay?" he asks softly, stroking my cheek with his thumb.

Out of the corner of my eye, Aiden gives us an unidentifiable look. He turns around and rips down the sign above my locker with ease.

"Yeah, I'm okay. Thanks." I wiggle out of his intimate hold and turn to Charlotte. "I'm so sorry if I just dragged you into this."

"I'm not scared of her," she clarifies. "Plus, you didn't even do anything. She's just crazy."

"Crazier than a PMSing girl with caffeine withdrawal who ran out of tampons and got locked out of her favorite coffee shop," Noah says. We all glare at him. "What? Too soon for period jokes?"

I shake my head at him. "Why are you even here? Aren't you supposed to be on bed rest for the week?"

"What? After you told me about what happened yesterday, there was no way I was missing out on all the fun!" he explains. "Best decision ever."

During this exchange with Noah, Aiden walks to the nearest garbage bin, throws the now-ripped-up sign into it, and drags the bin to my locker.

The five of us stand in a line beside each other, quizzically looking at my locker.

"Do you think it's real blood?" Charlotte asks.

Noah sticks his hand out, swiping his finger on a tampon covered with red liquid, and puts that finger in his mouth. The four of us stand there with hanging jaws, too shocked to process what just happened.

"Just as I thought," Noah announces. "It's ketchup."

"What if it was blood?!" Charlotte exclaims, looking slightly nauseated.

"But it wasn't," Noah deadpans.

"But what if it was?!" she repeats.

"But it *wasn't*," he emphasizes.

That concussion seriously messed with Noah's head. Maybe he shouldn't even be at school right now.

"Do you really think Kaitlyn and company would touch a dirty tampon?" he adds.

Or maybe Noah's a lot smarter than we give him credit for.

8

It's lunch, and the group is at our usual table. I'm sitting between Charlotte and Mason, with Annalisa directly in front of me. I told her, Julian, and Chase what happened, as they hadn't seen my locker this morning.

"I wish I was there so I had a valid reason to break her face." Annalisa stabs her pasta with her fork.

"I can't believe she's doing this just because she doesn't like you around Aiden," Chase remarks from the other side of Charlotte. Aiden's eyes darken but he doesn't say anything.

"Well, I did bitch at her a couple of times, but she started it!" I defend myself. "I just hope Charlotte isn't dragged into this now."

Chase's head snaps over to meet my eyes, suddenly very alert. "What do you mean?"

Noah fills him in. "Kaitlyn was all, *Ohh, since Amelia and Charlotte are best friends, imma go after both of you.*"

No one else notices, but I catch Chase subtly moving a little closer to Charlotte. Aiden's keen eyes didn't miss that small action either. He's perceptive, and I don't miss the fact that I'm the only one who catches it.

"She's batshit crazy anyway; she doesn't need a reason to torment someone," Charlotte states. "Plus, I was brought into this the second she decided to mess with my best friend."

"Me too," Annalisa states, and the others murmur and nod in agreement, and Mason throws his arm around my shoulder.

"No one fucks with my k-bear," Mason announces confidently.

My heart swells. Never has a group of people stood by me and supported me like this. I've had friends before, of course, but not like this—nothing that felt like they had my back, no matter what was thrown at them.

I lean my head affectionately on Mason's strong shoulder. "Thanks, guys, but there's no need for anyone to get involved. I just need to think of how to get back at her."

"Like hell we won't get involved! Fuck with my friend and you fuck with me!" Noah declares.

Annalisa nods. "Let's just corner her and break her nose."

"We don't hit girls, Anna," Aiden informs her, putting his phone away.

"I know you guys don't, but I don't have a problem doing that!" Annalisa clarifies.

Julian sighs. "You know you can't do that, babe."

Annalisa gives her boyfriend an irritated look. "You know just as well as I do that I'm perfectly capable of breaking her nose."

I lift my head from Mason's shoulder to look at him when he speaks. "No one doubts that you can break her nose, it's just that you *can't*."

"Her mom is the principal, which means Kaitlyn pretty much

gets away with everything," Noah explains, more for my benefit than anyone else's.

"Charlotte told me that the first day of school," I say.

"Basically, if you touch a hair on Kaitlyn's head, you're screwed," Mason explains.

"You're telling me I can't do anything about it? Not even get even?" I say.

Noah shakes his head. "Even the smallest thing she'll go crying to her mom."

"Once, this girl Kaitlyn didn't like accidentally spilt coffee on her shirt." Julian leans forward. "Kaitlyn ran to her mom and said the girl attacked her and threw scorching hot coffee at her for no reason. Kaitlyn's followers obviously backed her up. That girl got suspended."

"It's so unfair," Charlotte huffs.

I refuse to accept the fact that I can't do anything about Kaitlyn. If there's one thing about me that has never changed, it's that I don't take shit from anyone. It's what's kept me alive this long. I'm programmed to stand up for myself, and daughter of the principal or not, I will get even with Kaitlyn.

"Amelia?"

Aiden rarely contributes to conversations when Charlotte and I are around, so when he does, he gets our full attention. "What are you thinking?"

He didn't miss how I was deep in thought, calculating my revenge. And in that moment, I'm struck by how alike we actually are.

"I'm thinking that Kaitlyn's shit out of luck. I don't care who her mother is and there's no way in hell I'm letting her get away with this," I say.

Annalisa's diabolical smile fills her face. "That's what I'm talking about! What can we do?"

"You'll get suspended!" The always practical Julian tries to talk some sense into us.

"Not if it's so subtle she'll have nothing to rat about," I say, my mind already reeling with possibilities. And then I've got it, and a huge grin spreads across my face—my friends look at one another and then lean in . . .

✖

During our spare fifth period, Annalisa and I drive to the dollar store to get the supplies we need.

"We need one of those big envelopes that you practically have to claw open once it's sealed," I tell her.

We grab it and a few other things before paying and driving back to school.

"I love this idea. It's so harmless yet subtly annoying it's genius!" she exclaims from the passenger seat of my car.

"Best part is, if she goes crying to her mom, what's she going to say?"

"She can't! It doesn't hurt anyone, just annoys the hell out of you." Annalisa says. "You have such a way of subtly screwing with people. I tend to go right for the violence, which will get me in trouble one day."

I laugh. "What can I say? It's a gift."

Now that we have the supplies, I hope that Aiden will cooperate for part two; he wasn't keen when we talked about it briefly at lunch.

When last period starts, Noah and I turn around in our seats to face Aiden and Mason. We're huddled close. Fortunately, Mr. Rogers is one of the most disinterested teachers I've ever had. He just assigns homework and doesn't care if we work with others as long as we hand it in by the due date.

I'm currently leaning in close to Aiden so that no one will overhear our conversation. When I ask him for help, he flat out refuses again.

"Come on, Aiden! When have I ever asked you for anything?!" I plead.

He pretends to be deep in thought. "Well, you've asked me to fuck off a couple of times."

"Aiden, if we're going to do this, we have to do it now!" I say urgently.

Kaitlyn and her friends are currently oblivious to the rest of the class, sharing a laptop and scrolling through some website, their headphones plugged in.

"Come on, man! It'll be hilarious!" Noah prods Aiden.

"Fine," Aiden grumbles. "Give me the stupid envelope."

"Yay!" I take the envelope out of my bag and discreetly hand it over to Aiden along with a black sharpie.

He takes the marker and writes Kaitlyn's name on the front in his bold, identifiable handwriting. I quickly take the envelope back from him and shove it into my shoulder bag. Now, for the last part of the plan.

"Mr. Rogers!" I thrust my hand up in the air, grabbing the attention of the rest of the class.

He looks up from his laptop screen. "What?"

"Can I go to the bathroom?" I ask.

"What? Time to change your tampon already, Amelia?" Kaitlyn sneers.

Mason, Noah, and surprisingly even Aiden, all turn to glare at her.

"Go." Mr. Rogers dismisses me before looking back at his screen, and I quickly leave the class, and then the school.

Once outside, I head toward Kaitlyn's red Porsche, still parked right at the entrance of the school, in plain sight of the front doors.

It's a nice day, so she left the top of the convertible down, with the windows rolled up. Letting the adrenaline pumping through my veins guide me, I place the envelope on the driver's seat, making sure Aiden's writing is facing up and noticeable. She's so obsessed with Aiden, she'll know it's his writing.

I quickly run back into the school before anyone notices me and sit back down in class, trying to look inconspicuous and calm my racing heart. Now we just have to make sure we're there for the show.

✗

After school, I meet up with the rest of the group. We get into position, standing off to the side of the school with a clear view of Kaitlyn's red Porsche.

"She's going to freak! I think she'll be so mad she'll breathe fire from her nose! That'd be awesome," Noah exclaims.

"Shhhh." We quiet down when we see Kaitlyn open her car door.

"Oh my God, Makayla's getting a ride with her. This is even better!" Annalisa enthusiastically whispers when Makayla gets in shotgun.

Kaitlyn grabs the letter as she closes the door and rolls down her windows. She clearly recognizes Aiden's writing, showing it off to Makayla and eagerly but delicately trying to open the envelope. She can't; I sealed that shit.

Abandoning trying to save the envelope out of curiosity of what's inside, she violently rips it open, and the seven of us burst out laughing.

Kaitlyn and Makayla's faces are full of shock as glitter goes flying *everywhere*: all over their faces, clothes, skin, and especially all over Kaitlyn's beloved car. If you know anything about glitter, you'll know that it's basically the herpes of the craft world. That stuff is impossible to get off, and you'll be finding it everywhere for *months*. Harmless, yet so incredibly annoying.

Best part is, she'll never rat out Aiden if she's trying to get with him—there's no way she can spin this to her mom to get me suspended. *Mom, an envelope stuffed with a glitter bomb that may or may not have been from Amelia was in my car?* I don't think so.

Kaitlyn and Makayla get out of the sparkly car, frantically trying to shake the glitter from their hair. They're shrieking, and their frenzied movements are attracting weird looks from the students who walk by.

"How much glitter did you put in that envelope?" Julian asks, astonished.

"It may or may not have been packed so much that glitter was escaping from the seams," I giggle.

"They're going to look like sparkly strippers for weeks," Mason adds.

"Not to mention she'll be driving the sparkle mobile for who knows how long. That stuff doesn't vacuum easily," Chase chuckles. "Great idea, Amelia."

"Honestly, I can't take all the credit. I got the idea from some website back when I was at my old school, but I couldn't wait for them to mail her the envelope, so I just made my own version," I confess. "Still funny though."

Kaitlyn stops shaking around and her furious eyes zero in on me from across the parking lot.

"That's our cue to leave," I announce.

Aiden grabs my wrist and leads me away from Kaitlyn before anyone else can react. I turn back and wave to the rest of them as Aiden pulls me along. I hear them chuckling good-bye to each other, probably heading off their own separate ways before they incur the wrath of a glittery Kaitlyn and Makayla.

"What's the hurry, Aiden?" I smile and look up at him. "Scared of big, bad, sparkly Kaitlyn?"

He glares at me, not slowing down, but his lips pull up on one side to make his famous one-sided smirk. "So far, we've had a confrontation a day with her. We had today's this morning at your locker. Let's save some excitement for tomorrow, yeah?"

I laugh, slightly shocked that Aiden's actually joking with me. "It's probably for the best."

He lets go of my wrist and we walk side-by-side to my car. We don't say anything, but I'm too busy chuckling quietly to myself, recalling Kaitlyn's expression when she got a face full of glitter. I hope some got in her mouth. That'd be even funnier.

"Thanks for walking me to my car and making sure I don't get ambushed by Kaitlyn and friends."

"Be careful tomorrow," he warns.

"Yeah, yeah, she'll be on a sparkly warpath. I've got my insect repellent," I joke as I get into my car.

I look at Aiden standing outside my door and give him a smile, then start my car and drive away.

Despite how great it felt to get even, I was wary going to school the next day. I wasn't ready for another confrontation. I was starting to worry about the constant escalation—what it could lead to, how it could all end up. But it turns out, I didn't need to be concerned.

As soon as I get out of my car, Mason and Noah are immediately at my side. I literally didn't even close the driver's-side door before the pair are shoving each other, trying to determine who gets to be the first to hug me. Growing tired, I wrap my arms around both of them at the same time in greeting.

"Were you guys waiting for me to pull up?" I lock my car door, then walk in sync with the boys on either side of me toward the school.

"What are you talking about? It's not like we waited for you in Mason's car, saw you pull in, drove to where you parked, then"—Mason reaches behind me and smacks Noah upside the head—"*Ow!*"

I laugh. "I know you guys are worried about Kaitlyn and friends attacking me, but I'll be fine. I promise. I don't need you guys as my bodyguards."

"Aiden told us to make sure someone's always with yo—" Noah glares at Mason, who just hit him again. "*Ow!* Cut it out!"

Mason meets his glare, muttering something about why they never tell Noah secrets.

"I can so keep a secret! You just never told me that this was a secret!"

"Common sense, Noah."

I stop walking, and the boys keep going and bickering, not

even noticing I'm missing. Great bodyguards they make. They stop arguing long enough to notice that I'm not between them anymore, and turn back to look at me expectantly.

I cross my arms and rest my weight on my left hip, with my right knee propped out. Classic I'm-through-with-this-bullshit pose. They slowly make their way back to me.

"Aiden asked you to watch me?"

"Well, not just us—" Thwack! "*Dude!*" Noah rubs his head for the third time. "She already knows! Might as well just tell her straight up!"

Mason sighs. "He's got it down to a science. You pretty much have someone with you in every class. We're with you first period; we walk you to second. Aiden and Julian are in your second; they walk you to third. Chase and Charlotte are with you until lunch, where we all are, then fourth—"

"What if I have to pee?" I cut him off, bewildered.

Noah smiles. "I thought of that, so we got it covered too. You wait until you're in transition. Anna or Charlotte go in with you, the guy who's there waits outside to make sure no one comes in to ambush you."

"Aiden actually planned out the rotations of my bodyguards? And you organized my bathroom schedule?" I'm so overwhelmed I don't know what to think right now. "I didn't know he cared so much."

"I told you Aiden's actually a great guy. He's just—"

"Guarded?" I finish.

"Yeah."

"Prickly?"

"Like a cactus." Noah nods.

"Angry? Easily agitated? Permanently unimpressed? Always scowling—"

"He has his faults," Mason cuts me off.

No fair. I could've named at least seven more, not including gorgeous. Or brilliant. Or intuitive. Not that I would've said any of that out loud.

"But moral of the story is that he's a great guy," Mason continues. "You just don't know him like we do."

I do know that he's a confusing pain in my ass.

"Why all this precaution anyway? I'm sure Kaitlyn won't do anything so bad that I need to be chaperoned when I pee."

Mason sighs. "Kaitlyn's ruthless. We'd all rather prevent something from happening, than get a call that you 'fell' down the stairs or something."

My eyes widen. "She'd push me down the stairs?!"

That it wouldn't be the first time I've been pushed down the stairs, is what I don't say.

"Who knows what she's capable of? No one has ever stood up to her so blatantly. All we know is that she's seriously pissed and I don't want you to end up in the hospital. Again." Mason fits his hand in mine and starts walking, pulling me along with him.

"Do you think she'll leave me alone if one of you guys are with me?"

"Oh, no. Shit's gonna go down. At least if one of us is there, you won't have to face it alone." Noah beams at me. "I hope it's when I'm there. I don't want to miss any of the action!"

This time, Mason and I both glare at Noah.

"Aiden is behind all this? Why does he care so much anyway?"

Maybe, just maybe, Aiden considers me a friend? And that would explain the sudden protectiveness? I know I'll never be as close to him as the Boys are, but that's to be expected. Just making sure I don't get ambushed by his psycho stalker is enough in my books. He doesn't have to open up to me or tell me his deepest secrets, but he chuckles around me. For a guy like Aiden, whose emotional range is either bored or mad, that feels like a big step forward.

Noah makes a face. "I think he feels bad."

"About what?" I ask as we walk through the front doors and down the halls.

"Kaitlyn's only out to get you because she told you to stay away from her imaginary boyfriend: Aiden. I guess he kind of feels like she's attacking you because of him," Mason explains.

"He'd never say it out loud, though," Noah says, as if reading my thoughts. "You can kind of just tell. Or we can. We've known him since we were kids."

"He doesn't need to worry about it. It's not his fault his booty call from hell decided to go all psycho on me. I guess I kind of made it my own fight officially yesterday when I glitter bombed her," I reply honestly, and they laugh.

As we round the corner, we see Aiden at his locker, clearly identifiable by his tall, muscular frame, easily towering over the other students. He turns to look at us and meets my eyes. I smile at him. Maybe he'll smile back? His eyes zero in on my hand, held comfortably in Mason's. His scowl deepens and he turns around to finish pulling books from his locker. Okay, maybe no smile. We'll get there. Baby steps. Mason pulls his hand from mine as we continue toward Aiden's locker.

When we get there, Mason leans back against the locker beside Aiden's and crosses his arms across his chest. "Hey."

Aiden grunts in response.

"I'm going to get a breakfast bagel!" Noah announces. "The cafeteria lady who works Wednesday morning always gives me extra bacon!"

I laugh at his retreating form. That kid could get a telephone pole to like him.

"So, I hear you've taken up detail as head of my security brigade," I say casually, trying to hide my smirk and ignoring Mason glaring a hole in my head.

Aiden shuts his locker and narrows his eyes at Mason, who gives him a shrug, before looking at me.

This is gonna be good. He's going to admit he likes me—or at least doesn't hate me.

"I just don't want to have to explain to anyone why Mason had to drive you to the hospital. I've got enough problems."

Wow. His heartwarming concern is touching.

"*There you are, you evil little troll!*" The screech erupts from down the hall, and Mason and Aiden straighten up on either side of me.

Kaitlyn bulldozes through the hall, angry-looking friends on her tail, leaving a path of confused and intrigued students behind her. Looks like the drama's starting early today.

Resisting the urge to laugh as she gets closer to me, it's hilarious that she's still sparkly. Like *really* sparkly.

"Wow, Kaitlyn. Someone looks extra radiant today. Did you do something with your hair? No, no, your makeup is different. No . . . I don't know. You just seem to . . . shimmer . . . today."

The giggle escapes before I can contain it. The residue of my fun prank is still evident, and it's impossible to take her mean face seriously. Mason laughs beside me.

"You think this is funny?" she shrieks. "How dare you do this to me!"

"Do what? Oh, I get it. You're all sparkly because you're

embracing your future career. Good for you, Kaitlyn. I always thought you'd make a good stripper."

The crowd laughs, and Mason does as well. Aiden stands tense beside me, like he's preparing to jump in front of me in case she pounces.

"This didn't come out of my hair! I washed it, like, ten times yesterday!" Makayla whines.

"Good." I laugh harder.

"Shut up, Makayla!" Kaitlyn says harshly to her best friend. "I know you did this, Amelia, and you'll pay."

"Do what? I don't know what you're talking about."

"I know it was you, bitchface—" she starts.

"All right, listen here, you sparkly demon slut. I don't know what you're talking about so let's just hold today's confrontation to a few short minutes. Whatever it is you think I did,"—or what I actually did, but she's got no proof—"I didn't. I want to go to class today without causing a scene. If you have a problem with me, I ask that you please write it nicely on a piece of paper, fold it up, and shove it up your ass."

My smile is so obviously fake that it makes the vein in her forehead bulge and I mentally high-five myself. Instantly, she loses her composure completely and *lunges* at me. Tossing my arms up in an X in front of my face, with my eyes closed, I brace for impact.

There is none.

Aiden's got Kaitlyn's forearms, holding them out and away from him as she tries to swing at me. I resist the urge to laugh as I lower my arms. It just looks so comical: this sparkly five foot five blond, with a bright-red face and crazy eyes, urgently trying to get past the six foot three muscular wall who looks like he's extremely bored of the situation already and is not even breaking a sweat.

"You cocksucker!" she yells.

"No, I'm afraid that's you, sweetie." I smile sweetly at her as I peek around Aiden.

"ARGHH!" She lets out a battle cry, and Aiden holds her out a little farther from him.

She seems to realize who she's battling to get to me before going slack and stopping altogether.

"You!" she accuses Aiden. "You helped her with this! You participated in tormenting me?"

She yanks her arms from his hands and he lets her go easily. "We are over, Aiden Parker! You hear me? Over! I want nothing to do with you!" she announces, then looks at Mason. "*Any* of you."

Mason rolls his eyes. Aiden sighs and tells her for the umpteenth time, "We were never together."

Kaitlyn shouts, "UGH!" and leaves with her friends, a mist of glitter trailing along behind them.

With the threat gone, my stomach drops as I realize some people in the crowd are recording. Immediately, I cover my face and turn my back to anyone holding up a phone. Aiden notices and steps in front of me.

"Get to class," he orders, and like magic, the crowd disappears.

Right then, Noah bounds down the hall toward us, his smile fading as he realizes he just missed the drama.

"Shit! I told you I wanted to be here when the drama happens! All the fun stuff always happens when I'm not here." He pouts.

The three of us glare at him, but this time he ducks before Mason can smack him upside the head for the fourth time this morning.

9

For the first couple of days, we were all on guard, worrying that Kaitlyn would enact some kind of revenge. But it's been one whole week since Kaitlyn "broke up" with Aiden. Seven days of absolutely nothing interesting or significant happening. With the quiet lately, I don't know if I should be worried or not. But Kaitlyn moves on pretty fast; she already found another guy to latch onto and obsess over. She's been getting rides to and from school from some guy in a red Mustang. I don't recognize him, and he doesn't go to King City, but he looks around our age.

Kaitlyn may have moved on, but I don't think she's quite through with her vendetta against me. Good news is, the Boys have loosened up their watch on me since there appears to be no risk of an imminent attack, and I can now pee unchaperoned.

"Oh my God, have you seen this video?" Annalisa asks.

The eight of us are at our usual table, just starting our lunch period.

"What video?" Mason pulls his sandwich from his backpack.

"The one showing Kaitlyn going all ballistic and trying to attack Amelia in the hall after the glitter bomb prank." Annalisa laughs, pulling out her laptop.

"What?" My face drains of color.

"Someone must have recorded it because it's on Facebook. Kaitlyn made such a fool of herself, it's hilarious." Annalisa's now searching on her laptop to show us the video.

No, no, no, no, no, this isn't happening.

"Am I in the video? Like, do you see my face?"

Shit, shit, shit, shit, this is not good.

No one seems to notice that I'm having a slight panic attack as we huddle together to watch the video. It begins when I call Kaitlyn a sparkly demon slut, my voice and face clearly visible, and ends when Aiden commands everyone to go to class. Everyone laughs, making comments about how ridiculous Kaitlyn looked or how red her face was or how unconcerned Aiden looked. No one notices that I haven't spoken a word.

This video needs to be taken down before it screws everything up. No way in hell do I want to change schools again. My mom and I can't go through that for a fourth time this year, and certainly not as a result of something stupid I've done—putting our lives at risk for a bitch and a glitter bomb. There are only so many airlines my mother can work for before she'll start running into people she knows from *before*. Her resentment toward me is palpable every time she's home for more than twenty-four hours. Plus, I actually like it here. I have really good friends whom I don't want to lose.

"Who posted this video?" I demand in a serious tone.

Everyone stops talking and gives me a strange look.

"Ethan Moore," Annalisa says slowly. "What's wrong?"

"He needs to take it down."

The video *can't* be on the internet. Everyone has access to the internet. Anyone can see that video and see me in it and know where I am. And I bet Ethan hasn't even restricted the privacy settings.

"Amelia, calm down," Aiden says slowly, concern on his face.

Actually, everyone at the table is looking at me like Aiden is, their faces full of concern. What's their problem? Why do I feel dizzy? Oh, I'm hyperventilating.

"Amelia? Don't worry about the video. You look great in it, and it embarrasses Kaitlyn. She probably hasn't seen it yet that's why—ohh. You're scared Kaitlyn's going to see it and go ballistic?" Noah assumes.

Everyone takes Noah's assumption and runs with it, talking at once.

Mason: "She won't do anything, I promise."

Annalisa: "If she tries something, we'll kick her ass."

Chase: "We'll make sure you're not alone."

Charlotte: "She probably won't even see it."

Noah: "I better be there for the drama this time!"

Julian: "She won't confront you again."

"I don't care about Kaitlyn!" I snap.

Around me, concerned expressions turn into looks of confusion.

"Okay," Charlotte starts slowly. "What's wrong, then? We'll fix it."

I freeze, realizing that I'm overreacting, which would betray at least some of the secrets I'm trying to keep. Honestly, they don't know that it's not just a video of me looking fierce and telling off Kaitlyn—they don't know what's at risk. My friends think this video is a good thing; another weapon in our arsenal to slight Kaitlyn.

But I don't care about how I look in the video. I don't care that Kaitlyn looks ridiculous. All I care about is that my face and voice are clear as day, for anyone to identify. Honestly, my phone is void of selfies, and I haven't taken a picture of myself in nearly a year, nor let anyone else take one either. This petty high school drama *can't* screw everything up.

But I can't tell them that as they look at me expectantly.

"Oh . . ." I need to find Ethan Moore. Now. "You know, what's posted online haunts you forever. I don't want some future employer to find this video and not hire me because they think I'm some bitchy drama queen who has a fascination with glitter."

I'm rambling, not even fooling myself. Six pairs of eyes blink at me. The seventh pair narrows at me. *Stop analyzing me, Aiden.* I'll think of some better excuse later. My first priority is to find Ethan.

Standing up abruptly, I hastily collect my lunch, throwing my barely touched sandwich away. "I gotta pee, so I'll see you later."

Throwing my bag over my shoulder, I hurriedly start to leave without any further explanation. I get about halfway to the exit before realizing that I have no idea who the hell Ethan Moore is or how to find him. I pause midstep, do a one-eighty, and crash into the people behind me.

"Sorry," I mumble to the pissed off line of disgruntled students behind me, and book it back to our lunch table. "Quick question, what does Ethan Moore look like?"

My friends look at me like I've completely lost my mind.

Chase says, "He's a junior. Long black hair to his shoulders."

"Here." Annalisa turns her laptop to show me his Facebook profile picture.

I memorize the picture and turn back around without another word, on a mission to find Ethan. There's only twenty minutes left of lunch, so, with no time to waste, I march down the hall. Chase told me that he's a junior, so I stop the first people I recognize as juniors in the hall.

"Do you know Ethan Moore?"

About ten other kids give me the same blank stare before I end up at the right group. "Yeah," says a kid with a shaved head and braces.

He doesn't offer any more information. I stand there, nodding with my head to prod him to continue. The kid stares at me.

"And I can find him where?"

"*Oh!* Yeah, he's usually in room 136. I'm always there with him but—"

"Thanks," I mumble, and head to room 136, way too occupied in the task at hand to worry about social etiquette.

The door is cracked open, and I peek in first to see what I'm up against. There are about twenty boys crowded around two televisions hooked up to gaming systems. A few boys have controllers in their hands, thumbs moving quickly to kill the aliens on the screen. The ones watching crowd in closely, yelling instructions. I've clearly found the gamer room. From what I can tell, the majority of these boys are juniors, but some are younger. No one I know.

I spot Ethan—one of the boys with a controller in hand—instantly recognizing him from his Facebook picture.

Pacing outside the room, a game plan forms in my mind. How will they react to a girl in their gamer room? I think they're past that age where they value games over girls, right?

I look through the door again. The majority look socially

awkward, but who am I to judge? They could all have girlfriends or boyfriends for all I know. Being nice is probably the way to go. First, I take a calming breath. Forcing myself to put on a cute smile, I fluff out my hair. I take another calming breath, trying not to let my anger and the urgency of the situation show through.

Be friendly.

"Hi!" I lighten my voice to sound more polite and friendly.

All twenty boys freeze, then turn their heads to look at me, not even caring that the ones playing just died.

"Are you lost or something?" one asks, not rudely, but in a genuinely concerned tone.

My cheeks hurt from smiling this wide. "No, of course not! I'm actually looking for Ethan Moore."

Nineteen pairs of eyes gawk at Ethan, wondering how and why a senior girl knows his name. Ethan sits there with a slightly shocked face, but recovers quickly, trying to seem cool for his friends.

"That's me, babe," he says.

I resist the urge to drop the act.

"Could I talk to you for a second?" I ask politely.

"Anything for you, hot stuff."

Seriously dude? *Hot stuff?* The fake smile stays plastered on my face and I wait patiently as he gets up and walks over to me.

Up close I can see that his shoulder-length black hair is slightly greasy, tied back in a little elastic band. He's grinning and his brown eyes are alight with curiosity and boastful pride.

The corner of the room affords us some privacy from his friends, who are still gawking at me. When Ethan reaches me, I open my mouth to talk, but I'm unnerved by their stares. Plus, Ethan keeps looking back at his friends with a that's-right-the-pretty-girl-wants-to-talk-to-*me* kind of gloating face. His whole demeanor comes off way too cocky. I love confidence in a guy, but this is too much. Ethan wears himself like he has to work extra hard to prove that he's confident, instead of just being that way.

When Aiden walks into a room, it's filled with his presence. He naturally commands attention and respect without even having to do anything. Even the way he holds himself radiates confidence, and the way he—wait, since when did I use Aiden as a role model for anything? Why am I even thinking about him? It's definitely the stress messing with me.

Focus, Amelia!

I turn to Ethan's friends, who are blatantly checking me out. "You guys can continue playing your game now. Don't mind us."

Ethan looks at his friends, too, gloating. "Yeah, guys, she's here to talk to me." He looks at me and winks. "Don't worry about them, babe, I'm all yours."

"I don't know if you know me, but my name's Amelia Collins. I'm in that video you posted."

"Oh yeah! I knew you looked familiar! You're awesome! I saw you telling off Aiden too! You totally kick ass!" he exclaims.

I feel my smile become genuine. Maybe this kid isn't bad and this will go pretty smoothly. "Yeah?"

"Totally! We hate Kaitlyn! She deserved what you said to her. Your insults are hilarious too! Did you see how she reacted? I can show you; I got it on video!"

Maybe I was too quick to judge him. Maybe my first impressions of people are off. After all, I thought the Boys were all assholes and they turned out to be my best friends here. As much as I hate to admit it, even Aiden isn't horrible.

"Actually, I did see the video, and that's what I came to talk to you about."

"You want a copy? I can get you a copy!" I guess he dropped his cocky attitude and is now in I'm-trying-to-impress-royalty mode.

"No, the opposite actually."

He freezes, looking confused. "What do you mean?"

"I want you to take the video down and delete it."

He looks at me like I just told him I eat butterflies and he should try some. "Why would I do that?"

"I would just really appreciate it if you could take it down, please. For me?" I beg, trying the cute girl approach as I don't think he'll buy the future-employers-see-this excuse.

"No way in hell! You couldn't pay me enough to take that video down. Kaitlyn makes a complete fool of herself."

"Listen, I know no one likes Kaitlyn—"

"No. I'm not taking that video down." His voice turns hard, no longer happy that I'm talking to him. "She embarrasses herself, and it's hilarious. Plus, I'm getting mad traffic to my Facebook page."

"I'm sure she'll do something even worse. And you'll be there to tape it again. Please? Just take it down." My nice attitude is wearing thin. I thought this would be easy.

He crosses his arms and turns away from me, his cocky attitude back. "No way, sugartits. The video stays."

My nice façade cracks. I'm in his face now, blocking his exit, and putting authority in my voice. "Listen. I need the video off. Now."

"I said no," he says, eyes narrowing.

"And I'm telling you. Take. It. Down."

He pulls out his phone and scrolls through it, stopping at the video and playing it, holding it out for me. "See this? This is hilarious. It's staying."

It takes everything I have to restrain myself from reaching out and twisting his arm to grab the phone from him. I could easily just use my jujitsu on him and forcibly delete the video, but that would draw even more attention to myself. I already have enough attention on me by hanging out with the Boys and being number one on Kaitlyn's To Destroy list.

"It's staying." He puts his phone back in his pocket.

"I need it down."

Don't hit him, don't hit him.

"You want it down badly, huh?"

I nod at him. He gives me a creepy, cocky smile. Looks like try-too-hard-to-be-confident Ethan is back.

"I'll take it down. For a blow job."

Don't break his nose. Don't break his nose.

"Are you serious?"

"One hundred percent. Do that for me and I'll take down the video for you." He gives me a triumphant smile and brushes my hair off my shoulder with grubby fingers, his hand lingering on my shoulder. He actually thinks I'm that desperate. Well, I am desperate, but I'd never sell myself like that.

I can't hold it anymore. Reaching up to the hand he left on my shoulder, I grab his wrist and pull it in front of me, twisting it in the process. He stands up on his tiptoes, trying to lessen the pain I'm causing.

"Listen to me, you little perv." My tone is venomous. "Don't you *ever* try to blackmail a girl into sucking your dick. Don't ever try to blackmail girls, *period*. Treat girls with some respect and maybe you'll find some delusional chick who is willing to be your girlfriend. You don't coerce people into sexual favors." I twist harder, my anger stealing some of my control. "Who do I look like to you? Do I look like the type of person who would sell her dignity? I asked you nicely, now I'm not. Take the video down or I snap your wrist."

His eyes widen a little, considering my threat. He's a gamer. He needs his wrist. Despite the pain I know I'm putting him in, Ethan looks at me defiantly. "Do it and I sue you for all your worth. My dad's a lawyer and I have nineteen witnesses."

The word *lawyer* catches me immediately. There can be no court cases or charges, and we're not alone in the room—there are many, many witnesses. And so I loosen my grip on his wrist a little. Taking a deep breath and noticing the other boys in the room staring with wide-open mouths, I let go of Ethan's wrist completely. He brings it to his chest, rubbing it, his look triumphant. The bell rings, signaling that lunch is over and that we have five minutes to get to class.

"The video stays," he says, walking back to his friends, who start leaving the classroom, still giving me weird looks.

I was right about him being a douche when I first met him. My eyes narrow after the gamers' retreating forms, seeing endless possibilities of how to get Ethan to take the video down, most ending violently. This can't end that way for obvious reasons, so I guess it's time to start scheming.

10

The only thing on my mind when I hit the gym before school is the obnoxious look on Ethan's face from yesterday. Ever since what happened led to us being here in King City, I've been keeping up my workouts. Partly because I can't be caught off guard again, and partly because it makes me feel better to work it all out on the mats.

I take extra care on my makeup and give myself ample time to get to school early once I'm finished.

Last night I packed the most slutty-yet-still-appropriate-for-school outfit I own. It's a tight skirt and a fitted black T-shirt that's low cut and has a zipper down the front. I give myself one last approving look in the gym mirror before I leave for school.

I'm so early that the junior hallway is eerily quiet. I'm trying not to look suspicious standing casually beside the hallway closet. Eventually, a janitor goes in, and when he leaves, I quickly wedge my foot in to stop the door from closing. Taking a casual look around, I pull out a wad of paper and jam it into the side of the lock so it won't activate when the door closes. Still facing the hallway, I close the door to test it, making sure it doesn't lock, and then leave the door closed, ignoring my beating heart.

Now that the hard part is out of the way, I just have to wait. It takes a bit, but eventually I spot Ethan, walking with one of his friends. I note which locker is his, and leave the hallway, hoping that the jam holds throughout the day.

During my morning classes, I'm a little spaced out, still thinking about how that video Ethan posted has been online for a full day now. I haven't even told my mom. I can't risk her reacting and calling in a favor, deciding this is the last straw, and then we're moving again. None of my friends called me out on my vacant attitude until lunch.

Noah waves his hand in front of my face to gain my attention. "Earth to Amelia!"

"Sorry, what?"

"We asked how you did on your calculus test. The one we just got back," Noah says. Everyone's at the table except for Aiden.

"How do you think I did!?" I snap.

They all give me shocked expressions, surprised that I snapped at Noah for asking an innocent question.

I sigh. "I'm sorry, Noah. I'm just really stressed."

"Is this about yesterday?" Charlotte asks hesitantly.

"I guess," I say.

"About Ethan?" Annalisa asks.

They're not stupid. They know I acted all unhinged because of the video; they just don't know why. "I asked him to take it down nicely. He firmly said no. I threatened him; he reminded me that there were witnesses in the room. Long story short, he didn't take the video down."

"This is really bothering you?" Mason asks and I nod, picking at my lunch. "I'll talk to him, then. He'll listen to me. If not, I'll meet him somewhere where there aren't any witnesses."

"Don't worry about it. I got it covered." I smile at Mason, looking into his brown eyes. *I love chocolate.*

"Are you sure? It wouldn't be a problem," Mason insists.

"It's fine, really. Thank you, though." I'm ready to change the subject. "So, who else failed that calculus test?"

✂

It's the end of the day and I'm impatiently waiting for the final bell to ring. I'm sitting beside Mason in sociology class. Anxiously fidgeting in my seat, I'm staring down the clock like if I focused hard enough, I could will time to speed up. When the bell finally rings, I jump up and out of my seat, barely throwing a good-bye over my shoulder to the three boys. Getting to Ethan's locker is the only thing on my mind. I get a few feet down the hall before I feel a presence that's impossible to ignore walking beside me.

"I need to talk to you," Aiden says, his expression giving nothing away.

"Great. Later."

Escaping Aiden, I'm swallowed up by the crowded hallway. Ethan's almost at his locker. Just in time. He spins his lock and enters his combination: 13–35–08. I repeat this sequence multiple times, making sure to memorize it. He opens his locker and puts his laptop on the top shelf, making room for his other textbooks. It's time to make my presence known.

"Hey, Ethan."

He pauses, looking at me with a bored expression. "Oh, it's you again."

Deep breaths. You can do this.

"Listen, I guess we got off on the wrong foot. See, I don't really care about the video, I was just . . . nervous."

"Nervous about what?" he snorts, not really paying attention to me.

I've always been a good liar; I've been doing it for too long. Time to put it to good use. I stand closer to him, leaving about two inches of space between us.

"I don't really care about that video. I needed a reason to talk to you, and the video gave me one."

"What—what do you mean?" He gulps, forgetting about his books and open locker.

"What I mean is that I used the video as an excuse to talk to you. I've always thought,"—*don't puke, Amelia, you've got to sell it*—"that you were the cutest guy in this school. I just never thought you'd talk to me."

Don't puke, don't puke, flirty smile.

His eyes zone in on my girls, which are dangerously close to his chest, and his cocky smile is back. Must . . . resist . . . urge . . . to break his nose. He seems to believe me pretty easily, despite me threatening him yesterday.

"Well, I am pretty hot," he smirks, still not taking his eyes off my boobs.

"The hottest." I trail my hand down the side of his back, sub-consciously restraining myself from jerking away from him. Douche bag. *It's for the greater good, Amelia,* I tell myself.

"What do you say I take you up on that offer?"

His eyes widen. "What?"

I give him a flirty smile. "You heard me. It's after school. I'm guessing you have nowhere to go. I'll do it now."

He doesn't even question my change of attitude, practically fumbling to grab his backpack and put his lock back on, eager to get a blow job.

"Oh my God, oh my God, oh my God, this is actually happening, it's happening," he repeats slowly.

"I know a place; it's private." With a suggestive wink, I walk down the hall and he scrambles to follow me.

We get to the janitor's closet that I scouted this morning. The door opens with ease and I discreetly pull out the wad of paper, trying not to do a giddy happy dance that it held all day. The halls are practically empty by now, everyone wanting to get out of this hellhole as soon as possible.

I take a deep breath. Too late to back out now, Amelia. Trying to keep my racing heart steady, I push open the door.

"I can't believe this. I'm going to get a blow job from a hot senior girl." Ethan walks into the small closet.

Idiot.

With zero hesitation, I swing the door shut, which locks with Ethan still inside. I laugh as I hear Ethan banging on the door from the inside of the closet.

I mean, seriously. I gave him a whole speech yesterday about how I would never do that and how degrading it was to even suggest it. Walking away, I smile to myself in victory, looking down at his phone in my hands. I swiped it when I ran my hand down his back. He was too busy ogling my boobs to even realize I'd taken it.

I may be willing to use what I've got, but I'm not about to sell my soul to the devil.

Back at his locker, I quickly undo the lock. He was so distracted by me that he left his laptop in his locker, exactly what I wanted to happen. Grabbing the computer and turning it on, I slide down the locker to sit on the floor.

Perfect. He doesn't even have a password on his phone or laptop. I snort out loud. He made this so easy for me it almost isn't fun.

Almost.

Quickly scanning his open Facebook, I'm confused when I can't find the video anywhere. It's not on his profile; it's not on his computer's saved files. Why isn't it here?

"You won't find it."

The sound of his voice makes me jump. Caught off guard, I reflexively snap the laptop shut. Aiden's standing over me.

"Huh? Won't find what?"

He sits beside me on the floor and leans against the locker. I hate that I notice how close he is, and how good he smells.

"I got him to take it down and delete it. It's gone."

I drop the innocent act. "It's gone?"

The corner of his lips twitches into a smirk. "If you would've listened to me earlier when I was trying to talk to you, you wouldn't be sitting here right now with a stolen phone and laptop."

"I was going to return them—"

"Where is Ethan anyway? How did you get his stuff?"

"I locked him in the janitor's closet," I say casually, like we're discussing the weather.

Aiden laughs, and I have to force myself not to stare. It's the first time Aiden's genuinely laughed out loud around me. It's nice. He should do it more often.

"Wow," he says. "I can honestly say I didn't see that coming."

Just then, the extent of his words registers with me. "Wait, *you* got him to delete the video?"

He runs his hands through his hair, looking as close to embarrassed as Aiden—with his stoic face—could be. "You freaked out about it, so I figured it was important to you."

He knew how much it really meant to me before everyone else, and helped me without me even having to ask. He wasn't even there at lunch when everyone else realized I was still bothered by the video. I guess he isn't as hard or cold or has a heart made of ice like he wants everyone to think. He actually cares about his friends. Wait, he considers me his friend!

"How'd you get him to take it down? He was a total ass when I asked him."

"I told him that I didn't appreciate my face being on the internet."

My eyes widen. "That's all you said to him?"

"Sometimes, the reputation does all the talking for you," he says darkly.

Wow. I literally twisted Ethan's wrist and he didn't even budge. Aiden gives him a subtle hint and he scrambles to oblige. The curiosity is killing me. I have to ask. "Aren't you going to ask me why I freaked out like that?"

"No. I'll find out eventually. You can count on that." He stands up, brushing off his pants. "You should probably let Ethan out of the janitor's closet now."

With that, he walks down the hall without a good-bye, leaving me to stare at his retreating back. He's guarded and doesn't let a lot of people see who he actually is. He scares people away with his tough, uncaring act. Or maybe it's not an act and that's who he really is. But if he really doesn't care about anyone, like he wants us to think, why go through the effort to get that video deleted for me? I think that his permanent scowl and frosty attitude are defense mechanisms—a way of keeping people at arm's length. For some reason, he doesn't want anyone around him, and doesn't want them to get too close either. Only the Boys, who have practically grown up with him, actually know him, the *true* Aiden—the man behind the impassive, unimpressed mask.

Or I'm just completely overthinking everything and Aiden's just a huge asshole. But one thing I know that's true about Aiden is that he's very perceptive. You think I'm hiding something, Aiden? What are you hiding? I stand up and put the laptop back in the locker. I guess it's time I let Ethan out of the closet.

✘

I needed the video down, and I did what I had to do. I always do what needs to be done, but I do it on my own terms. Ethan screamed bloody murder when I let him out of the janitor's closet, but when I said that I'd tell Aiden if he ever talked to me or bothered me again, he shut up pretty quickly. Dodged another bullet, and again with Aiden's help—it was becoming a bit of a habit, and I wasn't sure at all how I felt about it.

11

It's been a week since I locked Ethan in the janitor's closet and I'm sitting cross-legged on Charlotte's bed, our chemistry and calculus books and notes scattered all around us.

She looks up from her spot on the bed. "Remind me why I want to get into science when I'm older?"

I look at the clock: it's almost midnight. I sigh. "Because you want to better the human race with your knowledge of science and medicine?"

"I'm seriously regretting that decision," she mumbles and flips through her notebook. "It's a Friday night and we're sitting here studying."

"You say that like it's unusual for science students to study on a Friday night."

I received another failed calculus test earlier this week, and we just had a quiz today. I was prepared this time, but I'm positive I flunked it too. Charlotte's in a different calculus class, but it's all the same material, so she's been trying to help me.

So far, we've been studying chemistry and calculus together every day after school until late, and I'm not any closer to understanding this gibberish than I was before. I don't think Charlotte really knows what she's doing either.

"I know, but I just wish our lives were a little more exciting. We could at least do something other than study *one* day out of the week," she complains.

"What? Investigating the qualitative and quantitative nature of chemical systems at equilibrium isn't exciting enough for you?" I tease.

"We could've gone to the movies or something. Even the guys are at that party."

"I know, I can practically hear the music from here."

Some jock from King City High who lives a few streets over from Charlotte was hosting tonight. Mason, Noah, and Chase tried to convince us to go with them, but after the last party I went to, I firmly decided I'd rather study. Charlotte agreed, and Annalisa proclaimed that since we weren't going, she wasn't either—she and Julian went out on a date instead.

When Mason, Noah, and Chase tried to get Aiden to come, he said "Busy," without elaborating, which I totally didn't understand. They do everything together, especially party. It was already bad that Julian wasn't going, but now Aiden wasn't either.

Mason and Noah bugged him to go, but Aiden gave them a stern drop-it look and said, "You know why."

When he did that, their eyes widened in realization, as if Aiden explained everything perfectly with that one look and three words.

"Well, I'm done studying, let's just go to bed. Sleep here tonight?" Charlotte asks me.

She's been inviting me to sleep over every time I'm at her house, and I'm running out of excuses why I can't. I want to sleep at Charlotte's, and my mom probably wouldn't find out if she wasn't home; it's just that I literally *can't* sleep at Charlotte's. My pills are in my nightstand back at my house, and without them, I won't be getting any sleep.

"Sorry, Char, my mom's expecting me to be home." My mom's on an overnight flight; she wouldn't even know if I went home or not.

I feel bad lying to Charlotte, but I don't want her to know that I need pills to get to sleep. Even with the pills, I don't do much sleeping. She'd think I was weird if I couldn't sleep, so I got out of bed and started working out at 4:30 a.m.

She frowns at me. "Are you sure? I don't snore or anything."

I laugh at her as I pack up my stuff. "I don't doubt that, I just need to get home," I say. "I'm not the greatest sleeper."

After I reassure Charlotte that I have to go home multiple times, she finally allows me to head downstairs. Her older brother is at a party and her parents are at some fundraiser, so we don't bother trying to be quiet as we head downstairs.

At the door, we talk a little more while I put my shoes on. As I reach for the doorknob, the doorbell rings. My hand freezes on the handle, and Charlotte and I look at each other.

"Are you expecting someone?" I whisper.

Charlotte shakes her head. The two of us stare at the big wooden door that separates us from whatever is on the other side of it. "It's past midnight. My brother's crashing at his friend's house and my parents wouldn't ring the doorbell."

The doorbell rings three more times. We take a step back from the door and stare at it, unsure about what to do.

Then, "Charlie! It's me! Open the door!"

Thank goodness: Chase. Charlotte opens the door quickly and he stumbles in. "*Charlie!* Amelia? What're you doing here?"

He slurs his words so much that we can barely understand them. He's disheveled, and sways back and forth in the doorway.

"How drunk are you?" Charlotte moves to catch him as he stumbles again.

"What? Me? I only had a little," he slurs, hiccupping at the end. "Okay-y-y. I might've drank a teensy bit too much."

"Damn it, Chase. I told you not to mix energy drinks and alcohol! It makes you think you can keep drinking and then you get drunker than ever." Charlotte scolds him as he leans on the wall, free of her support.

"You're right, Charlie. You're alwayyyss right. That's one of the things that makes you so great," he slurs, and looks at her with unfocused eyes.

"How did you get here?" I look outside. "You didn't drive did you? Or get in the car with someone drunk?"

A lazy smile spreads over Chase's face and his eyelids droop. "I walked! The party's, like, right over there." He makes a noncommittal hand gesture. "I may be drunk, but I know drinking and driving's a big no-no. Ha-ha. Nonno. I sound Italian. That's how they say grandpa, right? Noo-noo."

"Yes, Chase. Italians call their grandfathers *nonno*," Charlotte says slowly, like she's speaking to a child.

Chase laughs. "Even when I'm drunk I'm still smart! But not as smart as you, Charlie. You're the smartest person I've ever known. And prettiest. You've got the nicest smile I've ever seen. And you smell so pretty! Like vanilla and strawberries."

Charlotte gives Chase a confused look while he's talking, and I try to change the topic before he says something he regrets. "Why did you come here, Chase?"

"Weeeelllll, a bunch of Silvers crashed the partayyy—"

"*What*! Where are Mason and Noah?" I interrupt him, worried for my friends and thinking about the last time the Kings and Silvers clashed.

"Relaaxx," he slurs. "Nason and Moah are fine. The crashers were cool. The Silvers that we all hate are at the Tra—oops." He stops himself before he finishes.

"Where are the bad Silvers, Chase?" I ask him, not even sure if he's a reliable source since he got Mason's and Noah's names mixed up.

"I . . . I . . . what do I know? I'm drunk? Remember? Maybe you're the drunk one!" He laughs.

"What do the Silvers crashing the party have to do with you coming here?" Charlotte tries to bring him back on track.

"Oh yeah! Anywayy. These Silvers are cool, ya know? Like, they're just chill. But they brought their girlfriends with them. And I was lookin' around and thought, wow, ever'one has a girlfriend. Even Noah was hooking up with some chick and Mason was talking to some girl."

A little pit of jealousy rises in my stomach when he says Mason's with a girl. I don't know why, but I feel it. I know we're just friends. That we'll only ever be just friends, but the attention I get from Mason is nice; it makes me feel *normal*.

Chase continues, looking at Charlotte. "And I thought, they all look so happy. I could be happy if I just grew some balls and said how I really felt. I'm soo stupid for not telling you that I—"

"*Chase!*" I interrupt him, seeing how close he is to making a mistake that he'll regret in the morning, "I'm leaving now, anyway. How about I drive you home?"

I don't give him the option as I throw his arm over my shoulder and start walking him away from the door. He's so drunk he just goes along with it.

"Bye, Char," I say quickly. "Call you tomorrow."

We're at my car and I'm half shoving Chase into it when he notices where he is. "But, I can't go yet, Amelia. I finally decided I'd man up and tell Charlie that I love her."

Charlotte has already closed the front door. "I know you do, Chase, but you might want to think this through when you're sober."

How Chase feels about Charlotte is pretty noticeable if you look hard enough. He's always sitting beside her, teasing her about her name, and making sure she's okay. The one missing piece to the puzzle is how she feels about him. We've never talked about it, and so it makes sense to me that Chase should think it through, especially if he's about to announce to his best friend since childhood that he's in love with her when he's decidedly less than sober.

I deposit Chase in the passenger seat and jog around to the driver's side. "If you puke in my car, you're dead." I start the car and pull out of the driveway.

"I have thought it through. Not the puking. About telling her. All those couples are sooo happy. I wanna be happy. Charlie makes me feel that way and I wanna be with her."

"Chase, even if you did decide to tell her, you shouldn't do it while you're drunk." I sigh. "I'll just get you home and if you still want to tell her, you can do it tomorrow."

"I can't go home. I told my parents we weren't drinking since last time Noah got a concussion."

"Okay, then where were you supposed to stay?" I'm not patient enough to deal with a smashed Chase. "Where—"

I look over at the passenger seat to find Chase already passed out. "Ughh, why me?" I complain out loud to myself.

Pulling over, I grab my phone to call one of the Boys so I can drop Chase off at their house. Mason and Noah are probably still at the party—they don't answer my calls. Julian's phone is off, and Aiden's rang once then went straight to voice mail. Jerk. I call again, and this time it skips the ring entirely and goes into voice mail, meaning he turned his phone off. I guess I'm taking Chase to my house.

Once we pull into my driveway, I turn off the car and turn to look at my new predicament.

"Chase?" I shove him, and nothing. "*Chase!*" I shove him again, and again, and the boy barely even moves.

Fantastic. How am I supposed to get this giant, sleeping man into my house? Maybe I should just let him sleep it off in my car? But what if he pukes? I don't need my car to smell like vomit and regret. Getting out and rounding the car to his side, I open the door and take off his seat belt.

"Chase?" I try one last time, and his head lolls to the side as I shake him.

Pinching the bridge of my nose, I sigh in frustration. Looks like I'm putting that gym membership to good use. Reaching into the car, I put my hands under his arms and after several unsuccessful attempts, I manage to pull him out and lean him against the car.

"*Chase!*" I practically yell into his ear.

He murmurs something and slumps on the roof of my car. Standing behind him, I wrap my arms around his back and link my hands together across his chest, under his arms. When I move him away from the car, the sudden force of his full weight causes me to stumble, and the two of us practically slam into a tree, Chase taking the brunt of it.

"Sorry!" I automatically say even though he can't hear me. He'll definitely feel that later.

I manage to lead us to the front steps, his body leaning against me and his feet dragging on the ground. By the time we're leaned against the railing, I'm sweating and huffing from the effort. The boy is *heavy*. One step at a time, I pull him up the porch steps, his legs banging into each step as we go. I'm so lucky my mom isn't home right now or I'd be in a heaping pile of trouble.

I set him down rather roughly when we reach the top step, leaning his upper body against the wall. "Sorry," I mutter again, my arms practically shaking from exertion.

Of course my key's at the bottom of my purse, and after getting the door open, I can't even manage to pick Chase up. Grabbing him under his arms, I drag him into my house. I make sure to set his head down gently once we're inside, and close the door.

Kicking off my shoes and throwing my purse down, I catch my breath and study Chase, contemplating my options. He's inside, which was a mission in and of itself, but what now? Should I leave him here? Should I try to get him onto the couch? A phone beeps and I realize that it's Chase's. I dig in his pockets and see that it's the sixth message from his mom.

Well, that's not good.

I use his thumbprint to unlock his phone and quickly scan her messages. They're all along the lines of *Are you boys having fun? Are you sleeping over or coming home? Your phone better be dead cause you better not be ignoring me!*

I glance at Chase, who rolls onto his side, trying to get comfortable on my cold floor.

Sorry, Mom, my phone was charging, I text back to her. *Sleeping over tnght. Talk tmrw.*

I send the message and slip Chase's phone in my pocket. I feel a bit bad lying to Chase's mom, but I don't want to get him in trouble.

I glance at his face and know that I can't leave him on the floor, even though my whole body is tired from carrying him in here. Sitting him up, I half carry, half drag him into the living room and prop his upper body on the couch, then his lower body, and eventually, I get him onto the couch and into recovery position. I leave a lamp on for him and place his phone on the side table by his head, as well as a bucket on the floor in front of his head, just in case.

✘

"Urggghhhhh."

The sunlight is streaming through the kitchen window when I hear Chase wake up. I walk into the living room and hand him a glass of water and some aspirin. He takes it and sits up from where he slept on my couch last night.

"I feel like crap," he complains while swallowing the aspirin.

"It's called a hangover." I sit down on the other side of the couch, facing him and crossing my legs.

"How did I get here?" He looks around. "And why am I all sore?"

"You passed out in my car before telling me where you live. None of the guys answered their phones, and Aiden sent me to voice mail, so I brought you here. And you're sore because I may or may not have dropped you a couple of times trying to get you inside."

He gives me an accusing look.

"What? You're twice my size!" I defend myself.

"But I wasn't with you last night?" He rubs his face.

"You don't remember showing up at Charlotte's just after midnight and proclaiming your love to her?"

He straightens up at that, suddenly very alert. "*I did what?* I'm such an idiot. What did she say? Did I ruin everything? I wasn't supposed to tell her. Damn, I'm such a fuc—"

"Relax," I cut him off. "I stopped you before you spilled your guts. You were close though."

"Oh thank God." The tenseness in his shoulders reduces slightly.

His eyes are blank as I recount everything that happened last night from the moment he banged on Charlotte's front door.

"How did you know I was going to tell her how I felt?" he asks.

"I know how you feel about Char. I'm good at noticing things like that."

He sighs and runs his hands through his hair. "No one's ever noticed before—well, except Aiden."

That didn't surprise me one bit.

"Thanks for stopping me before I did anything stupid—well, more stupid than what I normally do when drunk."

"Why haven't you just told her how you feel?"

"I can't do that. Charlie and I have been best friends since she moved here in second grade. She was this cute little girl with pigtails and sparkly pink running shoes. This bully pushed her down during recess, shouting that she had cooties. She was crying when he left her on the ground, and I felt really bad. So I went up to her and told her that I didn't think she had cooties."

He laughs out loud. "She gave me this look. You know, the Charlotte look? The look like 'Well, duh, idiot.' And then she lisped through her missing teeth, 'Well, obviously I don't have cooties.'"

I laugh at his seven-year-old Charlotte imitation, but don't interrupt his story.

"I asked her why she was crying. She told me it was because there was mud all over her favorite shirt now." He shakes his head, still smiling. "It was this pink sparkly shirt that matched her sneakers. At the time, I thought the kid did her a favor, but I didn't tell her as much. She was still sitting there in the mud, crying. You know Charlie, always has been nonconfrontational, quiet, never stands up for herself."

Chase frowns at thought.

"So I offered her the spare shirt that my mom put in my cubby in case I ruined the one I was wearing. It was this blue shirt with dinosaurs on the front, and would've been too big for her. I promised her I didn't have cooties, either, so she could wear it. That way, she wouldn't have mud on her all day."

"Aw, how romantic, Chase," I gush, picturing seven-year-old Chase coming to Charlotte's rescue.

He laughs. "I was always a hit with the ladies. She changed into my shirt and it was too big for her, but I still thought she was beautiful. The mean kid saw her wearing my shirt and pushed her down again, said that she was giving my shirt her cooties. So I beat him up."

I laugh, fake gasping. "Chase! You beat up a seven-year-old?"

"It was a fair fight! I was seven too!" He chuckles. "Charlie and I have been best friends since then. I guess I should thank that kid. Because he had this irrational fear of cooties, he brought me closer to the girl I love."

That's so cute. I wish I had someone who loves me like Chase loves Charlotte. He still remembers the day they met, down to the detail of her missing teeth and shoe color. "I thought you went to elementary school with the Boys?"

"No, Charlie and I went to one school, Julian and Aiden went to another, and Mason and Noah went to another. In grade six, our schools started having meets for sports and stuff, and we all met at a basketball tournament. We became friends and hung out outside of school. Charlie never liked them, and honestly, she never hung out with all of us until you came along and made her sit with us at lunch."

"I think she likes them now. She even told me that Aiden isn't that bad."

"He isn't; he just has his own stuff going on that he deals with. He's a really tough guy, and doesn't let people in."

"Where was he last night? Why couldn't he go to the party?" It better be somewhere important if he sent me to voice mail during an emergency. I had his passed-out best friend in my car. And he was the one who put his contact info in my phone in the first place.

"What? How would I know?" The guilty look Chase is trying to hide says otherwise. "Anyway, where was I in the story? Oh yeah, so we all went to grade nine and started at the same high school, and we were happy because we could see each other at school, too, instead of just after and on the weekends. In the middle of freshman year, Aiden casually brought up how I loved Charlotte, and I couldn't believe how he noticed. None of the other guys noticed and I don't think I made it that obvious."

Aiden's observant like that, noticing *everything*.

"He said he wouldn't say anything and here we are four years later, with Charlie and everyone else still oblivious to how I feel."

"Why haven't you told her?"

He shakes his head and looks down at the glass of water in his hands. "I can't do that. She won't feel the same way and it'll crush me, hearing out loud how I'll never be with her."

My heart aches for Chase. I wish I could reassure him that Charlotte feels the same way as him, but I can't.

"I always try to put on this player image in front of her to try to make her jealous, which clearly hasn't worked. I try to go out with other girls to move on from her, but that doesn't work either. None of those girls are Charlotte." He laughs a sad laugh. "I've known the girl of my dreams for a decade, and I can't even be with her!"

This whole comforting-people-in-love thing is foreign to me. "I don't know how Char feels about you, but I know she really cares about you. Maybe someday it'll grow into something bigger—maybe she already feels that way about you. You'll never know unless you tell her how you feel."

His eyes widen and he shakes his head frantically. "No, no, no. I can't do that. And you can't either! Please don't tell her!"

"Hey, I already knew and haven't said anything." I calm him down. "I won't say anything, but this is going to eat you alive. You almost confessed everything to her in a drunken stupor in the middle of the night!"

"I'll be more careful, I promise. She just can't know. She'll reject me and we'll be all awkward." He frowns again and looks back at the glass in his hands. "I'd rather have her as a friend and silently love her than tell her and lose her forever."

12

Chase and I spend Saturday together, hanging out and lazing around my house.

My mom comes home not long after Chase wakes up, but she doesn't really say anything. It's practically lunchtime and we'd cleaned up so it didn't look like Chase slept here. She makes some small talk before going up to bed since she just got off work, but I don't miss her giving Chase the I'm-watching-you glare.

When he leaves later that night, my mom comes down and gives me "the talk."

"I know I'm not home all that often, Amelia," she says. "But I have to be able to trust you."

"You can trust me," I argue.

"I'm not so sure—parties and staying out late studying. It all seems awfully like your life before we were in King City." She looks at me, her eyes hard. "I can't move again. I can't go through it one more time."

"I'm being careful," I say. "I am, honestly, but being a normal kid is also a way of blending in. It'd be just as weird if I hid in the corner and didn't talk to anyone."

Our version of the talk has nothing to do with sex and everything to do with my mom blaming me for the state of our lives. She leans into this argument every time she sees that I'm getting close to someone in a new town. Chase is technically the first guy friend that she's met since we moved here, so I guess she feels like she has to say it again, but alter it to be more suitable for boys.

"On your best behavior, no screwups, no secret talks, let nobody in—you are Amelia Collins, you can't forget it."

It's the same speech, over and over again.

"Part of me realizes that you can't not be who you are, so I'm glad you're having fun, enjoying your life, but—"

"I know, Mom, I know. I can't get close to anyone. I *know.*"

My mom's face has aged disproportionately to her age—the strain of the last year or so weighing on her, causing crow's feet to appear next to her eyes, and the bags under her eyes never seem to go away. Seeing her like this makes me feel awful, and as she goes on about how I can't trust Chase even if he's just a friend, even if he's got the face of an angel and the body of a Calvin Klein model—he's not her, and she's the only one I can really trust.

Deep down she misses the house I grew up in—she misses my dad, our old routine, the familiar grocery store we could walk to, the school that was just behind our house, the ease of our everyday life. So she's away as much as possible these days: more overtime, longer flights, farther-away destinations. And lately, I've noticed her getting into a car with some guy in the driver's seat. Maybe she's dating? Either way, she's spending less and less time at home.

I always feel tense after our "talks." I hate that my mom feels like she needs to remind me to stay away from people. I hate how I know I'll never be able to be close to someone like Annalisa is with Julian. So, usually, I go to the gym to blow off some steam.

After hitting the punching bag aimlessly for a while I feel a bit better. I take a drink, then steady the bag and punch with all my might.

I hate him.

I always pretend the bag is the same person. The one responsible for everything.

I take a punch, the lifeless bag taking shape into *him*.

He ruined everything.

I punch.

I hate that I can't be close to people.

I punch.

I hate that I can't be my true self. That I can't get in the pictures with Charlotte and Annalisa. I hate that I can never just let someone *in*. I hit the bag with all I have until I'm standing there heaving, all my energy wiped, tears threatening to escape from my tired eyes.

As I'm leaving, I recognize another person at one of the punching bags, hitting with abandon. I see a part of myself in her. Her technique isn't very good, but she's here out of anger and frustration, not to practice her form.

When she takes a swig of her water, I tap her on the shoulder. "Amelia?" Annalisa's dark eyebrows draw together in confusion.

"Hey. I didn't know you came here."

"Yeah, sometimes." She shrugs. "It's a good way to blow off some steam, you know?"

"I know exactly what you mean." I laugh dryly.

She adds a few more punches, the chains holding the bag squeaking as her final hit sends the heavy bag flying.

"So, who pissed you off?" I ask her, half as a joke, and half genuinely wanting to know.

She wipes the sweat off her forehead and turns to face me with a haunted look in her eye. "Someone I thought was my brother, but who ended up ruining my life."

She readies her stance and starts hitting the bag again. I get the hint that she wants to be alone right now and leave her be, her words replaying in my mind.

✕

When we get back our calculus quizzes from Friday, I'm not even surprised when I see my failing grade.

What else is new? This is the second calculus test I've bombed since I started at King.

I just don't get it. And I can't pay attention to Mr. Fidiott when he teaches for the life of me. Honestly, if he put the lesson on that clock at the front of the room, I'd probably learn something. I spend all my time staring at it.

With seven minutes and thirty-four seconds left of class, everyone packs their bags.

Mr. Fidiott turns to the class. "Okay, I'll let you out of class now since it's is almost over anyway."

The class is filled with different choruses of excited yeses, and I'm not ashamed to admit that I might have been the loudest one. Mr. Fidiott is so cool, letting us out of this hell six minutes and fifty-two seconds early.

"Except you, Amelia. May I speak with you?"

I take that back. Mr. Fidiott is not cool. He's a dream stomper. He just stomped all over my dreams of escaping this hellhole.

The class is filled with immature oohs, and it's unfair that I have to stay while the rest of the class gets freedom.

"Amelia," he says as I walk up to his desk, "this is the second test you failed in my class. The other quizzes you just barely scraped by."

"I know. I've been working really hard trying to get my grades up. I study with my friend practically every night!"

"You need this credit to graduate," he says, deadpan.

"I'll get the credit, I'm working really hard."

"I don't want you to fail, Amelia. That's why I asked one of my best students to tutor you."

"I don't need a tutor! Charlotte is helping me!"

"Charlotte needs to focus on trying to raise her own grade, never mind helping a failing student."

"Who agreed to tutor me?" I ask hesitantly.

His next words shock me so intensely that I might've been electrocuted. "Aiden Parker."

"What?"

"Aiden will be helping you. Talk to him about the times you can get together. And I expect your grades to improve significantly."

"But what does Aiden know about calculus?!" I vaguely remember getting a glimpse of his calculus test one time when he handed it in. It was full of confident answers.

"Aiden is among the top students in the senior class in many subjects. He has first choice of most colleges. I can't think of anyone better to tutor you."

I knew Aiden was smart, but I didn't know he was *that* smart.

Maybe he doesn't want people to know that he's smart because it'll ruin his badass reputation? I mean, he intimidated Ethan with just a sentence, and people practically jump out of his way in the hallway. If there was a pebble in his path that he couldn't be bothered to walk around, it would grow legs and move out of his way with just a menacing glare.

"Can't we get one of the *other* top students in the school to help me?" I protest.

Mr. Fidiott gives me an amused look. "You must think you actually have a choice in the matter. I've already asked Aiden to help you and he's agreed. He helps you, or you fail calculus and don't graduate. It's quite simple."

The bell rings, indicating that second period is over and that we have five minutes to get to third. Mr. Fidiott gets up to erase the board. "You should agree on times as soon as possible." He pauses. "And *that* was the bell, get to class."

That's him telling me "that's final," and kicking me out of his class.

I sigh and leave the room grumbling. What does Mr. Fidiott know anyway? His name literally has the word *idiot* in it.

Why he thinks I'd benefit from Aiden tutoring me is beyond me.

Even so, why would Aiden agree to tutor me? Why would he show me this little-known fact about him—that he's actually a genius? We've established that we don't hate each other, and I've taken his actions to mean that he considers me his friend, but that doesn't mean he would willingly volunteer to spend extra time with me alone. I don't think he's that worried about me failing calculus and thus not graduating.

This is bull. Aiden can barely speak to me like a normal human being, how is he supposed to teach me to understand calculus? He'll probably get mad at me for not getting one of the theories, I'll say something snarky, and the cops will be called by my neighbors to investigate all the yelling.

At lunch, I sit down right beside the Student of the Year

instead of in my usual seat. "What the hell, Aiden?" I don't care that I interrupted Mason in the middle of his monologue about some football game.

"I guess you didn't enjoy your conversation with Mr. Fidiott?" Aiden says.

"What conversation?" Annalisa asks as she sits down, Julian and Noah behind her.

"Our calculus teacher told me that I need a tutor to raise my mark. If I don't pass, I don't graduate. He's making Aiden tutor me," I explain grudgingly.

None of the others except Charlotte seem surprised that Aiden is smart enough to tutor me. I guess being as close as brothers for years now, they'd know that Aiden is a genius.

"What the hell, man?!" Noah exclaims. "I ask you to help me with math all the time and you never do!"

"That's because you're helpless," Mason snorts a laugh. "Plus, he got that hot girl from fifth period to help you instead."

"I'm sure you enjoyed her company more than you would've enjoyed mine," Aiden adds, still looking bored, but slightly more amused.

"Oh yeah! Monica was great. We didn't do much studying though." Noah smirks.

"*Anyway*." I bring them back to the subject at hand. "Why would you even let yourself get roped into helping me? You don't strike me as the tutor type."

"Far from it," Julian adds under his breath.

Aiden throws a glare at him, and Julian unaffectedly adds, "What? It's true."

Aiden looks back at me with a neutral expression. "What? A friend can't help another friend out?"

What? Did he—? Did I just—?

"So you consider me your friend?"

My voice sounds more tentative than I hoped. Aiden's piercing gray eyes lock on mine, the intensity of his gaze making my heart speed up slightly. With his eyes holding mine hostage, he says in his steady, deep voice, "I don't volunteer to give up my time for just anyone."

I've stopped breathing. Unable to take the intensity of his gaze anymore, I look away, praying that I'm not blushing.

"Oh." I curse myself for being unable to think of anything else to say.

The conversation veers back to Mason's rant on football, and I sit there quietly, thinking about Aiden's words. Beside me, I feel Aiden lean over, his face dangerously close to my ear. I feel his hot breath when he says in a low voice, "Plus, I still have to figure out what it is that you're hiding."

I turn my head to watch him lean back in his seat, a neutral expression on his face, like he never said anything. My eyes narrow at him while he takes a swig of his soda. No way in hell will I let Aiden crack me.

✖

The day flies by pretty fast after that since my mind is occupied with the whole calculus tutor thing. Maybe Aiden tutoring me won't be that bad. Lord knows I need all the help I can get.

Shutting my locker and then shoving my way through the body of students, I'm hoping to catch Aiden before he leaves. Out of the front doors, and scanning the parking lot, I'm relieved he's still here, standing beside his black Dodge Challenger. He's talking to Mason and Julian, who are parked on either side of him.

"Aiden!"

I crane my neck up as I reach the three towering frames. Mason beams and Julian smiles as well. Aiden crosses his arms, eyes scanning the parking lot with his signature scowl before his eyes meet mine.

Seeing him now—his tall, muscular frame in front of his awesome car, his muscles straining as he crosses his arms over his chest, a scowl on his face—it's easy to see why he's so intimidating. I suddenly remember the Aiden who fought off all those linebackers at Noah's party by himself; the Aiden who can intimidate anyone with just a hardened glare. I blush as I remember that he did both of those things for me.

"We didn't decide on when you can tutor me. We have a test next week." I look him squarely in his steely eyes.

"I'll be at your house tomorrow at seven." He moves toward the driver's side of his car.

My mom is leaving tomorrow afternoon for work, so we'll have the whole house to ourselves. For some reason, the thought of Aiden at my house, the two of us alone, makes the butterflies start up in my stomach. It's then that I remember he wants to find out what I'm hiding. He's been to my house before, but never inside it. This is a perfect opportunity to get a better glimpse into my life.

"Why don't I come to your house? Or, like, the library or something?"

He turns back to me and says, "Your house. Seven."

"Is he ever—" I'm cut off from insulting Aiden's stubbornness when a loud engine, getting louder as it nears, roars by.

Mason and Julian both stiffen, looking around the parking lot for the source of the engine. The sound calls Aiden back to us, muscles tense and a murderous expression on his face. The red Mustang that Kaitlyn's been getting rides in pulls up and stops right in front of us. The driver turns off the engine and a guy gets out of the car.

He's tall, but not as tall as Aiden's six foot three. The sides of his blond hair are shaved but the top is long, pulled back into a short ponytail. He's also pretty toned, and I'll admit that he's hot, except for that malicious gleam in his hostile brown eyes.

He slams his door shut and walks toward us, a vicious grin on his face. Aiden immediately steps forward, pushing me behind him. He firmly stands his ground, arms crossed, muscles tensing for a fight. Mason and Julian take position on either side of him, mirroring his stance.

I shift over a little so that I can see the guy from behind Aiden.

"Ryan," Aiden growls.

So *this* is Ryan, the infamous Silver who has a rivalry with Aiden. His smirk sends shivers down my spine. "Relax, boys. I'm not here for a fight. Yet . . ."

"We'll kick your ass as usual, Simms," Julian replies.

"Baby!" Kaitlyn throws her arms around Ryan, kissing him before looking back at us, still hanging onto him. "Oh, Aiden. Play nice with my new boyfriend," she sneers.

Pfft, I doubt she even likes Ryan. All eyes turn to me as I realize that I scoffed out loud. "This the slut who ruined your car?" he asks Kaitlyn, keeping his gaze locked on me.

"That's her," she snarls, her eyes alight with victory.

Aiden steps closer to Ryan, blocking his view of me. "I suggest you just get out of here, Simms."

Ryan gestures for Kaitlyn to get in the car, and she walks around to the passenger-side door. "I suggest you keep a watch on that bitch of yours, Parker." Ryan leans over to look at me again. "Be a shame if something happened to her."

Who does this asshole think he is, threatening me? I'm about to push Aiden out of the way so that I can insult this guy myself, but suddenly time seems to slow down and everything happens in slow motion.

Not even a moment after Ryan stops talking, Aiden draws his arm back. In less than a split second, I remember something Noah said a long time ago, the day I came back to school after my time off at the hospital. He said that Aiden can't get suspended again. Knocking a guy unconscious on school property would do more than get Aiden suspended. I grab his bicep and swing around him so I'm in front of him. I slide my hands down from his bicep to his chest, trying unsuccessfully to push him back slightly as I look up into his blazing eyes. His gaze meets mine, and his eyebrows draw together as if wondering what the hell I'm doing.

"You'll get suspended," I warn him.

He studies me for a few seconds before dropping his arm and looking back at Ryan, whose eyes are wide with the realization that he was seconds away from being a bloody mess.

Yeah, bitch. Aiden almost broke your face.

"Leave. Now," Aiden barks.

Kaitlyn gets in the car and Ryan takes a few steps backward to his car door, eyes locked in a stare-off with Aiden.

"This isn't over, Parker," Ryan threatens.

"I'm counting on it."

If I wasn't friends with Aiden, I would've been seriously afraid of him. I don't know how Ryan is openly challenging him without shitting his pants. He gets in his car, and we watch as he obnoxiously speeds out of the parking lot. Only when Ryan's car is out of sight do I look back at Aiden, and belatedly realize that my hands are still placed on his toned chest. Taking a step back, I awkwardly drop them.

"I hate that guy," Mason grumbles.

"Who is he exactly?" I ask.

I'm not given an answer. Instead, I get an accusatory glare from Aiden. "What were you thinking? I could've hit you!" he growls loudly.

"But you didn't."

"But I *could've*!"

I step a little closer to him and crane my neck so that I can look him directly in his agitated gray eyes, trying to communicate my trust in him. "But you didn't."

"I can't believe this is the second time I'm telling you not to get in the middle of a fight," he says.

"I jumped in for *you*, Aiden," I say, hoping my cheeks don't look as warm as they feel. "Look around—there are students and teachers everywhere."

My words register when he looks directly at one of the vice principals, getting into her car a few rows away from where we're standing. He looks back down at me, an unknown emotion running through his eyes. "It would've been worth it."

"You'll get another chance," Julian cuts in.

I'm brought out of my little Aiden bubble by the sound of Julian's voice, and step back from Aiden for the second time in the last five minutes.

"Will someone tell me who he is now?" I ask.

"Ryan Simms. He's a Silver, and someone you don't want to get involved with," Mason says.

"Please. If Kaitlyn's got her grubby little hands all over him, I don't want anything to do with him."

"She called him her boyfriend. She sure moves on fast," Mason jokes.

"It makes logical sense. She feels rejected by Aiden, so naturally she'll move on to the guy who hates him as much as she does," I explain, pieces clicking together as I speak.

"They're perfect for each other, then," Julian adds.

"Are you going to tell me why you hate that guy or . . . ?"

"It doesn't matter, just stay away from him," Aiden says, his impassive face back, but still looking annoyed from the encounter. He walks back over to the driver's side of his car. "Go home and study, Amelia."

He gets into his car and the loud engine comes to life, then he pulls out of the parking lot and disappears down the road.

"Did he seriously just leave without telling me who that guy is? He threatened me!" I explain to Mason and Julian.

Mason gives me an exhausted smile. "Come on, k-bear, I'll walk you to your car."

We say good-bye to Julian and head to the other side of the parking lot.

"Mason, seriously. Ryan threatened me. I think I have the right to know why you guys hate him."

He sighs. "He and Aiden go way back. They've always hated each other."

I'm about to open my mouth to ask why, but Mason cuts me off. "I can't tell you why, just trust me when I say that he's the biggest asshole on the planet, and that you're better off not knowing him."

We get to my car, but I don't make a move to get in. "Is he going to be a problem?"

Mason gives a humorless laugh. "He's always a problem."

"Kaitlyn's up to something. She hasn't done anything since she 'broke up' with Aiden, and now she's with his enemy?"

"Nothing's going to happen to you, k-bear. I'll make sure of it." The strength and determination with which Mason makes that statement makes me blush.

"I'm not worried about Kaitlyn. I can handle myself, remember?"

I've been up against worse than Kaitlyn's petty pranks and harassment. Besides, if it comes down to a fistfight, I'm sure I can take her.

"I believe you, k-bear." He gives me a charming smile but it doesn't quite reach his eyes.

13

It's close to seven, and I fidget with my sweater, nervous about Aiden's arrival. Should I have changed? Cleaned up a bit? What's he going to think about my house? Wait, why do I care?

Five minutes before seven, the doorbell rings, and when I open the door he's there, looking as handsome as ever.

"Hey," I say as Aiden steps inside.

"You ready to learn?" he says as he kicks off his shoes.

"That depends. Are you ready to actually teach?" *And not be an asshole* is what I don't add.

He shoots me a smirk and follows me into the house, setting his stuff down on the kitchen table. Before I can wonder if Aiden is going to take this seriously, he gets right into it, pulling up a common problem and explaining how to solve it. I have to resist the urge to do a double take. He explains the problem patiently and calmly, nothing like the Aiden I'm used to.

I follow his steps like they're a map to a hidden treasure chest, but every time I try, I still don't get the answer at the back of the book.

"Aiden! I did exactly what you told me and it's not the answer!" I shove my calculator in his face, showing him the wrong answer. "I knew it! I knew you were just screwing with me! Are you even going to help me or do you get your kicks watching me fail? This is such a waste of time—you're not even taking it seriously!"

He calmly looks at my calculator screen, then at me, his face blank of emotion.

"Amelia," he says, "your calculator is in the wrong mode."

"What?" I'm sure the color drains from my face as I look back at my calculator, and what do you know? It's in the wrong mode.

I expect some sarcastic comment or asshole remark from him, but he doesn't even mention it. He simply outlines the steps I should follow again.

"But—but this actually makes sense!"

Aiden leans back in his seat and crosses his arms, a triumphant smirk on his face. "That's because it's easy."

"But I got a question similar to this wrong on the test."

"You never had me helping you before."

I actually laugh. What do you know? Aiden's actually a very good tutor. He's patient and understanding and nothing like the asshole I've come to know. I even ordered us a pizza around the hour mark and we ate like we were long-time friends. About three hours after that first embarrassing outburst, I actually understand the last few lessons from class over the past couple of weeks.

Now, just past ten thirty, we decide to call it a night.

"Thanks for this. And sorry for yelling at you." I stand up and start clearing the pizza box.

He stands up with me and grabs the discarded plates. "You're improving."

"You're surprisingly really helpful." I smile. "I never thought that you of all people would be able to help me."

He leans against the counter, his muscles straining as he crosses his arms across his chest. "What? You didn't think I was smart enough?"

"No, it's not that. Well, maybe. Mostly I didn't think you'd be patient enough. But I guess I am kind of surprised that you're actually a genius. Not because you don't look smart, just that you have that I-don't-care-about-anything-now-get-out-of-my-face kind of vibe," I rant, letting the worlds spill out of my mouth before I have the chance to realize what I'm saying.

Instead of being offended by what I said, Aiden just looks at me seriously. "Having good grades is the only thing that'll help get me out of this hellhole."

"Oh." I never stopped to consider Aiden's home life. He drives a pretty expensive car, but he's never talked about his family. Then again, neither have I.

He straightens up and grabs his bag from the floor. "I should get going. When are your parents getting back home?"

"My mom will probably be home sometime tomorrow afternoon."

He raises an eyebrow a fraction, enough to let me know that he realizes I didn't mention my father. He doesn't say anything about it though. "You're here alone tonight?"

I tuck my hair behind my ear, feeling a little vulnerable. "Yeah, I usually am."

"That explains the baseball bat."

"Oh yeah. I hoped you'd forgotten about that." I blush.

"You'll be okay here by yourself?"

"Is someone concerned?" I joke, trying not to think too hard about if that means Aiden actually cares about me.

"You said your mom's rarely home. Where's your dad?" he asks.

Of course he'd ask. I left a loose string when I didn't mention my dad, and Aiden's going to pull at each one until he unravels the secrets of my life.

I don't know if it's the progress we made today as friends, or his openness with me when he said he wanted to get out of this town, or maybe it's the fact that I know he doesn't apologize for anything, but something compelled me to tell him the truth.

"Dead."

I guess that was one of his theories because he doesn't look that surprised. He surprises me, however, when he replies solemnly, "My mom too."

I figured he wouldn't appreciate an apology, so I didn't give him one. I'm just surprised he's being open with me. Aiden's the poster child for closed-off, impassive expressions, and I can't believe he's letting me into his life.

"When?"

"When I was ten. Cancer. You?"

"Just over a year ago. Drunk driver." I look away.

He's silent for a moment, then, "Did they catch the guy?"

Again, I don't know what's compelling me to be so open and honest with Aiden tonight, but it still doesn't deter me from looking him straight in his intuitive gray eyes. "He *was* the drunk driver."

I've never told anyone before. I didn't tell any of my other friends from the other towns. I've always tried not to get too close to them in case I screwed up and we had to move again. Maybe

I'm tired of distancing myself from people I know I could trust. Maybe I'm tired of lying for the past year. Maybe I just need someone to talk to, since I never had time to grieve properly after everything happened. Whatever it is, it makes me look Aiden straight in his eyes and say for the first time out loud the truth about my father.

He shocks me when he steps closer to me, his eyes revealing his concern. "What happened?" he asks softly, a stark contrast with his normally harsh tone.

"I was there."

I look away, eyes watering a little as I remember that awful night.

I was at the mall and had missed my bus, the last one of the night. My mom was attending on an overnight flight to Italy, trying to stay out of the house for as long as she could. Trying to run away from her problems as usual by throwing herself into her work. Flights away from her crumbling marriage and suffocating husband—a husband who turned to alcohol instead of facing the reality of his failing marriage. My parents had been drifting apart for as long as I could remember. They never touched each other. They never ate together. There was tension when they were in the house together. Years of neglect on my dad's part, maybe, or my mom finally realizing they married way too young—they never told me, but they didn't have to, I knew their relationship was a mess. People should trust their kids more—they see more than they reveal.

The luminescence from the moon painted the deserted parking lot in an eerie glow as I sat on the curb waiting for my dad. It was an hour since I'd called him to come and get me, and I was growing more and more unsettled. I shifted uncomfortably, cursing myself, promising that if he showed up I wouldn't be late for anything ever again, like I was for that damn bus. I probably could've walked home by the time my dad's SUV pulled up beside the curb, but it was late, and dark, and he'd never not shown up before.

Already agitated and unsettled by my creepy surroundings, I hopped in the car without a second thought, and my dad practically took off before I even closed the door. The smell hit me immediately. Still, I clicked in my seat belt and turned to my father, noting how he was swaying slightly and squinting as if he couldn't see straight.

I knew he was angry. He never really used to drink before he and my mom started arguing so much, so I'd never known his drunk personality. But when the fights had gotten louder and more frequent, and he'd been drinking more often than not, I'd come to learn that he was an angry drunk.

What the fuck, kid? Why'd I have to get you? Can't you take the fucking bus like every other normal fucking kid?

Then I knew he was drunk—other than the slurring, that was the only time he ever called me kid.

He was gripping the steering wheel tightly as he let his anger fuel him, already going thirty over the speed limit.

Of course not. You fucked up the bus schedule just like you always fuck everything up!

My father wasn't a bad guy. Never hit me, always took me out and bought me what I wanted. He just wasn't good to be around when his life was in shambles and he was drunk.

Dad. Pull over. I gripped my seat belt, not feeling safe in the passenger seat with a drunk driver.

Don' you tell me what to fucking do. I'm the adult here! The car accelerated even more and my father's anger radiated off of him in waves.

I panicked. *Dad! Slow down!!*

I told you to stop fucking telling me what to do! I get enough of that from your mother! God, you're just like her!

The car jerked as he forced the accelerator down again, and the scenery melted into a big blur.

Dad! I yelled

What? You don't trust your ole man?

I started crying. *You're drunk! Just pull over! Please, Dad! I want to get out!*

Of course you don' trust me! Just like your mother! I'm perfectly able to drive, see?

The car lurched to the left suddenly as he jerked the steering wheel in that direction, and my body moved with the sudden movement. Then just as quickly, the car swung back to its proper lane with another jerk, causing me to hit my head on the window from the harsh, sudden movements.

See? I know what I'm doing!

We were still traveling at lightning speed. Tears rolled down my cheeks from being so frightened, and now my head was pounding from hitting the window so hard.

Pull over! I screeched. *Let me out! Right now!*

Instead of listening, he just repeated his actions, his "proof" that he knew what he was doing. He swung into the oncoming lane, then jerked back into ours. He did it again, only that time we were about to go through a dark intersection. There was a loud crunching noise as the back of the driver's side of our SUV hit the traffic-light pole. Time stopped. Noise was cut off and replaced with white static. The car spun a few times through the intersection before we were blinded by a pair of headlights.

It was like that collision pressed play again. Time seemed to speed up as the white static was replaced with deafening noises: glass breaking, metal scraping, and a girl's terrified screams.

Thinking back, that was probably me.

I was airborne as the car flipped over and over and over, but it all happened so quickly I didn't even know how many times, or how long it lasted. When the car finally stopped moving, the intersection wasn't even in sight. We landed on the tires—right side up.

I was disoriented, confused. My head pounded and I felt so incredibly dizzy. There was a shooting pain in my arm, my whole body felt sore, and there was a lot of blood. My dad wasn't in his seat; he wasn't even in the car.

The police told me later that he hadn't been wearing his seat belt and flew through the windshield after the collision with the other car. They said he was dead, though, even before he flew through, his neck having snapped when his head hit the steering wheel on impact.

His body had landed half a block away. When the paramedics rolled me through the street strapped on the gurney, I turned my head in time to see them covering his battered body.

I wish I hadn't. That image will haunt me until the day I die. So will the other image I saw before I passed out: beside an upside-down, butchered car, the paramedics were placing a sheet over the now lifeless body of a six-year-old girl.

"Amelia? Are you okay?" Aiden's soft tone brings me back to the present.

He puts his hand on my shoulder, and I can feel his heat practically burning through my thin T-shirt. I bring my hand up to my face and wipe away the traitorous tears that have escaped.

How long was I zoned out for? Aiden doesn't seem annoyed; he looks genuinely concerned. I nod mutely, answering his question, and wipe the last few tears that stream down my cheek. I feel his thumb on my shoulder move slowly back and forth, comforting me in a way I never imagined such a small action could.

"Were you—were you hurt?"

I look back at him and nod again. "Broken arm, broken ribs, sprained wrist, concussion, some cuts and bruises. I was really lucky though. My dad—" I choke up again and look away.

It's been so long since I actually thought about my dad—about the trauma of what I went through that night. It was always overshadowed by everything else that happened after that day. I never actually thought about the fact that I was there when my *dad died*. I could've done something, done anything differently to have prevented that. He could still be here. I could still be at home instead of constantly moving. And Sabrina . . .

"My dad." I try again, staring at the wall. "He went through the windshield before the car rolled. They told me he died quickly, and that he was probably too drunk to feel anything." I chuckle humorlessly. "As if that's supposed to make me feel better."

Aiden's hand is clenched in a tight fist at his side, as if he's visibly trying to restrain himself. It's then that I also notice that his whole body is tense, and when I look back at him, his expression is hard again. Despite his whole manner suggesting his fury, the hand on my shoulder stays gentle, his thumb still caressing soothingly.

Aiden exhales from his nose, his jaw relaxing slightly. He drops the hand that was on my shoulder, that comforting hand, and looks at the wall behind me.

"My father, he wasn't that great either. When I was nine, we found out my mom was pregnant with twins. Two little boys.

"It's really rare for a woman with cancer to get pregnant, and she didn't even think she would be able to have kids again," he continues as both of his fists clench again, a thinly veiled expression of fury in his normally apathetic eyes. "My father told her that with the medical bills and other payments, she couldn't keep them."

I'm holding my breath, so captivated by Aiden and his words. It's rare that he opens up to people and I don't want to do anything to discourage him. He's trusting me.

"She refused to get an abortion," he continues, "and he just walked out of our lives. Haven't seen him since."

This time it was my turn to comfort Aiden, putting my hand on his bicep reassuringly. That's horrible. His dad left his nine-year-old son and his wife, pregnant and with cancer, because he didn't want to deal with the bills.

"My stepfather wasn't any better."

"What—" I swallow, my mouth dry, kind of already knowing what his answer will be. "What did your stepfather do?"

My words seem to remind him where he is and what he's saying, and his eyes snap back to mine, his impassive expression back in place. "You said collision. Was anyone else hurt?"

I drop my hand. I know he's changing the subject back to me, and I can respect that. He already opened up so much to me, and for someone who never lets anyone in, he's told me so much.

I could've lied. It would've been easier. It would've been better. But I just couldn't do it. I couldn't betray him like that after he's been so honest, letting me see him more vulnerable than anyone ever has. Lies are expensive, and I'm already living a giant one.

Some part of me just felt like I had to be honest about this, just this once.

"A little girl. Her name was Sabrina," I confess quietly. "She was only six when she died. And it was all my fault."

"No. Amelia! You can't—"

"It was, Aiden!" I cut him off. "I missed my bus! I called my dad to get me. I got in the car with a *drunk driver*! Aiden, I killed a little girl!"

I'm crying in earnest now, letting the emotions I haven't allowed myself to feel flow free for the first time since Sabrina's funeral. Aiden doesn't even hesitate. His arms wrap around me as he pulls me in close, my body fitting perfectly in his sculpted arms. I wrap my own around his back, snuggling in closer to his comforting heat while he holds me as I cry.

This one hug, this affectionate action from a guy who's normally so impassive and callous means more to me than anything. I've never felt so secure before, so okay to be vulnerable, that it makes me want to stay nestled in his embrace forever.

He rests his chin easily on the top of my head, one hand rubbing my back slowly, soothingly, the other in my hair. "It's not your fault. You didn't shove the alcohol down his throat. You didn't put the keys in his hands. You didn't tell him to put his life and the life of his only daughter in jeopardy. It's *not* your fault, and don't you ever fucking forget it."

"But Sabrina's dead. Her father, Tony, lost everything that day. His wife had recently passed, and because of me his only daughter is dead too."

Aiden puts his hands on either side of my face and pulls me back to look at him, holding me hostage with his intense gray eyes.

"It was not. Your. Fucking. Fault. Sabrina's father can't believe that it was."

He does. I know for a *fact* that he does.

"You weren't there, Aiden. I snuck into her funeral and sat in the back of the church and tortured myself with all the sad people gathered to mourn her; all the people gathered to hate me for being the person who caused her to be taken from them."

"Stop it, Amelia!" He lets go of me and steps back in frustration, and I can't help but immediately miss his comforting warmth. "It wasn't your fault and that's fucking final. Anyone says otherwise and I'll beat the shit out of them myself."

He might have to. He didn't see Tony that day. He looked so broken, so unsure of what to do with his life now that his princess was gone, the last living reminder of his wife.

His eyes. They were haunted; so heavy with sorrow, so full of pain. I'll never forget those eyes, since their transformation is the reason my life is so messed up.

Over time those eyes changed from hurt to despair.

From despair to hopelessness.

From hopelessness to anger.

From anger to revenge.

Still, I nodded, agreeing with Aiden.

✄

I really didn't see anything wrong with opening up to Aiden—at the time, I'd never felt so comforted before. I had some of the best sleep I've had since the accident.

But waking up the next morning, my panic rises. And it keeps going all weekend. My overactive mind whirls over every single reason I *shouldn't* have told Aiden.

It wouldn't be so bad if I'd just left it at "My dad was the drunk driver," but the more we talked, the more I felt compelled to tell him the truth. Something about him just made me feel so comfortable, so okay with being vulnerable that I forgot to keep my guard up and stick to my script.

I've never opened up to anyone about any of that before, and out of nowhere I decide to spill some of my darkest secrets to the school's biggest badass? What the hell, Amelia? Get it together!

My mom's going be so pissed when she finds out. We're going have to move again and then she'll have to find another job again and every day she'll grow to resent me even more and—no.

I stop pacing. She's not going to find out. I won't say anything to her because Aiden isn't going to tell anyone. I mean, normally Aiden would probably tell the Boys, since they do everything together, but he's not going to. Not this time. Aiden and I connected on a deeper level last night. He told me about his mom and his brothers. I wonder what happened to them?

But either way, I think he's intuitive enough to know that I wouldn't want anyone else to know.

I mean, he didn't tell anyone about Chase loving Charlotte, so it's not like the Boys share one brain; they keep their own secrets too. I'll catch Aiden first thing and confirm that he won't tell anyone. He won't. I just know it. I can trust Aiden. Sure we started out hating each other, but now we're friends. He opened up to me. He trusts me. He understands me.

I shower and fix my messy hair, putting it into a French braid down my back, attempting to hide the dark-brown roots growing in. I put on a bit more makeup than usual, masking the dark bags under my eyes.

Since I don't have to straighten then loosely curl my hair, I finish getting ready really quickly, giving me about twenty minutes until I have to leave.

I open my closet door and pull out an old shoebox disguised among my other shoeboxes. I sit down cross-legged on my bed and pull it in front of me.

Aiden got too close to finding out the whole truth last night. Looking through this shoebox, I'm reminded of why he *can't* find out anything else. Why no one can know anything, and why keeping my secret safe is important.

The first thing I pull out is a bunch of newspaper clippings about my dad's accident, detailing the accident and showing pictures of our totaled SUV and Tony's destroyed car. Aiden's plan worked in the end. He wanted to tutor me to find out some of my secrets, and he did. He found out more than I ever intended anyone to know. And it really wasn't that hard for him.

What he doesn't know, though, is to what extent Tony's grief overtook him.

I pull out another newspaper clipping, running my fingers over the bold title: 16-YEAR-OLD THEA KENNEDY KIDNAPPED.

I pull out another one: PRIME SUSPECT IN KENNEDY KIDNAPPING IDENTIFIED AS TONY DERANDO.

They go on and on, and I flip through them unconsciously, stopping at one in particular: THEA KENNEDY FOUND SAFE; DERANDO NOWHERE TO BE FOUND.

I put it aside and grab the next thing: a note, with the simple words *You Will Die* written in a harsh, crazed scrawl. I pull out another similar one, and another, and another—more death threats phrased in different ways in the same menacing handwriting.

Sifting through them, I come to an object with a picture stapled to it. This is the only picture that exists of this girl. She's got blond hair cut into a short bob and wears thick-framed glasses that no one knew didn't have an actual prescription. This picture was taken without her knowing, like a surveillance photo, as she was leaving school.

It had been stapled to a doll—one that had been altered to look like the girl, except for one difference. The doll originally came with a knife shoved cruelly in its head. The note that was attached to the brick that came through the window read: *You can run* Isabella, *but I will* always *find you.*

I shiver, moving the doll and picture to the side. I pull out another newspaper clipping: TEEN ATTACKED AT PART-TIME JOB: THREE PEOPLE DEAD.

Another: WITNESSES SAY MALL ATTACKER'S PRIME PURPOSE WAS TO KIDNAP TEEN HAILEY JOHNSON.

Another: POLICE STILL LOOKING FOR MALL ATTACKER WHO LEFT THREE DEAD AND AS MANY INJURED.

Another: TEEN HAILEY JOHNSON RECOVERING IN HOSPITAL FROM ATTACK THAT LEFT THREE OTHERS DEAD.

Running my fingers over the picture taken of Hailey as she was leaving the hospital, I recall the color contacts that made her eyes blue and the straight, black hair that framed a bruised face. She was holding the left side of her ribs, recovering from the fight with the mall attacker.

I shiver again and quickly throw the artifacts back into the shoebox.

Aiden knows that Sabrina's father, Tony, lost everything the day of the crash, but he doesn't know that he's been out to get me ever since. He doesn't know that I've been running from Tony for the last year, and that's the reason that I've moved so many times. He doesn't know that Tony has found me and tried to kill me three times in the last year. He doesn't even know that my real name isn't Amelia.

No one is going to find out any of this. But Aiden is smart. He's observant. He knows how to connect the dots.

I've told him more than he should know—I told him more than it's *safe* to know. No more letting my guard slip.

Stick to the script was drilled in my head by the police and federal agents trained in this stuff.

You're not Thea Kennedy anymore. You're Isabella Smith, they told me.

When that didn't work, they told me I wasn't Isabella Smith anymore, that I was Hailey Johnson.

When that didn't work, I knew what was coming. I didn't even wait for them to give me a name—I picked Amelia Collins, and they filled out the documents.

This only works if you keep the secret, they told me. *You are Amelia Collins. No one can know otherwise. If they find out, Tony finds out.*

He's dedicated his life to finding me. One slipup on my part and he's at my door. One slipup and he's here again, sending me death threats or breaking into my house, or finding me at a part-time job and trying to kidnap me at gunpoint again.

Tony will not find out. No one will find out. I like it here. I'm not slipping up.

14

After parking near the back of the lot, I make my way toward school just in time to catch Aiden pulling in.

"Aiden!" I call out to get his attention as he climbs out of his gorgeous Challenger.

"Hey, about Friday night—"

He leans against his car and takes the now-familiar stance: arms crossed, eyes intense. "What about it?"

"It's just, you know that . . . could you maybe—"

"Do you seriously think you have to ask?"

"Pardon?"

"Were you not just going to ask me to keep my mouth shut about Friday?"

"Maybe?"

He gives a low, humorless chuckle and straightens up from where he was leaning on the car. "You really think you had to ask me to keep your secret?"

"Well, I mean—I figured I wouldn't, but it's kind of important, and I wanted to make sure."

"You really thought I'd tell people? Jesus, Amelia, I should just get you a trampoline since you love jumping to conclusions."

"Who are you and what have you done with Aiden Parker?" I laugh.

"What?" He smirks.

"I didn't know that you were familiar with the art of teasing," I say.

I can't believe how much he's opened up to me in such a short amount of time. If you told me a few days ago that Aiden Parker would joke around with me, I would've asked you which mental institution you escaped from.

He's guarded: he keeps his emotions locked up and only lets people see his anger, boredom, or indifference. But he opened up to me, told me about his mom and dad, and now he's joking with me. I'm getting to know the true Aiden Parker, not the tough asshole he wants everyone to believe he is, and I like him.

"Being an intimidating asshole all the time gets boring. I like to spice it up sometimes," he jokes.

I laugh again before stopping and staring at him in awestruck amazement. Aiden is giving me a real, full smile. Not a smirk. Not a sneer. But a real, full, happy smile. My heart beats faster as I realize that it's directed at me. And it's the most gorgeous thing I've ever seen.

He realizes that I'm staring at him and raises an eyebrow, a ghost of his smile still on his face. "What?"

"Nothing. It's just—I've never seen you smile like that before," I tell him honestly, quietly adding, "You should do it more often."

Any traces of his smile disappear, and he looks away from me and out into the parking lot. "I guess I don't have much to smile about."

The Aiden I'm used to is back because of my big mouth: the guarded, hardened Aiden whose closest thing to a smile is a smirk or unimpressed scowl. "Anyway, you don't have to worry. I won't tell anyone about what you told me."

"I know. I'm—I'm sorry for even having to ask you. I know you won't."

A lot is riding on my image. If people start digging into my past, they won't really find anything. Amelia Collins didn't exist until a few months ago.

Aiden once asked me why there weren't any pictures on my phone, and that's because there can't be any evidence of me. Not even on my personal phone—we can't take any risks until the police find Tony. Having more people know the truth about who I am just complicates things, and the more people who know, the greater the odds that Tony can find out.

Even if I do trust Aiden, I hope he doesn't dig any further into my past. Realistically, all it would take is a simple internet search to find out that there was never an Amelia Collins in a life-threatening car accident that left a little girl dead.

He doesn't do anything to soothe my fears when he adds, "Are you sure there's nothing else you're hiding though?"

"What?"

"Some things just don't add up. There's more to the story. You can talk to me, if you want."

Trying not to look worried, I take a page from his book and change the subject. "How about you? You never told me what happened to the twins. Are they . . . ?"

"Alive? Yeah. A pain in my ass, but alive and healthy.

"We managed for a while without my dad. My mom gave birth to the twins, and life was okay for a while."

"What are their names?"

"Jason and Jackson. They're nine now." A trace of his smile is back as he thinks about his little brothers. I can tell that he loves them deeply. Just remembering the anger and hatred he had when telling me that his dad was pressuring her to abort them reaffirms this.

"You mentioned a stepfather? Your mom got remarried?"

Any love in his eyes for his brothers is replaced by pure hatred at the mention of his stepfather. He reaches down for his bag, which is on the ground by his feet, but I'm not finished. I need to know. Not just for curiosity's sake, but because I'm genuinely interested in Aiden and his life, and need to know more about him.

I reach out and grab his sculpted bicep, stopping him from picking up his bag and effectively ending our conversation. "Come on, Aiden. I was honest with you."

"Fine, but the same thing applies. This stays between us."

He looks back out into the parking lot, breaking eye contact. "We were okay for a while, but the cancer came back, and it was getting harder for my mom to pay for everything and take care of three boys. When Jason and Jackson were a couple of months old, she remarried—probably more out of necessity than anything else." He pauses, frowning. "My mom died a couple of months later. The twins were barely one and I was ten."

"Did you live with your stepfather?"

He tenses when I ask that question. "And his son, for a while. Not anymore."

"What do you mean?"

He scoffs. "Greg's in jail."

I don't miss how he doesn't like to refer to them as his step-father or stepbrother.

"So you just live with your brothers now?"

"Yup. We lived with a neighbor for a while, but now it's just me and the kids." Thinking of his brothers seems to put him in a slightly better mood.

The warning bell ringing through the parking lot breaks our little bubble, reminding us of our surroundings.

He straightens up, lifting his bag from the ground and swinging it over his shoulder. "Come on, we should go before we're late."

I reluctantly walk with him to the school entrance. I still have so many questions to ask him, so much I still need to know.

Is he taking care of his brothers all on his own? How does he get money to pay for everything? Is someone helping him out with the boys or the bills? Is he their legal guardian? How does he feel about all of this?

The more I find out, the more I need to know about him. Everything that Aiden does fascinates me, and I find myself craving more of him. Aiden and I have more in common than we think: We both have a past that we'd rather not have anyone knowing. We both have family issues, and we definitely both have our own dark secrets.

✖

At lunch, I pull out my Nutella sandwich and Mason eyes it. "That looks delicious, Amelia."

"We remember what happened last time you stole my Nutella sandwich, right?"

He rolls his eyes and lightens his voice a few octaves to imitate me. "'You take my sandwich, I take your life.'"

"I so do not sound like that!" I protest.

"Definitely have to work on your Amelia impression," Chase jeers at him.

"But I do remember her saying something like that," Charlotte adds.

Mason chuckles. "Yeah, that's my k-bear." He ruffles my hair and I giggle as I whack his arm away.

"Damn it, Mason! I'll have to redo this French braid now!" I scold him.

He ignores me and chuckles. "I'm going to buy lunch anyway, be right back." He gets up from the table and walks toward the cafeteria line, but not before trying to mess up my hair again.

I giggle at Mason as I run my hands over my hair, trying to smooth it back into place, but Aiden's giving Mason an indecipherable look, a slight scowl on his face.

I suddenly remember that there's a calculus test in a week, and I could really benefit from some extra study sessions with Aiden before then.

"Hey, Aiden. Do you think you can tutor me a couple of times before the test next week? Maybe tonight or tomorrow?"

He pops the tab on his soda can. "Can't until Thursday."

He didn't even hesitate before offering up his time, and I'm sure there are a million other things he'd rather do than teach me calculus.

"Thursday it is. Friday too?" I ask hopefully. Lord knows I need all the help I can get.

"Busy Friday," he says cryptically, not bothering to elaborate. "I'll be there for seven."

Oh shit. I totally forgot that my mom is home on Thursday before her flight. I don't want Aiden there while she's home. I don't want her to meet any more of my friends. I don't need another lecture on not letting the truth out to anyone, no matter how much I like them or how hot they are. That'll just be awkward because I already told Aiden more than I was supposed to.

"Actually, can we go to your house?"

"Library?" he counters.

"Library works for me," I say.

"Oh, how sweet. Aiden's doing charity by tutoring the less fortunate." Kaitlyn comes up to the table and stops beside me. "It must get hard being that stupid all the time."

"I wouldn't know, you tell me," I snap.

Her eyes narrow at me. "Just wait. You'll get what's coming."

She backs up and turns around, walking toward her friends sitting at another table. Mason passes her as he walks back to our table, giving her a confused look.

"What was that about?" he asks as he sits down with two plates of mouthwatering chicken fingers and fries.

"Oh you know. Insults and threats. The usual," Chase clarifies.

Mason chuckles. "I'd be concerned if it was anything different."

Wordlessly, Mason slides one of the plates of fingers and fries in front of me, and I simultaneously give him half of my Nutella sandwich, as if we'd choreographed this exchange.

We laugh and dig into our meals. Charlotte catches my eye and gives me a questioning look. I just shake my head at her. Of course I've thought of Mason in a more romantic way, but nothing can happen between us. He always makes me laugh and I love hanging out with him, but he's a player. Plus, my life is complicated enough without throwing in boyfriend drama. Double plus,

I can't have a boyfriend since our whole relationship would be a lie. My own boyfriend wouldn't even know that my name is Thea, not Amelia.

✖

The rest of the week is pretty long and boring. Now, at almost seven o'clock on Thursday night, Aiden and I are sitting against the lockers in the school hallway. We were in the school's library, but it closed around five thirty and I was in the middle of a break-through, so we just migrated to the hallway, where we've been ever since.

The school is dark and deserted except for the occasional jan-itor wandering by, but no one seems to mind that we're still on school property.

We're making a lot of progress, and I'm still surprised every time Aiden proves himself to be an amazing tutor. His endless patience with me and ability to explain the concepts without smashing his head on the wall at my incomprehension astounds me.

"Aiden, this is amazing! One more session with you like this and I can definitely get a C on the test Monday!"

"We're not aiming for a C. We're aiming for an A," he corrects me.

"Aiden, you're good, but you're not a miracle worker."

"You can do this, Amelia. You're picking up the concepts really fast, and you're a lot smarter than you give yourself credit for."

The honesty and conviction that he says that with causes me to blush and look away.

"Yeah, well, I have a good—"

The sound of a blaring car alarm coming from the parking lot echoes through the hallway. The only cars in the quickly darkening parking lot, other than the janitors', are mine and Aiden's. We look at each other, and he pulls me up with him from off the floor. In an instant, we're outside, the school door slamming shut behind us.

The lights of my car are flashing as the alarm goes off. Aiden takes a couple of steps closer to my car, pulling me by our intertwined fingers. Now a little closer, I can see that the two visible tires are slashed, and from the way my car is sitting, I can tell that my other tires met the same fate.

I look at Aiden to gauge his reaction, but he isn't even looking at me or my car.

His burning gaze is fixed intently on the platinum-blond passenger sticking her middle finger out of the open window of the red Mustang speeding away. What the fuck? Slashing tires? Is this the 1970s?

I pace beside my vandalized car, trying and failing to contain my anger.

"Who the hell does Kaitlyn think she is? And Ryan Simms? Of course they make a great couple, they're both sociopaths!"

Aiden walks back toward me from seeing if his car was vandalized, the sound of his footsteps echoing in the dark parking lot.

"Is your car—"

"It's fine," he cuts me off, walking around my car to inspect it again.

"They didn't touch it?" I'm kind of surprised. Ryan hates Aiden more than Batman hates the Joker, and Kaitlyn isn't his biggest fan either.

"Simms knows it'd be pointless slashing my tires; I get new ones practically every few weeks."

"What? Why would you need to get new tires every—"

Aiden waves me off. "Never mind. Plus, I'd kill him if he touched my car."

I wouldn't doubt that.

"Also,"—he nods at the security cameras at the top of the school—"I park in perfect view of the security cameras. Your car is parked out of reach of any of them."

I scowl. "I can't believe they were smart enough to figure that out. Maybe together they have half a working brain."

In retrospect, Kaitlyn's mom *is* the principal—Kaitlyn would know where the cameras don't reach. Aiden inspects my car as I pace around him, worrying. I really have enough stuff to think about, and now I have bitchzilla and her psycho boy toy to add to the mix?

"Amelia?" The hesitation in his voice makes me pause my furious pacing and look over at him expectantly.

"All four tires were slashed—" He states the obvious.

"*I know*, Aiden," I snap.

"And the driver's side of the car was keyed," he finishes.

It's dead silent for a single heartbeat.

"She keyed my car! She fucking *keyed* my car. That son of a bitch slashed my tires while Ms. Manicure keyed my fucking car!"

I don't know what to do with the anger filling me up. My fists are clenching as if they can't decide if they want to punch someone or strangle them, maybe both.

Aiden hesitates. "It gets worse."

"How can this get any worse!" I explode. "They fucking *vandalized* my car!"

I march around to the driver's side to see what Aiden was talking about, and halt as I take in the damage to my car.

In big, crude but legible print, the words MAN-STEALING WHORE are scratched into the paint on the side of my car.

Man-stealing whore? How the hell am I a man-stealing whore? Who does she think she is calling me a man-stealing whore? I haven't done anything! Who have I stolen from her? How can she justify calling me—

"Amelia?" My internal tirade is cut off by a concerned Aiden.

Aiden. Of course. This all comes back to him. All my problems since I started this stupid school are because of him. I wasn't supposed to draw attention to myself. I was supposed to lay low and just finish senior year.

But no. Aiden had to be an emotionless, authoritative dick and start problems. He's the one who brought all the attention onto me. He's the one who couldn't keep it in his pants and screwed psycho-stalker Barbie. He's the one Kaitlyn warned me to stay away from or she'd start shit with me. He's the one thing that Kaitlyn wanted, and because he was so intent on being an asshole to me, she figured that I was who he moved on to.

I don't want any of this.

And now the ruthless, untouchable Queen Bee has it out for *me*, and she's paired up with the one sleazebag who already has it out for Aiden, and clearly they have no problem *breaking the law* in order to hurt me.

I'm already facing one relentless psycho who disregards laws and is hell-bent on hurting me.

And. Now. I. Have. Three.

I can't do it. I can't handle this. I want to go *home*. I want to be Thea Kennedy with happy hazel eyes and curly brown hair, whose biggest worry is which nail polish color she should choose or if she'll look good in her prom dress. Whose only boy trouble is whether Daniel Russell likes her back or not, or if Eli Woods would ever notice her. I want to live my life without pretending to be someone I'm not, without having to look over my shoulder for people determined to hurt me.

My head is dizzy with all these revelations. Or maybe it's the fact that I'm hyperventilating.

"Amelia! Calm down! Breathe!" Aiden looks panicked, like he doesn't know how to get me out of this panic attack.

"It's okay," he soothes, his fierce gray eyes boring into mine. "I'll handle this. You'll be okay. I'll take care of everything, I promise."

He wraps his powerful arms around me, but in my frantic state I shove him away from me.

"*No*, Aiden! You can't take care of everything!"

"I will—"

"No! Don't you think you've done enough damage?!"

"What ar—"

"This is all your fault! I was swept into this drama because of *you*! Kaitlyn hates me because of *you*. Ryan hates me because of *you*. I have enough shit to worry about without those two thinking of ways to torture me!"

His concerned expression reverts back to the expression he shows the rest of the world: impassive, emotionless, unreadable, hardened.

"I'm tired! I'm tired of all this bullshit! I'm tired of being swept into *your* drama with *your* enemies. And I'm especially tired of you pretending to care about me when you really just feel guilty about getting me into all this shit in the first place! You don't care about me, Aiden! Your conscience is just telling you to fix your screwups."

If Aiden is hurt by anything I'm saying, I would never know— his impassive, stoic expression never changes and his hard eyes never give anything away.

"Don't think you're doing me any favors by pretending to care. I'm going to go back into the school to get my phone and call someone who *actually* cares about me to come pick me up! I won't inconvenience you anymore by forcing you to pretend to actually care about me."

I stubbornly turn around and march back to the school doors without another thought, even though a small part of me is aching, telling me I'm stupid and begging me to turn around and run into the safety of Aiden's protective arms. It's telling me that I'm overreacting, that I know that absolutely none of this is Aiden's fault. I'm sad, hurt, and frustrated, and took it out on the first thing available. I know that it's not Aiden's fault I can't be Thea Kennedy anymore. I know it's not his fault that Kaitlyn and Ryan vandalized my car. And I definitely know that Aiden wasn't pretending to care about me: his countless past actions have proven otherwise.

But a bigger part of me is saying it doesn't matter, that I'm fed up with drama and pain and emotional roller coasters. It's saying I'm better off without Aiden, and that maybe Aiden is better off without me. All I've ever done is cause pain and suffering to the people I've grown close to. It's saying that I'm so emotionally damaged that I'm better off alone.

When I reach the school doors, I pull on a handle, but the door doesn't budge. I try the other door and get the same result.

No. No. No. No. This isn't happening. I frantically pull on both handles at the same time.

Locked.

✖

"Open the door!" I yell for what feels like the hundredth time, banging on the locked school doors.

Aiden leans on the wall to my right, his arms folded across his muscled chest, looking immensely bored.

"I know you're in there, you stupid janitor!" I bang on the door again, my frustration clearly evident.

I'm still reeling from fighting with Aiden, my vandalized car, Kaitlyn and Ryan, and everything in general.

"We've been here for twenty minutes." Aiden sighs indifferently. "He's clearly jerking off somewhere with his headphones on. No one's going to open the door."

He leans his head back on the wall, his eyes closed and arms still crossed; the complete picture of relaxed disinterest.

"No one asked you to stay!" I snap at him, turning back to the doors and banging on them again.

But the bigger part of me is too busy being overcome with anger toward this stupid. *Bang.* Door. *Bang.* That won't. *Bang.* Open. *Bang.*

"URGHHHH!" My primal scream of frustration echoes through the dark parking lot.

Aiden gets off the wall. "Amelia. It's late. Let's just go home and get our stuff in the morning."

"All of our shit is in there! My purse. My phone. My house keys. My car keys—not that they'll do me any good, but still— your car keys. How the hell am I supposed to get home! It's a twenty-minute drive! That's like an hour's walk! And what time is it? Like, ten thirty? Eleven? My mom left on her flight at nine! How am I supposed to get inside my house if my keys are sitting in this godforsaken school and no one is home! I need to call someone and nothing's open around here where I can use a phone! Are there even pay phones around here anymore? I doubt I'd even know how to use one. I don't even have a quarter or nickel or whatever the hell those ancient things use and *oh God*! My car! I have to get it out of here before the whole student body sees the message Kaitlyn scratched into it and—"

"Amelia!" Aiden shakes my shoulders. "Breathe."

Doing as I'm told, I take big gulps of air. Aiden rubs his hands soothingly up and down my arms, encouraging me, and my traitorous body instantly relaxes at his touch.

"I'm fine." I push his arms off once I recover, immediately missing his reassuring contact.

"Look," he starts, putting his therapeutic hands in his pockets. "Clearly, screaming and banging on the door isn't working. It's probably a fifteen- to twenty-minute walk to my house from here, closer than yours. I have a spare set of car keys, and we can call Mason or someone to give us a ride back. That way, we can sort out everything with a tow truck to get your car out of here."

"But isn't everything closed—"

"I have connections." He cuts me off smoothly. "The driver owes me some favors, too, so it'll be free of charge."

"But where—"

"He'll bring it to my mechanic. I have connections there, too, so they'll get you new tires and see what they can do about the paint job."

"But how do you—"

"You can call Charlotte or Anna and stay at one of their houses tonight. I'm sure they won't mind. I'll come back first thing in the morning when they unlock the doors to get our stuff before anyone touches it."

Snapping my mouth shut, my mind replays what he said to me before I freaked out and placed all the misfortunes in my life on him. *I'll handle this, you'll be okay. I'll take care of everything, I promise.*

It seems like he is. He figured everything out and covered all of the bases without even missing a beat. While I was over here attacking the door and screaming my lungs off, Aiden came up with an *actual* plan that isn't just *okay*, but the best one that you could possibly come up with for a situation like this.

After I was a bigger bitch than the mayor of Bitchville to him just a few moments ago, I wouldn't have blamed him for just leaving me here to yell at the door while he did the logical thing and just walked home. Hell, even *I* would've left me here to be a bitch on my own after what I said to him.

Yet he stayed. He waited with me while I threw a tantrum and he's still figuring out ways to help me out. He's pulling his connections and favors to help *me*. And I totally don't deserve any of it.

"Why?" I ask before even realizing that I did.

He furrows his brows. "I don't want anyone touching my stuff and I'm sure you don't eith—"

"No, not that." I cut him off. "Why are you still here? Why didn't you just leave?"

"I wasn't going to desert you in the middle of a parking lot at night," he says, like it's the most obvious thing in the world.

"Even after what I said to you?"

"Despite what you may think, I actually do care about you."

My body's confused. Like it doesn't know whether to melt at

his confession or erupt into butterflies or float away to cloud nine. My brain settles on the most basic and unrefined thing as a reply.

"Oh."

"Come on. The sooner we start walking, the sooner we can get this mess cleaned up."

He walks down the front steps and through the parking lot, not bothering to check if I'm following. I stare at his back, frozen to the spot, my brain still trying to connect the dots.

He stops walking and turns to face me, looking irritated. "Are you coming or are you just going to stand there all night?"

Snapping out of my reverie and jogging to catch up, I throw one last glare over my shoulder at the school doors. Falling into step with him, the only sound comes from our faint footsteps echoing through the quiet streets.

"Aiden?" I ask quietly, keeping my eyes trained in front of me as we walk.

"Yeah?"

"I'm sorry about what I said. I didn't mean it," I admit, still not looking at him.

He gently takes my hand, his fingers intertwining with mine. Electrical sparks run up and down my arm from where we touch, my hand secured in his strong and comforting grasp.

His reply is instantaneous. "I know."

✗

The walk to Aiden's house from the school didn't take long. The farther away we got from the school, the more I realized that we were walking into a sketchier part of town. It wasn't so rough that you'd want to pull your children inside and shut the curtains at the first sign of darkness, but it wasn't as comfortable as my cozy suburban neighborhood.

Despite walking through an intimidating neighborhood late at night knowing that a madman is hell-bent on killing me and two psychotic teenagers have made it their mission to make my life hell, I'm strangely relaxed. My comfort has everything to do with the powerful and fearless Greek god holding my hand, his presence silently promising my security.

Still, the annoying, nagging voice inside my head tells me that I shouldn't be relying on Aiden to feel safe and comfortable. He's not always going to be around when there's trouble, and I definitely don't want him around if Tony crashes back into the scene.

History has proven once I get too settled something goes horribly wrong, and I'm forced to flee, starting over from a blank page and leaving behind pieces of my heart in each town I've moved to. This time, I know that when I'm inevitably forced to go, I'm going to be leaving behind a much bigger piece of my heart, and that scares me almost as much as Tony does. But a much louder voice in my head snaps at that voice to shut the hell up and hoard the warm, comforting feeling I get when I'm around Aiden.

He leads me toward a gray, two-story house with an attached garage. It's on the average-to-small side, but it's a good size considering it's just Aiden and his brothers. The door is right in the middle of the façade, with large paneled windows between it and the end of the house on both sides. Despite being in a rougher neighborhood, the house is remarkably welcoming.

Aiden inconspicuously looks around as we walk up to the front, and he releases my hand, leaving it cold and deprived of his comfort. He bends down and removes a brick from the pathway, taking out the key hidden beneath before putting it back.

We walk the few steps to the sturdy oak door. Aiden unlocks it and swings it open, letting me walk in first. He follows behind me, closes the door, and turns on the lights.

I'm not sure what I expected to see, but shocked is a bit of an understatement for how I feel.

Aiden is a high school senior with sole custody of two nine-year-old boys. I guess I kind of expected his house to be a bit of a mess, or chaotic, or dirty, or something other than what I'm seeing right now. It's clean and organized. The dark hardwood floors and modern furniture make the house look inviting and comfy. I can't help but feel safe and welcome, and ignore the fact that this might have less to do with the house and more to do with the gorgeous, resourceful guy fidgeting beside me. The usually calm and impassive Aiden seems a little uneasy with having me here, and I remember that he always wanted to tutor me somewhere other than here, even when I asked.

"Your house is really nice," I say.

"You shouldn't be surprised, everything about me is nice. I'm practically the poster child of niceness," he states seriously, with a straight face.

We make eye contact before I burst out laughing, and he chuckles.

"You have your moments," I say, and any tension that might've been lingering from tonight or from his worries of having me here are gone.

I suddenly remember the twins and slap my hand over my mouth, trying to stop my giggles from escaping. Aiden raises an eyebrow at me questioningly.

I remove my hand and whisper, "I'm sorry for being so loud. It's, like, super late—aren't your brothers sleeping?"

"They're staying at a friend's house tonight," he says dismissively, and leads me deeper into the house.

We emerge into a lived-in but clean kitchen with a few dishes in the sink, some notes and photos on the fridge, and an open box of Froot Loops on the table.

"You do eat Froot Loops!" I exclaim and laugh again, remembering our first encounter when I asked him who pissed in his Froot Loops.

He smirks at me. "Lucky guess."

Taking a seat on a stool by the counter, I laugh and watch Aiden open the fridge and pull out a bottle of water. "Do you want anything? Food, a drink?"

"Water is fine, thanks."

He passes a bottle of water to me and closes the fridge. "I'm going to make some calls, make yourself at home."

I fidget in my seat, but the urge to snoop is too great, so I hop off the stool to inspect the notes on the fridge. There's a fourth-grade math test stuck with a magnet to the fridge with the name *Jackson* written at the top beside a big red A+. Beside that is an identical test with an identical grade, but with the name *Jason* written at the top instead.

My heart melts and it takes a lot to resist the urge to *awww* out loud. Aiden puts his brothers' tests on the fridge to show how proud he is of them. He's such a good brother and guardian; it's obvious how much he loves those boys.

Just underneath the tests is a grocery list, and I'm not that shocked to see that it's mostly healthy food; you can't have a body like Aiden's and eat total crap. I resist the urge to giggle when I see that the twins added things like Twinkies, Pop-Tarts, and Cheese Puffs to the grocery list in bold lettering.

There's also a picture of who I assume are the twins. They look similar to Aiden, except where he is more closed off, stoic, and serious, the twins look more open, happy, and carefree. They have dirty-blond hair that sweeps over their foreheads, shining bright-blue eyes, and mischievous smiles. They're almost identical, but there are some telling features that would make pretending to be one another hard to an analytical eye.

There's also a picture of Aiden with the boys. One is climbing on his back and he's holding the other one upside down. I smile at the genuineness and playfulness of the three brothers in the picture, committing the rare, carefree smile Aiden's sporting to memory.

The more I learn about Aiden, the harder it is for me to think of him as that asshole who crashed into me on my first day of school and fireman-carried me up the stairs. Every day I spend with him, the more I think of him as this loyal, intelligent, and resourceful guy who's a fierce protector of the people he cares about.

I pull off the photo of the smiling, carefree Aiden and his brothers, and smile fondly at it.

There's still a lot I don't know about Aiden, but I do know that I trust him more than I've ever trusted any other guy, and that he's dangerously close to breaking down all of my armor and leaving me more vulnerable than I've ever been. It's all different, and I haven't felt this way before—any secrets I shared with friends back home feel silly now, worrying about gossip or petty, cliquey school politics. Tony is real. The twins are real. And Aiden and I are both totally different people because of them.

✄

BANG! BANG! BANG! The pounding at the door jolts me out of my thoughts.

"Amelia! Can you let Mason in?" Aiden yells from the other room.

"Got it!"

As soon as I open the door, I'm enveloped in a protective and warm hug.

"K-bear, are you okay? Aiden didn't tell me any details, just said something went down at the school and you were involved."

I wrap my arms around him and rest my cheek on his solid chest, heartened by his concern and protectiveness over me.

"I'm fine, Mason. My car, however, is not." I step out of his embrace and he looks at me questioningly.

"What happened?"

We close the door and walk back to the kitchen, where we sit as I explain about my keyed car, slashed tires, and accidentally leaving all of our things in the locked school.

"That bastard!" Mason spits, his knuckles white from how hard he's clenching his fists.

"I can't believe the two vilest teenagers on planet Earth found each other. It's weird how life works sometimes."

Ryan and Kaitlyn *are* actually the perfect couple: they both have dark, maniacal, demonic creatures where their souls should be.

"What's the next step? We have to get him back. No one screws with my k-bear and walks away from it!"

"There is no next step," Aiden announces as he walks into the room and tosses me a sweater of his.

"What do you mean there's no next step?" Mason asks, growing angrier as he states the facts. "They slashed her tires and keyed her car! That's not a small thing! That's vandalism and damage of property!"

"There is no next step because I'm going to handle it," Aiden clarifies.

He ushers us to the door, which he closes and locks, and we head to Mason's Range Rover, parked in the driveway.

"We're going to drop you off at Charlotte's, I already called her. Mason's going to take me to school so I can pick up my car and wait for the tow truck, which should be on its way," he says.

"What do you mean you'll 'handle it'?" I pull his sweater around me as he opens the back door for me and closes it once I'm seated. It's cold outside, considering it's probably almost midnight, and I'm instantly grateful that Aiden thought to give me a sweater.

He gets in shotgun and Mason starts the SUV. "I mean what I said. I'll handle it."

"They messed with *me*. I should help, or have a part in your plan to '*handle it.*' Or at the very least *know* what it is," I assert, getting slightly annoyed with his reluctance to let me help, or even tell me what his plan is.

"I want to help too." Mason sticks up for me. "And I'm sure Anna is just dying for an excuse to break Kaitlyn's nose."

I smile at the mention of Annalisa. She would so love to do that.

Aiden glares at Mason, clearly peeved that he didn't take his side. "I'll handle it, *tomorrow*," he emphasizes.

As if Aiden just revealed his grand plan from those few words, Mason's eyes widen in realization. "Oh."

"Why? What's tomorrow?" I ask, oblivious to whatever just happened.

"Nothing." Aiden dismisses my question.

"Clearly there's something!" I exclaim, getting frustrated.

"Don't worry about it, Amelia," Mason adds.

"No, tell me!" I demand.

"Leave it, Amelia."

"Just tell me, Aiden!"

"It's better if you're not involved."

"Mason?" I plead.

"He's right. We'll handle it."

"What?! Now Mason gets to be involved? Are the other boys going to be involved too?"

They share a look. Their action and silence confirming my question.

"Great! So everyone gets to be involved except the person their vandalism directly affected!"

We pull into Charlotte's driveway, and she opens the door, waiting for us on the porch.

Aiden gets out of the SUV and opens my door for me, his intense gaze meeting mine. "Messing with you affects all of us."

I ignore the butterflies and stand my ground, sliding out of the SUV. "But it still—"

"We'll talk more in the morning, okay?" Aiden smoothly interrupts me, probably more to shut me up than anything.

"But—"

"I'll get to the school early to get our stuff and I'll meet you at your locker," he says as he closes the door once I'm out of the car.

He gets back into the passenger seat. "Good night, Amelia," he says, and Mason repeats this as well before Aiden closes his door and Mason reverses out of the driveway.

I watch them drive away as Charlotte comes down to meet me.

"What's going on?" she asks, concerned.

I narrow my eyes at the receding Range Rover. "I don't know. But we're going to find out."

15

Despite being exhausted from the day's events, I don't sleep much at Charlotte's. Not only do I not have my sleeping pills, but my mind is whirling with possibilities of what Aiden and Mason meant by "tomorrow."

Which is today. Meaning something is happening today. And I still don't know what it is. But I do know that I'd rather have nothing happen. Of course, deep down, I really wish I could tear Kaitlyn and Ryan a new one for messing with me, but I can't. I had all night at Charlotte's to think about it while I couldn't sleep, and I'm positive that the best thing to do is to leave it alone and let it go.

There are bigger things at play here, and I don't want a stupid high school rivalry to ruin—and quite possibly literally end—my life.

If I retaliate and do something to Kaitlyn and Ryan, they'll just hit back bigger and harder. It'll become a never-ending cycle until I lose; and I know for a fact that I won't win this war. There are hundreds of things they could do to end me, especially since I'm not even Amelia Collins. Then it'd be only a matter of time until this stupid teenage drama drew Tony to me, and then it wouldn't be just stupid teenage drama anymore. It would be a serious battle for my life, and innocent people could get hurt.

The last time Tony hunted me down, he was so hell-bent on destroying me that three innocent people died. That's three innocent lives ended because of *me*, and I will live with that heavy burden on my conscience for the rest of my life. It's so painful even the passing thought of it is too much, so I push the past out of my mind and concentrate on the here and now—this isn't a game. This is bigger than some teenagers getting caught up in a heated rivalry. It's bigger than my hatred for Kaitlyn and Ryan and their hatred for me, Aiden, and the Boys. This is my life and the lives of the people I care about. So this has to end now before Kaitlyn and Ryan retaliate with something worse than slashing my tires and keying my car.

Determined to tell Aiden to drop any idea about retaliation, I meet him at my locker like he instructed, and just as he said, he got here bright and early to get our stuff before anyone else could touch it. Despite his promise that we would talk in the morning, we did no such thing. He hands me my stuff and practically sprints away from me before I can even think about pestering him for answers. Fine. But he can't avoid me all day.

I plan on bothering him in second period calculus, but Mr. Fidiott gives us a sample test of the one that we'll be getting on Monday, so no talking allowed. Plus, Aiden gets out of there before I can catch him, leaving Julian behind to give me an apologetic smile on Aiden's behalf.

By now my friends all know about what Ryan and Kaitlyn did,

and they are all pretty pissed. Their show of solidarity and level of anger on my behalf really make me feel like I belong. Like these are my true group of friends, and when one thing hurts one of us, it hurts all of us. Except no one really knows who I am; I'm lying to everyone. Like the thoughts of Tony and my life before, I push this out of my mind, too, and try to concentrate on the conversation flowing around me.

"I still think we should go with my first suggestion and just break her nose," Annalisa states, licking yogurt off her spoon.

Everyone but Aiden and Mason is sitting at our table in the cafeteria, talking about what happened to my car.

"Babe, we've been through this many times. You aren't allowed to break her nose." Julian chuckles at his girlfriend.

She mumbles something about Julian not letting her have any fun.

I look longingly at the seats usually occupied by Aiden and Mason. Does their absence have something to do with "tomorrow"? Or did they mean tomorrow as in tonight? I hope I'm not too late to tell them to drop it. Shit. I should've tried harder to get their attention. I knew something was happening today and here I am, not making finding Aiden and Mason my top priority.

"Oh, hey, Amelia," a sarcastic, nasally voice says.

We all look at Kaitlyn, who's walking past our table with her mindless followers. "I noticed you didn't drive here today. Still having car problems?" They laugh as they continue on their way.

Annalisa abruptly stands up, looking ready to start a fight, but Julian immediately pulls her back down into her seat.

She glares at Kaitlyn's retreating form. "If karma doesn't hit her soon, I fucking will."

"I'm really counting on that." Noah chuckles.

"What are we going to do?" Charlotte asks.

"Honestly, guys, I think—" I try to tell them to leave it alone, but no one's paying me any attention.

"Something that would really piss her off," interrupts Chase.

"No, guys, really I think—"

"It has to be worse than what she did to Amelia's car," interrupts Noah.

"But I'd rather—" I say.

"We should break into her house!" Annalisa suggests.

"And put hair remover into her shampoo bottle!"

We all look at Charlotte.

"Really, Charlie? We just suggested breaking and entering, and the worst you can think of is hair remover in the shampoo?" Chase jokes.

"Sorry, I'm not good at this revenge thing," Charlotte admits shyly.

"Hey, hair remover in the shampoo bottle is pretty diabolical." Noah defends Charlotte's idea. "I mean, can you just picture Kaitlyn's face when all of her hair falls out?"

"We are *not* breaking and entering. As much as I hate her, I don't want to break the law," I assert, finally getting a word in. "Guys, I don't want—"

"Whose house are we not breaking into?" Mason interrupts as he arrives at the table with Aiden.

I instantly perk up when I see them. If they're here, that means I'm not too late to call this off.

"We were just talking about how to get back at Kaitlyn and Ryan, which *Aiden* was supposed to tell us about," Charlotte says while Mason takes his usual seat on my left, and Aiden sits on his left.

"Why is Aiden in charge of revenge?" Noah protests. "Why can't I ever be in charge of revenge?"

The table erupts into laughter at Noah's suggestion, still too excited about this to pay attention to my protests.

"Noah, honey, you're way too sweet to be the mastermind of a revenge plan," Annalisa explains.

"Fine. I won't be in charge. But we should come up with a plan together. We should have, like, a group vote! It's only fair!"

"No, guys. I don't—"

I'm interrupted again by everyone talking together at once, all throwing out suggestions and ideas.

"*Guys!*" The conversation stops and we all look at Aiden, waiting for him to continue. When I look at him, his observant eyes are trained on me, as if he can read my mind and personally feel my frustration.

"Amelia's been trying to say something."

"To be honest, I'm really just sick of all of this. I don't want revenge. Think about it. I get her back. She gets me back. It's a never-ending cycle. Someone has to be the bigger person and end it somewhere."

The table erupts, everyone protesting and talking at once. The only person not saying anything is Aiden.

"You can't just let her get away with what she did!"

"That'd be letting them win!"

"We have to do something!"

"At least let me break her nose!"

"They deserve to pay!"

"Guys! I'm touched. Really. But I don't want to start a never-ending war. Ryan already hates Aiden, Kaitlyn despises me. Together they make a ruthless team without boundaries. I don't want to have to be constantly looking out for the knife they plan to shove in my back. Can we please just be the bigger people and drop it before I'm the target of even more torment?" I plead, disclosing at least half of the truth.

Charlotte's the first to break the silence. "But don't Aiden and Mason already have a plan? Aren't you guys going to handle it today?"

"Tonight. We'll handle it tonight," Mason clarifies.

The boys' eyes all light up with realization, and even Annalisa seems to get what they're talking about.

"What's tonight?" Charlotte asks.

"Friday is when Aiden goes to the Tr—" Noah is cut off when he notices Aiden sending him a death glare.

"Friday is when Aiden goes *where*? Aiden? What is Noah talking about?" I ask.

"The Tracks," he says. "Friday is when I go to the Tracks."

"The Tracks? What do you mean?" I ask.

"I race for money. Illegally."

"But—how? Like, how does it all work?" I can't stop picturing scenes from *The Fast and the Furious*: large crowds, sketchy people, loud music, practically naked girls walking around everywhere. I mean realistically, if that went on every Friday night, especially with such loud cars all gathered together, how did other people and the cops not catch on?

"We call it the Tracks, but it's not really a drag strip or anything. It's about an hour out of town, up north, on the deserted country roads." Mason fills me in.

Noah continues, "It's not like a huge, professionally organized thing. Nothing like you see in the movies and stuff about racing. Yeah, it's big, but not that big. It's just a bunch of people who get together and make bets on the racers."

"The two or three people racing put money down against each other, but the spectators also make bets on the racers. It's a great way to make fast money," Julian explains.

That makes a lot of sense to me. Of course Aiden would do that. He's a senior in high school and guardian of two boys. He has no job but still has to pay for bills and gas and food and other expenses.

"How much do you make from one race?" I ask.

"Depends on how much you want to bet," Aiden says vaguely.

"How much did you make last Friday?"

He was there that Friday—that's why he ignored my call when I needed to get Chase somewhere.

"Around two grand."

"Two thousand dollars! In one night?" Charlotte choruses in disbelief as I almost do a spit take, barely containing the water in my mouth.

She and I are the only ones who clearly have no idea about any of this. Annalisa doesn't seem shocked, but I can't see Julian hiding something like this from her. I'm surprised Chase didn't say anything to Charlotte. But from how they all act when the subject comes up, I'm assuming it's something Aiden doesn't want anyone to know about.

"Do you guys race too?" I look at the other boys at the table.

Julian, Chase, Noah, and Mason all shake their heads no.

"We're nowhere as skilled as Aiden," Chase admits.

"But that doesn't mean we don't go to support him or back him up," Julian adds.

"Plus, betting on Aiden is a great way to make sure I never have to get a part-time job," Mason jokes, and the other guys laugh in agreement.

"How good are you?" I ask Aiden, already knowing the answer.

"The best."

"You ever lose?"

"Rarely."

"More like never," Mason adds.

Of course he wins; he has other people depending on him to win. He's been forced to grow up. He has a lot of responsibilities; more than any teenager should.

"Who goes to these things?" Charlotte asks.

"Us and a few other Kings, the Silvers, and some groups of people from some other schools around here," Noah informs us.

"When you said you were going to handle it tonight, what were you going to do?" I ask.

Clearly if the Silvers go to the track, then obviously Ryan does. That might explain why he and Aiden hate each other so much.

Aiden shrugs. "Make him pay. Still am."

"Aiden, I don't want you to—"

"This isn't just about you, Amelia. This is about Simms. He messed with me and mine, and for that, he's going to pay." Aiden interrupts me, a steely determination in his eyes.

Me and mine.

"But, Aiden, I don't want this to get out of hand. I don't want you hurt or to give them any reason to hit back harder next time. Adding fuel to an already blazing fire won't fix anything," I say.

I'd still rather leave it be and not kick the sleeping lions. I don't want to give them a reason to find out about me. Observant Aiden, the only person at the table to sense my hesitation, seems to understand that I don't want this getting back to me.

"Don't worry, Amelia," he says. "It won't look like revenge. It'll just look like any other day at the Tracks."

I must've given him a skeptical look because he adds softly, "You'll be kept out of it. I promise."

Aiden doesn't take promises lightly, and despite my uncertainty, I'm unable to do anything other than put my trust in him. I believe that he knows what he's doing. There's a reason people are scared to cross Aiden, and that's because he always comes out on top.

"Fine. But I'm coming," I declare.

Aiden doesn't even take a second to think about it before he growls out, "No."

"Yes, I am." I stubbornly hold my ground.

I need to be there to make sure he's okay, and to make sure he doesn't do anything stupid. Mostly, I want to see and experience the Tracks—to understand what makes up this huge part of his life, see him in his element. Really, though, I want to support him.

"You're not." He narrows his eyes at me.

"Why not?"

"Because I said so."

"Don't use that on me! I'm not *five*!"

"Face it, Amelia. You always end up finding trouble. Or it finds you. Either way, I won't be around to make sure you're okay," he replies honestly.

"Please, Aiden? I'll be good, I swear!" I beg.

"No," he states, deadpan.

"But what if—"

"No."

"But how about—"

"No."

"But when I—"

"No."

"UGH!" I throw up my arms in exasperation. "You're impossible! You know that? Like, if I was Kaitlyn, I'd say that I literally can't even right now."

At the mention of Kaitlyn, the boys exchange a knowing look.

"Wait, Kaitlyn's going to be there, isn't she?"

Aiden sighs. "It doesn't matter. It doesn't change the fact that you're not coming."

"Of course it matters!" I explode. "Aiden, you're being stubborn. Tell him, Mason!"

Mason, who's currently sitting between Aiden and me, looks back and forth between us, seeming unsure of whether to go against Aiden or back him up.

"I'll stay with her the whole time," Mason cautiously suggests.

"Yes! I'll stay with Mason! And Noah and Julian and Chase can stay with me too! That's *four guys* making sure I don't get into trouble. Plus, Anna and Char will keep me out of trouble. I'll be good, I swear!" I send Mason a grateful look and look up at Aiden with pleading eyes.

He studies me with his indecipherable gray eyes before sighing and running his hand through his hair in defeat. "Fine. But you stay with Mason the *whole time*. I mean it, Amel—"

"I will, I promise!" I cut him off, sharing an excited smile with Mason.

"Seriously, Amelia, I have enough to do already and I can't be worrying about you the whole time."

"Pinky swear." I reach across the table and grab his hand. He allows me to lock my pinky finger with his, sealing my promise in order to ease his worries, all the while ignoring the growing sense of dark foreboding knotting through my stomach.

16

It takes about an hour to get to the Tracks, so we decide to meet at my house. Charlotte's parents don't know where we're going, so she said she's sleeping at my house. It's not a complete lie because she is, in fact, spending the night.

"They sure are taking their sweet time. It's getting really cold out here," Noah complains, having arrived here twenty minutes ago wearing jeans and a fitted T-shirt.

"Didn't you bring a jacket?" Annalisa asks Noah.

"No."

"We can stop at your house to grab it before we head up to the Tracks," Charlotte suggests.

"No way. My mom is home."

"So?"

Noah scoffs, as if it's the most obvious answer in the world. "I could *never* admit I'm cold to my mom who told me to bring a jacket 'because it's November.'"

I can't help but laugh at Noah's impression of his mom. *Yeah.*

I totally get that. But I text Mason to bring Noah a sweater. Hopefully he hasn't left yet.

Our banter is cut off by the beautiful sound of Aiden's black Challenger pulling into my driveway, his headlights illuminating the porch we're sitting on. He turns the car off and gets out, then walks over to us.

He looks as gorgeous as ever in his fitted black T-shirt, black leather jacket, and dark jeans, his masculinity and dominance unmistakable. However, he doesn't look too happy about this whole thing; all day he subtly tried to get me to change my mind, but I'm too stubborn for my own good sometimes. Mason's Range Rover pulls up, and he shuts off the SUV and gets out. He looks confident and charming as always in dark jeans, a fitted white long-sleeved shirt with only three buttons on the top, which are undone, and a black leather jacket.

"Finally! You took forever," Noah exclaims. "You better have the heat on in the truck!"

"Sorry, I had to turn around and get some idiot a sweater." Mason smirks and throws Noah a black sweater, which lands right in his face.

"Dude! You're the best!" Noah laughs as he puts the sweater on.

"Don't thank me. Amelia's the one who told me to bring it."

Noah looks at me before tackling me in a bear hug, planting overexaggerated slobbery kisses all over my face. "Oh thank you, thank you, Amelia!"

I laugh and push him off me, wiping his spit off my face. "No problem, Noah. I wouldn't want to face my mother's wrath either."

Aiden and Mason suddenly wear matching scowls.

"All right! Let's get this show on the road!" Chase stands up from where he was sitting on my front steps and walks toward Mason and Aiden. "Who's going in which car?"

"Anna and Char are with Julian. Amelia—"

"She's with me," Aiden finishes for Mason in an authoritative tone that leaves no room for protesting.

Everyone turns to look at me. I have absolutely no problem with that—not a single objection. I like spending time with Aiden, especially one on one, and to be completely honest, I feel the safest when I'm with him.

"Okay. Then Noah and Chase are with me," Mason finishes, his voice a little disappointed.

"Great. Now that that's settled, can we please *get in the heated truck*?!" Noah exclaims, jogging over to Mason's Range Rover and impatiently waiting for us to follow his lead.

Sitting in Aiden's car, I put my seat belt on and wait for him to push the start button so that I can turn on my butt warmer. Best. Invention. Ever.

"Last chance to change your mind," he says as the engine revs to life.

I shake my head. "No backing out now."

"You stay with me tonight. When I'm not around, you stay with the guys. Okay?"

"I don't need a babysitter," I say, just to see what he'll say.

"I know you don't," he says, surprising me. "But you can't be alone tonight. There are a lot of sketchy people there. A lot of Silvers we don't get along with. Plus, kids from some other schools that aren't too great either. Most people are pretty cool, and I'm not expecting that much trouble other than Simms and his asshole friends. But with your track record of finding trouble, I'll feel better knowing you're with someone I trust."

"What about Char and Anna?" I ask, trying to move my train of thought away from how amazing Aiden is to me.

He takes his eyes off the road for a second to glance at me. "You really think Chase would leave Charlotte's side?"

"I guess you're right. Plus, I doubt Char would do anything to get herself into trouble."

"And Anna's been a couple times, but she won't get herself in trouble."

I look out the window at the scenery, the trees blurring together in the distance. "What are you going to do tonight?" I ask quietly, referring to his resolution to get back at Ryan.

"Just what I said I'd do. Make him pay."

Aiden has a look of determination on his face, the scowl back in place from just thinking about Ryan. This anger is from more than just what Ryan did to my car—this goes way back. There's more to the story, but I don't want to press Aiden. No matter how much he hates Ryan, I still don't want him getting hurt over any of this.

"I don't want you to get in a fight," I admit softly, running a finger gently over the knuckles on his right hand, which is resting on the gear shift, the spot rough from being busted and bloodied from fighting. His face softens, an unknown emotion running across it. He flips his right hand over and catches mine, intertwining his fingers with my own.

"I'm not going there with the intention of fighting," he tells me.

"But what do you mean when you say you're going to make him pay?"

I try not to feel disappointed when he releases my hand to shift gears, trying to convince myself that I don't already miss his warm touch.

"I'm *literally* going to make him pay. Race him and up the initial racer's bet. By a lot."

I smile, understanding his plan, and my worries and stress lighten slightly. I should've known. Aiden isn't stupid.

He knows that fighting them won't do anything. Of course, Aiden would most likely win and he'd probably feel better getting some punches in, but then what? Yeah, he would have kicked Ryan's ass, but is that really an effective way of getting them back? I mean, it'd probably feel *fantastic*, but handing Ryan's ass to him in a race in front of his friends and peers and walking away with a shit ton of his money would probably feel a whole lot better.

I can't wait to see Aiden wipe the floor with Ryan's smug, arrogant face.

✗

By the time we get to the Tracks—after we all went to a drive-thru for coffees and teas—it's around ten o'clock. There are crowds of people gathered in groups around different cars that are spaced out on the grass. From what I can tell, the majority of the people here are in their late teens to mid-twenties. The space itself is just as Mason said it was at lunch: deserted country roads. The actual road is still in good shape, but it's clear that this place is so out of the way that no one would wander onto it unless they knew what it was used for.

Despite being dark, the roads and space are still dimly illuminated by the brightness of the moon and from the headlights of the various cars. It's obvious that not all cars are used for racing; many people are here with their regular vehicles to support their friends, bet on the racers, and just have somewhere to go on a Friday night.

Aiden parks on a stretch of grass and turns off the car as Mason pulls up beside him. I get out of the Challenger and stretch my legs, seeing Julian pull up beside Mason.

There's only one run-down building close by that looks like it's still kind of used, but other than that one, there aren't any structures around. It's mainly an open field with roads intersecting and turning for miles. The sound hits us, engines from a blue and an orange car racing each other grinding away.

The distance and speed they're traveling make it hard to make out the models, but the bright colors make it easy to tell them apart as they travel farther away from the main part of the track. There are some sparse areas of trees in the distance that block the view of the road, but for the most part, if you have good eyesight you can see the racers, even at the farthest point they look like tiny toy cars. People are standing on top of cars and trucks, trying to get a better view of the race. They're shouting and cheering for the cars, hoping that the person they bet on wins.

As I scan the crowd, my eyes stop on a bright-red Mustang in the distance, a group of people and parked cars around it. Ryan's leaning against it, his arm draped around Kaitlyn as he talks to a bunch of other guys who I'm assuming are his friends from Commack Silver High. Kaitlyn isn't the only girl in the group, but she is the only one dressed like she's ready for a night at a club.

Isn't she cold? Can people from hell even get cold? I notice that Makayla is the only other one of her friends here; the other girls must be from Commack. Some of the guys with Ryan are the party crashers from Noah's Halloween party. One of them catches my eye and glares directly at me, sending a shiver down my spine.

Dave.

I subconsciously step closer to Aiden, who's in the middle of a conversation with Mason and Noah. Dave follows my action and notices Aiden, clearly remembering how he handed him his ass without even breaking a sweat, and he unconsciously brings his hand up to rub his jaw.

"I shouldn't be here. What if he's here?"

I look away from Dave to look at Annalisa, who's speaking to Julian in hushed tones off to my right. I shouldn't be eavesdropping, but her nervous tone worries me. She's usually so strong, confident, and fierce—it's odd to see her so worried and unsure.

"We haven't seen him here in a while." Julian comforts her as he wraps his arms around her. "Even if he is, you know I won't let him anywhere near you."

I look away, not wanting to intrude on their private moment.

"Amelia."

I'm brought back to reality when Aiden calls my name, and I look up at him standing beside me. "I'm going to talk to some people. Stay with the group, okay?"

"Friendly people?" I ask, a worried expression on my face, hoping he didn't notice my stare off with Dave. He has enough to worry about without needing to think about that asshat.

"Yeah, they're friends," he says with an entertained smirk, seeming to enjoy that I'm worried about him. "I'll be back."

He heads off in a different direction, his dark outfit making it easy to lose sight of him in the crowd. The group of us talk for a while and watch the various races before I start to squirm. *Damn it, Amelia. You just* had *to get the extra-large green tea, didn't you?* I think to myself.

"Hey, Mason?" I ask and he looks down at me. "There isn't a bathroom I can use around here, is there?"

Noah laughs. "Yeah. It's called *the trees*."

I must look mortified because the guys break out laughing.

"Calm down, k-bear," Mason says. "There is one, but I'm warning you, it's kind of gross since no one really takes care of it."

I contemplate holding it before ultimately deciding that I can't. "I don't care. I need to go."

Mason shakes his head in amusement. "I'll take you. We'll be right back."

He leads me on a two-minute walk through groups of people—nodding hello to some on the way—to that run-down building I saw when we first got here. It's only one story, and there are cars parked around here too.

Mason opens the door to the dimly lit building and points to the first door on the left. "I'll be right here when you're done."

I nod and hurry inside, gagging from the smell. He was not kidding when he warned me that it was gross. I lock the door and hurry up.

"'It's cold outside,' you said. 'Extra-large will warm you up,' you said. Stupid, tiny bladder," I mumble to myself as I quickly use the gross bathroom, wash my hands, and pull the door open.

As I walk out of the building, I slather my hands with the sanitizer that I always keep in my purse. Where's Mason? He was right here. Where did he go? I scan the area, looking for him. I find him in the distance, flirting with a dark-haired girl in knee-high boots and booty shorts. Even from where I'm standing, I can tell that he's charming the socks off of her. I can't believe he can't keep it in his pants for two minutes! Seriously, he left me alone at an illegal racetrack to talk to a random girl. And after that whole thing of how I shouldn't be left alone.

I'm torn between whether I should go over to him or not. I don't want to be *that* girl—the one who acts all jealous and possessive over someone she isn't even with, but I promised Aiden I'd stay with Mason. Stupid boy letting his stupid hormones be the priority.

Before I can decide anything, a rough hand clamps down over my mouth and an arm wraps around me in a steel grip, trapping my arms at my sides and pressing my back tight against a hard body.

Holy shit. Holy shit. Holy shit.

I try kicking the person behind me but it's no use as they drag me backward with force. I'm frantic, mentally begging Mason to look over, hoping that he noticed someone grab me. The last thing I see before I'm dragged around the corner to the back of the building is the back of Mason, who is still flirting with the booty-shorts girl.

I can't help but panic, and feel my eyes water.

He found me.

This is it.

I'm going to die.

This is not how I end. I did not go through everything I did just to die alone, weak and afraid, behind a bathroom at some illegal racetrack where no one will find my body. I absolutely refuse to go down without a fight.

Just you and him, Thea. You're not a scared little girl anymore. You train and work out in preparation for this exact moment— you needed and wanted to be ready for when Tony found you.

You are Thea Kennedy and you are a survivor.

As we get to the back of the building, I force my mouth open against the hand practically smothering me and clamp down on it as hard as I can.

"*Bitch!*" My attacker hisses as they yank their hand away from my mouth, and I taste the metallic tang of blood.

Their other arm is still wrapped around me, trapping my arms at my sides, but I don't waste time. While they're still caught off guard, I promptly lean back into them and swing my legs forward, gaining momentum before slamming my heels into their shins as hard as I can. It works, and as they release me, I go sprawling to the ground, landing face-first in the dirt.

I don't even waste a tenth of a second to catch my breath before I'm scrambling to stand up to get away, adrenaline pumping through my veins. Before I even have both feet under me, they grab my wrist and spin me around to face them.

Dave.

I'm so shocked that it isn't Tony that I freeze. I never thought I'd be so relieved to see Dave's hostile, ugly face in my life. My ease is short-lived, however, when he pushes me up against the brick wall of the building, and I'm reminded that while Dave may not be Tony, he clearly intends to hurt me.

"Such a stupid little bitch!" he snarls at me, his grip on my arms tightening. "You're not worth the trouble, but your boyfriend basically dislocated my jaw. I've been eating soup and banana mush for weeks because of you. He ruined my face, and I'm very fond of it, so how about we break something that he's very fond of?"

Dave tosses me like a rag doll away from the wall, and a pair of arms catch me. With barely a chance to get a glance of the guy, I notice he's one of Dave's friends from the party, one of the original linebackers who blocked me from escaping after I took Dave down at Noah's party.

This new guy spins me around so that my back is to him and

I'm facing Dave. New guy practically yanks my arms out of their sockets as he grabs each of my wrists and pins them behind my back, forcing me to stay in place. Dave smiles an evil, satisfied grin, watching me pinned helplessly by the inhumanly strong linebacker behind me.

"This is going to hurt me as much as it hurts you," Dave says with a sadistic smirk. "But just remember, what's about to happen to you is all because of your little bastard boyfriend."

Dave draws back his arm and punches me right in the stomach. I swear my lungs collapse and I double over in pain. My eyes water as I desperately gasp for air, and the only thing preventing me from falling to the ground is the monster holding me from behind. My ribs . . .

The linebacker yanks my arms back, forcing me to stand up straight and face Dave again. He has a sadistic gleam in his eyes as he puts his face near mine and runs his hand over my hair, smoothing it out. "Don't quit on me just yet, darling, this is just the warm-up."

Despite still trying to catch my breath, I spit right in Dave's gargoyle face. It contorts into an expression of pure rage. The guy holding me tightens his grip, forcing my arms impossibly close together and practically dislocating my shoulders. Dave winds up his arm to drive his fist back into my stomach, but a blur of black suddenly tackles him to the ground before he can deliver the hit. The guy holding me from behind releases me and goes to help Dave, and I buckle over, holding my stomach, trying to recover.

I'm too focused on trying to catch my breath to pay attention to the fight. Out of my peripheral vision, I see Dave and the other guy scrambling away, realizing that they'll lose this fight.

My breathing returning close to normal, I straighten up and

turn to thank Aiden for saving my ass once again, only to stop short when I'm met with a guy who definitely isn't Aiden.

In fact, I've never seen this guy before in my life.

This guy is tall and tan, with bright-blue eyes and buzzed brown hair, and looks like he's in his early twenties. He's on the skinnier side and doesn't look very muscular, but he must be strong if he made Dave and his giant friend retreat with their tails between their legs.

I awkwardly stand in front of him, not knowing what to do.

"Thanks?" I say suddenly, remembering that I probably have blood on me from when I bit Dave's hand, and wipe it away.

"He's a dick, anyway," the guy says nonchalantly.

I appreciate that he saved me from Dave and his friend, but I have this nagging feeling that something's off about him. Plus, I don't want to stay behind this building where no one knows where I am for any longer. I'm tired. I'm sore. I'm rattled. And to be honest, all I really want right now is Aiden.

I begin to walk back to the front of the building. "Right. Well, thanks again."

"Wait!" he says quickly, coming closer to me but not invading my personal space.

I regard him warily. He's not threatening, but I'm drained after what I've just been through, and I just want to get back to my friends.

"What's your name?" he asks gently.

I at least owe him my name after he jumped in to help me out. "Amelia."

"I'm Luke." He smiles. "I wish we could've met in different circumstances."

"Yeah, no one really likes being manhandled and punched so

hard in the stomach that they taste colors," I say, while trying to smooth out my hair.

"Been there, done that," Luke jokes, before growing serious. "Listen, you're friends with Annalisa White, right?"

My eyes narrow at him and my mind shouts *Red flag! Red flag!*

He must sense my alarm because he quickly adds "I saw you guys pull in together and you were talking to her."

That doesn't make me feel any better. I'm grateful that he's here, since he's the only reason I'm not a bloody mess right now—well, at least not a bloody mess with my *own* blood instead of Dave's. Seriously, I think I tore a chunk of his hand out; there are blood-stains on my leather jacket from when he grabbed my arms. But if this guy is enough to make the always fierce Annalisa nervous, then maybe I should be careful around him too.

"Who? Oh, that girl with the red headband? No, she came up with some friends of my friends. We just met tonight. Well, thanks again," I ramble as I slowly back up and then turn to run to the front of the building, leaving a very confused Luke behind.

Turning sharply, I run straight into Mason. He reaches out his arms and steadies me, preventing me from landing on my ass from ricocheting off him.

"Amelia? Where the hell have you been?"

Swirls of different emotions flood me when I see him. I don't know how to feel about him right now. On one hand, Mason is a great friend and I love spending time with him. I want him to be happy, and it really shouldn't be his job to protect me twenty-four seven. It's not his job to make sure I don't find trouble, which is inevitable anyway. On the other hand, *he left me alone* in a sketchy bathroom surrounded by even sketchier people who are into illegal shit. He literally had one job: to make sure I wasn't left alone. He knew that Ryan and the Silvers who *hate* me and already did illegal things to me are here, and he left me.

What makes it worse is that he left me so that he could *flirt with a girl.* Like his booty call couldn't have waited until I was done and back with everyone else? I don't expect him to give up his life and devote himself to a life of service and protection. He just had to wait *five minutes* and then flirt with her when I was with Julian or Chase or someone.

I know I can't blame him for what happened. It's not his fault that Dave hates me and Aiden. But if Mason was with me, Dave would've never grabbed me in the first place, and I wouldn't have just been beaten up and have a giant bruise forming on my abdomen. I'll eventually get over it and forgive him, but right now, I need to be mad. That shit was traumatizing and I wouldn't have had to go through it if he didn't ditch me. He wasn't even the one to save me. Like, did he not even notice that I was gone? He should know it doesn't take that long to pee.

"K-bear? What's wr—" He stops when he takes in my appearance.

I'm sure I look a mess. I know that my hair is tangled, and I can only hope that I got the blood off my face. My clothes are disheveled, not to mention the blood smudged on my jacket.

"Holy shit, Amelia. What the fuck happened to you?"

He grabs my chin and analyzes my face for damage, but I push his hand off, my anger brewing.

"It's not my blood," I answer coldly, and walk back to that awful bathroom to get cleaned up before anyone else sees me. I don't want to answer any questions and I definitely don't want Aiden to find out.

Mason quickly follows. "Amelia, stop. Tell me what happened."

I get to the bathroom and step in before turning to regard him with cold and angry eyes.

"Why don't you ask your booty call?" I snap, unable to help myself, before slamming the door closed in his face.

That was low of me, I know. It's not that girl's fault and it really isn't Mason's either.

There's more blood smudged around my mouth and neck than there should be. With my adrenaline and anger dying down, I notice that my tongue's throbbing in pain. I probably bit it hard. I wet my hand and start to get the blood off my face, out of my hair, and off my clothes. Before opening the door again, I double-check that I look close to normal. Satisfied, I swing the door open only to come face to face with a pissed off Mason, leaning on the wall across from the bathroom door, with his arms crossed.

He pushes himself off the wall when he sees me. "What the fuck, Amelia?"

I instantly go into defense mode. "Don't 'What the fuck,' me, Mason! If anything, I should be 'What the fuck'-ing you!"

I walk out of the run-down building and into the fresh air, and he quickly follows, stopping in front of me.

His face softens despite my outrage and he steps closer, reaching out to me. "Just tell me what happened."

"What *happened*," I snap, getting angrier with every word, "was that you *ditched* me to talk to some *girl*. I was left *alone*, which was what we were working so hard to *avoid*, and then I was kidnapped and dragged behind the building where two assholes proceeded to hassle me and one *drove his fist into my stomach* before some guy who *wasn't you* saved my ass!"

I purposely decide not to tell him who it was. I may be pissed at Mason, but I still don't want him to do something stupid like try to confront Dave.

Mason's face drains of color as I snap at him, guilt spreading over his features.

"God, Amelia, I am so, so, sorry. Are you okay? Of course you're not okay, what a stupid thing to ask! I'm so sorry; I never meant for this to happen. I never wanted you to get hurt! I'm the worst friend in the whole entire world; please forgive me. I promise not to leave your side ever again."

His apology starts to melt my cold façade, but then that girl in the booty shorts and knee highs that he ditched me to talk to calls his name and waves him over enthusiastically, and I harden again. Mason looks over at her when she calls him and another wave of guilt washes over his face.

"Just go," I say emotionlessly, stepping around him and walking back to where I think we parked when we got here. "Oh, and Mason? No one finds out about this. *Especially* not Aiden."

I don't wait for his response as I continue on my journey. I'm hurt, there's no doubt about that. What aches the most is that I considered Mason one of my best friends, and he let something so horrible happen to me. I know it's not his responsibility to protect me, but I still can't help but blame him. I'll forgive him . . . eventually.

The whole time I'm walking back to the group, Mason is trailing slightly behind me; I can feel his regretful gaze burning holes through the back of my head. When the group is within eyesight, I stop and wait for Mason to catch up to me so that we can walk up together.

He looks down at me expectantly with pleading brown eyes, waiting to see what I'll say. I hold my ground despite my wavering resolve to stay mad at him, selfishly choosing to let him stay guilty for just a bit longer before I break and forgive him.

"No one finds out about what happened, *ever*. Got it?"

Mason hesitates. "Only if you tell me who did it. Was it Ryan?"

I don't say anything and anger fills his brown eyes as he thinks about who could've possibly hurt me. "Just tell me, Amelia. I won't say anything if you just give me their names and let me deal with them."

"Drop it, Mason," I say, my anger toward him practically gone.

"No, Amelia." He holds his ground. "Someone thinks it's okay to keep messing with you and get away with it. Hell, I'll even tell Aiden and face his ass-kicking if it means he'll fuck up the people who hurt you."

My heart melts. "How am I supposed to stay mad at you when you talk like that?"

"I mean it, Amelia. Just say the name—"

"Why?" I interrupt. "So that you can go fight him? So you can get yourself unnecessarily hurt to defend my honor? That's a stupid reason to fight. I don't want anyone getting hurt on my behalf, Mason. It's done. Luke saved me and I'm grateful, but I just want this to be over and done with and—"

"Luke?" Mason asks. "Where do I know a Luke from?"

"It doesn't matter," I say, steering his thoughts away from Luke, whom I shouldn't have even mentioned in the first place. "Just promise me you won't say anything."

"But I really want to kick their—"

"Mason! If you promise me you won't tell anyone and forget about this, I'll forgive you," I plead.

He looks at me skeptically, seeming to have an internal fight between his need to get revenge or to get my friendship back.

"It *is* always easier to ask forgiveness later, than permission now," he reasons with himself.

"Mason! I swear, if you go around starting unnecessary fights I'll be really mad at you! Would you rather get in a fight and lose a friend, or help me out and be besties again?"

He weighs the pros and cons for a few moments before finally giving in. "Fine. But if something else happens, I get to drive my boot up some asses."

"Deal!" I exclaim, and wrap my arms around him, my anger already dissolved.

He pulls me in close, resting his chin on my head. "I really am sorry, k-bear," he breathes in my ear.

"I know. It's okay." I reply honestly before we break apart and walk back to the group together.

Now everything's fine between me and Mason, and no one will get in a fight over this. I don't want this situation escalating any more than it has to. No one else is getting hurt on my behalf. We get back to the group, who are clustered around Julian's and Mason's trucks, and they all turn to us.

"Where the hell have you guys been? It doesn't take that long to pee—unless . . . you guys were gettin' it on in the bushes, weren't you?" Noah jokes, moving his hips. "Bow chicka bow wow."

We can't help but laugh at Noah as Mason smacks him upside the head.

"He wishes," I joke. "Mason kept stopping to talk to everyone." I lie smoothly, knowing that Mason is well rounded and likeable enough that it's believable.

"Yeah, right," Mason adds, not sounding too convincing.

"Aiden was looking for you. I think he doesn't want to set up the race with Ryan until you're here," Charlotte tells me.

A tingling sense of warmth spreads through my body when I hear Aiden's name. After everything I've been through tonight, I want to revel in the comforting safety of his strong arms. But then reality hits and I realize that I can't do that without seeming like a total weirdo.

"Why?" I ask.

"I think he knows that you don't want him to punch Ryan in the face upon first sight, and the only way he can respect that is if you're there with him to keep him grounded," Annalisa intuits.

Annalisa's statement causes two different sets of emotions to rise within me. On one hand, Aiden is just . . . Aiden, amazing as ever. On the other, seeing Annalisa makes my stomach turn with anxiety and indecisiveness.

Seeing her reminds me about Luke and how he's probably the guy she was so nervous about when we got here. Should I tell her I saw him? But that would mean admitting I heard her private moment with Julian, as well as to the incident with Dave. I don't want to admit either of those, but what if Luke's, like, her abusive ex-boyfriend or something? I thought he could be her brother, but he doesn't look anything like her, so who else could he be? If she's nervous about him being here, she should know that he is. I don't want her being bombarded and caught off guard when or if she runs into him.

"Actually, Anna, there's something I need to—"

"There you are," Aiden says. "I was just looking for you."

He pauses for a minute, looking at me while seeming confused, as if trying to figure out what's different about me.

"What did you need?" I try to divert his attention.

He shakes his head as if to clear it. "Come on, we have to set up the race."

I hold my sigh of relief, grateful that I cleaned up well enough to pass his inspection.

Seeing Aiden so self-confident and fearless makes me want to run into his arms and be comforted knowing that it's him who's holding me. But sadly, I can't.

"Why do you need me with you?"

He looks at me with a sliver of an unknown emotion in his normally cool eyes. "Because if you're not, I'll do something that I promised you I wouldn't."

A warm, tingly feeling spreads throughout my body at his words, and I try not to turn to mush when he grabs my hand and intertwines his fingers with my own.

"Mason, grab Jonesy and bring him over to Ryan's car," Aiden instructs Mason, and then pulls me away from the group.

I look back longingly at Annalisa, knowing I should tell her about Luke right now, but Aiden's pulling me away from her. Julian won't leave her side and he'll protect her. She'll be safe with the group, and I'll tell her the second we get back from setting up the race.

"Who's Jonesy?" I ask, ignoring the effect Aiden's touch has on me.

"He kind of runs this thing. He's the neutral guy who holds the betting money for the racers. The racers put the cash down up front so that no one gets ripped off. Jonesy holds it while we race and gives it to the winner after. That way, everything's fair and no one can short anyone money they owe."

"Makes sense. But where are we going now?" I ask, already knowing but dreading to hear the answer.

"To challenge Ryan and take his money," he says simply.

What if Dave's there and says something? I don't think he will, because if he wanted to fight Aiden, he would've gone to him directly instead of beating up his girl to get to him. I freeze and Aiden looks at me funnily before I shake my head to clear it and continue walking beside him.

I said *his girl.*

And the weird part? I like it. I like the sound of "his girl."

Oh my God, I like Aiden. Like, more than a friend. Eff. My. Life. What is happening to me?

Aiden looks down at me and tenderly strokes my hand with his thumb, thinking that my racing pulse and tight grip are due to my nervousness about being near Ryan and the Silvers, not because of my terrifying revelation.

As we get closer to them, I know that I should feel more worried or nervous, especially since Dave and his friends assaulted me moments ago, but I'm not. I'm comforted by Aiden's presence, and somehow I know that if shit gets crazy, Aiden's first priority will be to keep me safe.

Ryan leans against his Mustang, talking to some other Silvers. Dave is there, sporting a newly split lip and freshly bruising black eye, courtesy of Luke, and I feel my blood turn to fiery lava in my veins. I want to strut right up to him and castrate him where he stands. What kind of coward has his friend restrain a girl so that he can beat her up? Plus, he's an even bigger coward because he only beat me up to hurt Aiden, since he's too scared to face him one on one (which he should be, Aiden would totally kick his ass). Kaitlyn is there as well, talking to Makayla, and a few other girls who go to C. S. High.

As we approach the group, they notice our presence and turn their hostile gazes on us. A malicious smirk grows on Ryan's face the moment he sees us. The sides of his head look freshly shaved and he's wearing a tight-fitting long-sleeved gray shirt with black sleeves that accentuate his muscles and dark-blue jeans. Again, I'm struck by how hot he would actually be if not for the fact that he's a total dickwad.

Ryan confidently strides toward us, followed by his pack of loyal followers. Kaitlyn marches right up to his side and he swings his arm around her. Both have venomous gleams in their eyes and stand confidently, like they own the whole world. I wish I could wipe the smug look off her face.

"Parker," Ryan addresses Aiden, then turns his intense gaze to me. "Parker's slut."

Aiden's eyes narrow and he goes to take a threatening step closer to Ryan, but I pull him back with our joined hands.

"Satan," I address Ryan without missing a beat, then look at Kaitlyn. "Satan's whore."

Kaitlyn scowls at my hand resting comfortably in Aiden's. "What do you wannabes want?"

Aiden looks questioningly at Dave's newly damaged face before turning his attention back to Ryan.

"You always want to race me, here's your chance," Aiden says impassively.

"You want a shot at *me*?" Ryan asks, acting like he's the big man on campus.

"Is that a yes?" Aiden keeps his tone even and his face in his regular confident and impassive expression.

"You sure this is a good idea?" Ryan asks, trying to act like it's no big deal, but it's obvious that he's excited. "We all know that the men in my family are notorious for beating you."

This time I can't hold Aiden back when he lets go of my hand, closes the space between them, and takes a swing at a wide-eyed

Ryan. A few feet behind him, shocked and frozen in place, Kaitlyn screams as Ryan is knocked to the ground from the force of Aiden's single punch.

The heat of Aiden's anger radiates off of him to where I stand. Ryan spits out blood from his position on the ground and his loyal dog pack take a second to register that their leader was just knocked to the ground before setting their gazes on Aiden.

Oh shit.

Aiden is greatly outnumbered, and this is not going to end well . . . for them.

Aiden's taken on a crowd of guys his size and even bulkier and heavier, and still kicked ass while he wasn't even that mad. This time it's personal, and if Aiden's anger alone is any indication, he's not just promising an ass-kicking, he's promising to *destroy* them.

Just when the dog pack is about to pounce, we hear a loud and authoritative voice. "All right, that's enough, boys."

The dog pack freezes and Ryan slowly stands back up. I take the opportunity to run around to Aiden and get in front of him, putting my hands on his muscled chest and pushing him back, trying to get distance between him and the Silvers.

He registers that it's me touching him and he doesn't resist when I push him back, since I wouldn't be able to move him if he didn't allow it. His breathing is heavy and his whole body is hard and tense, ready to attack on a second's notice. We move back a few feet, but he keeps his infuriated eyes locked on Ryan the whole time.

"Aiden," I say calmly and put a hand on his cheek, trying to get him to look down at me. He keeps his angry eyes locked on Ryan for a few more moments before slowly meeting my gaze. "Please don't fight," I whisper, staring into his darkening gray eyes, feeling his chest rise and fall with anger with my other hand.

He studies me for a moment before releasing a heavy breath through his nose and closing his eyes. I bring both my hands around his waist under his leather jacket and hug him to me, resting my cheek on his chest.

Aiden's body starts to relax and he puts his arms around me. I distantly register people having a conversation behind me, so I pull back slightly but keep my arms around Aiden's waist. I look questioningly in his eyes and he nods slightly, indicating that he's okay.

Reluctantly, I pull away from him, but he keeps one arm around me and firmly holds me to his side. My touch seems to have a calming effect on him, and I subconsciously sink into his side, loving the sparks I feel when I touch him.

We face everyone else, and I see that the raspy voice that broke up the fight belongs to a short, bulky guy with tattoo sleeves and short, dark hair. He must be at least five foot two, shorter even than me, but looks to be in his mid to late twenties. He's talking to Ryan in a professional manner, Mason standing beside him. This must be Jonesy, and Mason finally brought him over like Aiden instructed. Although short, Jonesy has a commanding air that makes it clear that he's capable of sort of running this thing.

We walk back to the group, Aiden already having slipped into his businesslike attitude.

"So, is there a race happening or what?" Jonesy asks.

Aiden's eyes lock back onto Ryan's. "If he's not afraid of facing me."

"You're on, asshole."

"All right!" Jonesy announces excitedly. "You know the drill, cash up front before the race. How much is it going to be tonight? Standard entrance fee of three hundred?"

Ryan gives an empty, cold laugh. "The entrance fee is for pussies. How about we up it a couple grand?"

Aiden's face doesn't reveal anything. "You sure you can afford that?"

Ryan scoffs and gives a malicious smirk. "I'm going to enjoy taking two grand from you."

I tug on Aiden's shirt with the hand that's resting on his back beneath his leather jacket, trying to signal not to bet that much money. I know the Boys said he never loses, but there's always a chance. Plus, he's doing this in part to get back at Ryan for vandalizing my car. I know that this rivalry goes way deeper than just me and my car, but I still don't want Aiden to risk that much money because of me.

He ignores me and says, "Let's do this then."

"*Great!*" Jonesy says, visibly excited. Aiden told me that Jonesy doesn't get anything from the racers' entrance fee, but he gets a cut from everyone who bets on them. He's probably going to make a lot of money from having the two rivals finally face one another.

"Go get ready and meet me at the starting line in your cars, with your money, in fifteen minutes! Let's have a clean race, boys!" Jonesy hurriedly turns around, going back to hype everyone up and take bets for probably the most anticipated race of the year.

Walking back to the group with Aiden and Mason is tense, to say the least. Aiden is seriously out of his mind. The difference between being *two thousand dollars* richer or poorer depends on a five-minute race against Satan's spawn.

Before we get to the group, Aiden tugs on my hand and brings us to a halt. "I need a minute with Amelia. Tell everyone what's going on and we'll be there soon," Aiden instructs Mason, who nods and heads back to the group.

Aiden releases my hand and looks at me with a . . . guilty expression? I've never seen him with a guilty look before. The difference in his whole demeanor is strikingly obvious now that we're in private, and I forget how he acts differently with me than with everyone else. He has his guard down, letting me read his emotions, which is remarkably different compared to the guarded, stoic, impassive Aiden he was just now in front of the Silvers.

This is real. This is Aiden. He feels comfortable enough around me to let his guard down and let me in. And the scary part about it? I'm not even sure if he consciously knows that he's doing it.

"Are you mad at me?" he asks softly.

"I'm not mad, but two grand is *a lot* of money, Aiden! That's money you could use for university or your brothers or—"

"No, not that." He waves me off. "I mean that I broke my promise."

I freeze, finally registering what he means and why he looks guilty. "I told you I wouldn't fight and I almost caused one anyway. I just—he just—I had to."

I can't. I can't handle this. If he gets any more amazing my heart will explode. My body moves on its own accord, and I step closer to him.

"Of course I'm not mad at you," I reply honestly. "I don't need to know all the details to know that he deserved that one."

"Ryan's dad is my stepfather, and he's my stepbrother, and I hate him, but you probably already guessed that."

Deep down, I knew, but thought if I didn't acknowledge it, it wouldn't have to be true—like if you ignore something long enough it will just go away. The thought of Aiden having to deal with a monster like Ryan because his mom married Ryan's dad when they were kids makes me ache for him. I nod, never breaking eye contact with him, never letting go.

I especially don't want to think about their history or what Ryan meant when he said that the men in his family are known to "beat" Aiden. I don't want to acknowledge the possible double meaning, and what that would mean about Aiden's childhood. I don't want to think about the fact that Ryan's dad, Greg, is in jail, and the possible atrocities that a young Aiden would have had to face to make him the guarded, stoic man he is today. It just hurts too much to think about that.

"So we're okay?" he says, gently.

"We were never not okay," I say.

He takes my hand again, a small action that I've become quite fond of, and we start heading back to the group.

"Aiden."

This time it's me who tugs his hand and brings us to a stop. He raises an eyebrow questioningly.

"You know you can talk to me about anything, right?" I say, ignoring the stab of guilt I feel for being such a hypocrite.

"The same goes for you, Amelia. I'm here for you," he replies.

And I believe it. Aiden is genuinely here for me. His past actions have done nothing but solidify that statement, and I want nothing more than to be able to open up to him. I wish I could just tell someone my full story for the first time and just be able to be *me*. To have even one person know the truth would take such a heavy burden off my shoulders.

Aiden could be that guy—the perfect guy. I just know, deep down in my heart and bones, that Aiden would be able to help me. I'm so tempted to just blurt out everything that I've kept bottled up for so long and cry in Aiden's open arms.

But I can't. And I won't. Because I'm Thea Kennedy. And my reality sucks.

I'm not destined to end up with such an amazing, understanding, and loyal man like Aiden. So instead of pouring out my soul like my heart is screaming at me to do, I just send Aiden a small smile and nod. He looks at me skeptically for a second before letting it slide, and we continue walking back to the group.

"Aiden! Two grand in one race? When you get that money, there better be some labeled *Noah's burger*," Noah exclaims when we get to the group. "Wait, what am I saying—it's two grand . . . make that two burgers!"

Charlotte and Annalisa notice my hand held comfortably in Aiden's, and they each try to catch my eye, but I avoid them. They're going to ask what's going on with us, and I don't even know the answer to that. I definitely don't want to spill and tell them about my crush on Aiden. We don't need to complicate things further.

"When does the race start?" I ask.

"I'll go to the starting line in five minutes," Aiden says, just as we hear the rumble of a loud car driving past us.

Ryan's red Mustang slowly cruises by, the driver's-side window rolled down so that he can talk to us from where he is.

"You know, Greg's due for parole soon. Maybe if he gets out early he can visit with Jason and Jackson. They need a strong father figure with a heavy hand," Ryan teases, and Aiden's face contorts with pure rage.

Aiden quickly moves forward, as if he could bare-handedly strip the metal off of Ryan's Mustang just to get to him, but Mason and Julian jump in front of him and hold him back as Ryan speeds away to the starting line. Aiden keeps his burning gaze on Ryan's car and roughly shakes off Julian and Mason.

"Change of plans," Aiden growls. "I want more money from this douche bag."

Aiden's furious. His little brothers are his life. No one is going to get away with threatening his family.

"You know the rules. Once you agree on the amount with Jonesy it's locked in," Noah sadly reminds him.

Chase nods, a thoughtful look on his face. "Plus, when you beat Ryan, he'll be so ashamed that he'll probably just throw a fit and leave."

"Can't you just smash his kneecaps in with a tire iron or something and get it over with?" Annalisa suggests.

Aiden meets my eyes for a second, then looks back at Annalisa and shakes his head. "As much as I'd love to, that won't do anything in the long run."

Aiden's smart. He'll always have the opportunity to beat Ryan's face in with his own two hands, but right now, he has the opportunity to screw him out of more money than Ryan could even count.

"I agree with Aiden. That piece of shit needs to learn a lesson about not being a complete fuckface. If it takes screwing him out of four grand to do so, then so be it," Julian declares, everyone else nodding in solidarity.

Did he just say four grand? Like a four, with three zeros after it?

"Great. So what's the plan?" Mason speaks up.

Aiden looks at us with a serious expression on his face. "You'll know it when you see it."

Chase checks his watch. "It's time."

Julian opens the tailgate of his pickup truck and hoists Annalisa into the bed of the truck, giving her a better standing view of the track, and jumps up after her. Chase does the same with Charlotte as Mason speaks in hushed tones to Aiden.

Noah heads over to Mason's Range Rover, parked beside Julian's truck, and hops in, his head emerging from the sunroof seconds later as he hoists himself up and sits on the roof, his legs dangling down the side of the SUV. Mason finishes with Aiden and goes over to his vehicle as Aiden walks back over to me. He stops in front of me and puts his hands on my hips, the warmth from his hands spreading throughout my entire body.

"Be safe," I whisper, my mind too focused on his warm hands to come up with anything else to say.

He nods, an unspoken agreement in his eyes, before he tightens his grip and easily lifts me onto Julian's pickup.

I stand with Charlotte and Annalisa, still not recovered from Aiden's closeness and the tingling feeling his hands left on my body. He gets into his Challenger and the engine roars to life, and we watch him drive to the starting line to embarrass Ryan and screw him out of more cash than I've ever seen in one sitting. To say that I'm nervous would be an understatement.

Aiden drives to the starting line to race his enemy and stepbrother for two thousand dollars—his enemy, who vandalized my car, probably made Aiden's life miserable as a child, and threatened to sic his abusive father on Aiden's little brothers. Ryan deserves a lot more than losing two grand in a race. Aiden and Ryan stop their cars side-by-side at the starting line, and Jonesy walks between them. I see Ryan hand him an envelope of cash. Aiden does the same, and Jonesy takes a second to quickly count all the money. Apparently satisfied with the envelopes' contents, Jonesy shoves them in his pocket and takes a few steps back.

"Who's ready to race?" he yells over the music blasting from someone's car, and the crowd cheers in anticipation. People are standing on cars and crowding the starting line, trying to get a look at the two greatest known enemies going head to head. From where we're standing in the bed of Julian's pickup, we have a pretty good view of the track. The headlights from the numerous scattered cars illuminate the pitch-black winding country roads, the bright moon only giving off so much light.

"*Parker?*" Jonesy yells and points at Aiden, who revs his engine in response.

I wipe my sweaty hands on my pants.

"*Simms?*" Jonesy does the same for Ryan, who answers in the same way as Aiden.

The crowd cheers louder, hoping that the person they bet money on wins.

"Let's start in *three* . . ." Jonesy holds up three fingers as he steps backward.

My heart pounds in my ears.

". . . *two* . . ." He puts a finger down and continues backing up.

I hold my breath.

Jonesy stands still and points at the drivers with both hands. "*Go!*"

Ryan takes off seconds before the word is even out of Jonesy's mouth, Aiden an instant later. The cars speed through the deserted country roads, traveling away from the main part of the track, making it hard to really see what's going on in the dark. For the most part, if you have good eyesight and are higher up, like we are while standing on Julian's truck, you can make out the cars, even if they look tiny because of the distance.

Despite Ryan's short head start, Aiden catches up pretty fast, and I cheer for Aiden despite the nerves twisting up my stomach. They're driving right beside each other when Aiden suddenly pulls forward and cuts Ryan off on a turn, leaving Ryan some distance behind him.

"Yes, Aiden!" I'm yelling and jumping up and down in excitement.

"He's got this!" Charlotte shouts beside me, the others cheering in agreement.

Aiden remains in the lead through two more turns, but then Ryan suddenly advances on him and now they're driving side-by-side. My heart is pounding so loudly I wouldn't be surprised if Julian could hear it from beside me.

"Come on, Aiden!" I cheer with Charlotte.

They get to an area in a distance where there are some sparse trees blocking the road from our view. We can only hear the loud roar of their engines, and I can only make out some blurs of the red from Ryan's Mustang shining through the trees.

"What's happening? I can't see shit," Annalisa says as she tries to get a better view around the trees.

Suddenly, a pair of headlights comes out of the area with trees, another pair following just behind it.

"Who's in the lead?" I yell.

As if answering my question, the cars turn, and we see Ryan's red Mustang trailing barely a foot behind Aiden's Challenger.

They continue through the rest of the track with Aiden slightly in the lead.

"This is the last turn before the straight shot to the finish line,"

Julian tells me and Charlotte without taking his eyes off the race.

It's a tight, windy turn, definitely hard for drivers to make at such fast speeds. To make it you'd either have to slow down a bit or drift, otherwise your car would spin out into the fields.

They get to the turn, and it looks like Aiden slows down a bit to make it while Ryan takes it fast, slightly spinning out into the field.

"What's he doing?" Julian mutters to himself beside me.

"What? What's he doing?" I ask nervously.

"Aiden always makes that drift perfectly. Why didn't he drift this time?" he muses out loud, more to himself than as an answer to me.

The crowd roars and people start running toward the finish. Ryan recovers from slightly spinning out and shoots for the finish line, Aiden barely a foot behind him from not drifting the turn. I'm jumping up and down, unable to contain my anxiety. Charlotte, Annalisa, and I are all yelling for Aiden to win, but the guys are all calmly sharing a look, as if they figured something out that we didn't.

About five seconds after the turn, the cars pass the finish line, the crowd cheering and yelling and booing. I stand there, completely stunned. Aiden lost.

My mind is unable to process what just happened. I jump off of the truck without a word to anyone and race over to where Aiden and Ryan are slowing down their cars and stopping. Other people are trying to crowd in as well, either to congratulate or yell about how that was complete bullshit. I shove my way through the people, not caring that I'm being totally rude, just knowing that I need to get to Aiden.

"Amelia!" Mason calls from behind me.

I turn my head but don't stop moving through the crowd, and see the Boys, Charlotte, and Annalisa hot on my trail. We get to where the cars are parked and go right up to Aiden, who's getting out of his car.

"Aiden." I act instinctively and throw my arms around his waist, pressing my cheek to his chest and hugging him close.

"It's okay. We can figure something out on how to make up for that two grand. I swear I'll help you get it back. I'm so sorry you lost it because of me," I rant, my heart heavy.

He stands there confused, but slowly puts his arms around me and holds me close.

"You know it's not your fault," he comforts me quietly.

"I still feel responsible," I mutter.

"Trust me, you're not."

I see Julian looking at Aiden and sharing a knowing look. I wish I could see Aiden's face but I'm too busy reveling in his warm embrace that I never want too—

Wait. I just threw myself at Aiden. In front of all our friends. *Get a grip, Amelia!*

I reluctantly but abruptly let go of Aiden and take an embarrassing few steps back. He probably thinks something's wrong with me now. God, why do I always make such an ass out of myself in front of people who are important to me?

Aiden makes eye contact with Ryan, who's standing beside his car surrounded by his friends and Kaitlyn and Makayla.

"Guess I put you in your place, you little bitch," Ryan boasts, a victorious smirk on his face. He picks up Kaitlyn and laughs. "Now his little whore can do what she's good at and spread her legs for money to make up for what he lost."

Aiden takes an aggressive step forward with his hands clenched in fists, but Chase puts a hand on his shoulder to stop him, and gives him a small nod.

Jonesy chooses that time to come over and hand Ryan the two envelopes of two grand each.

"Congratulations," he tells him.

"Yeah, congratulations on your *win*, Ryan," Mason exaggerates.

Dave picks up on Mason's sarcasm and gets defensive. "What? Why'd you say it like that?"

I can't help but glare at Dave. If I wasn't being held back by someone twice my size, I totally would've kicked his ass. If Luke didn't come along—shit, *Luke*! *Annalisa*. I need to warn Annalisa about Luke before she sees him!

"It's pretty obvious," Noah answers Dave, looking bored of the whole conversation.

"What is?" one of Ryan's friends asks.

Julian rolls his eyes. "Well, it's obvious you only won because you messed with Aiden's car."

Ryan's face turns red and contorts into a look of disbelief and rage. "I can beat that piece of shit without having to mess with his car!"

"Clearly you can't," Chase provokes him.

"I can, and I did!" Ryan yells.

Mason crosses his arms. "You should take the money and run, Ryan. We all know you wouldn't beat Aiden again."

Ryan takes the bait, getting worked up and defensive. "Of course I could beat him again. I could drive circles around his dumb ass."

Noah scoffs. "Yeah, right. Think that if it helps you sleep at night."

Ryan visibly gets angrier. "Fine! I'll prove it! Another race. Let's make it four grand just to prove that I'm not fucking around!" He throws Aiden one of the envelopes of two thousand dollars. "I'll even be generous and give you the two grand back, just because I know you wouldn't be able to afford another race with the champ."

Aiden looks at him as if he couldn't care less. "I didn't think you could afford to lose that much."

My head snaps toward Aiden, eyes wide. Shut up, Aiden! *You* can't afford to lose that much!

"I won't be the one losing it," Ryan answers.

Jonesy claps once to get our attention, rubbing his hands together and reminding us that he's still here. "All right, then, let's put your money where your mouth is. You know the rules. All cash up front."

Ryan takes his original envelope and shoves some extra money into it. He growls at his friends to give him any money that they have until he gets the remaining two grand, and hands the full envelope to Jonesy.

"All right, everyone! Rematch! Place your bets with Gabe now!" Jonesy announces to the crowd, excited about making more commission from the bets.

I grab Aiden's arm and pull him aside. "Are you crazy? What are you thinking? Let's just go; you don't need to bet more money."

He looks over my head and narrows his eyes at Ryan in the distance, trash-talking with his friends.

"I told you I want more money from him."

"But what if you lose? That would be four grand that could've been spent in so many better ways!"

He looks me straight in the eyes, melting my worries with his powerful gaze. "It'll be okay."

"But—"

"Hey!" Ryan yells from where he's standing with his friends, "You gonna talk all night with your slut, or we gonna race?"

If Ryan was anyone else, the look that Aiden shot him would've made them shit their pants in fear. Aiden goes back over to his car and gets in, then emerges with another envelope and hands it over to Jonesy.

"All right, everything looks good," verifies Jonesy, shoving the new envelopes back in his pocket. "Let's head over to the starting line and see who wins round two!"

The crowd cheers and many run over to Gabe, Jonesy's business partner, while others head back to their spots to get a view of the race.

"Aiden, you don't have to do this," I plead one more time.

"The deal was made with Jonesy, it's locked in," Mason tells me.

The loud roar of an engine interrupts us. "Ready for me to make you my bitch again?" Ryan calls from inside his car, before laughing and driving to the starting line.

"Don't worry, Amelia." Aiden smirks. "This will be the easiest four grand I've ever made."

With that, he gets in his car and follows Ryan to the starting line, hopefully the last time his car will ever be behind Ryan's. We run back over to Julian and Mason's trucks and get back in place, just catching Aiden and Ryan getting to the starting line. I didn't think it was possible to be even more nervous than I was the first time I watched Aiden race, but the heavy hammering in my heart is making it abundantly clear that this time is much worse.

"Are we ready for round two?" Jonesy announces, hyping up the crowd.

I must've audibly inhaled, because Annalisa looks at me. "He'll be okay."

"Anna, there's something—"

"Going on with you and Aiden? Yeah, yeah, we know," she finishes for me, totally catching me off guard.

I freeze, hearing Jonesy saying something to the crowd in the background but not paying attention. "Wait. What?"

"Don't think that Char and I haven't picked up on it! But give us details later; the race is starting!"

"No, Anna, that's not—"

"Don't worry, we'll wait until the Boys aren't around to interrogate you," she says playfully, without taking her eyes off of the track.

"Okay, but, Anna, you need to—"

"Stop talking, they started!" she shouts at me and physically turns my head toward the track, where Aiden and Ryan are speeding along the dark roads.

All thoughts fly out of my mind and my heart moves into overdrive from the stress of watching Aiden race. They're driving right beside each other when Aiden suddenly pulls forward and cuts Ryan off on the same turn as last time, again leaving Ryan some distance behind him.

Come on, come on, come on. Ryan takes the next turn tight, almost pulling ahead of Aiden, when suddenly it's like a total switch happens that's palpable in the atmosphere. Aiden easily pulls ahead of Ryan, making the next few turns with ease and leaving the Mustang farther and farther in the distance. They get to that area with the trees blocking the track, but this time it's obvious to see who's in the lead. Aiden drives back into view first, keeping an easy lead. The crowd goes wild, cheering for Aiden to stay out front, and my energy feeds off that of the crowd, my confidence and excitement growing with it.

"The last turn!" Noah announces, indicating the sharp turn that Aiden didn't drift last time.

Aiden's still in the lead, but you can tell Ryan's getting desperate to beat him.

They reach the turn, Ryan hot on Aiden's trail, and Aiden leaves me staring at him in lustful awe. He manages his Challenger perfectly, gray smoke billowing up from the skidding tires as he drifts the turn, straightening himself out easily.

I've never been so turned on.

Ryan attempts to drift a few seconds after Aiden, a skill much too advanced for him, and we watch with shocked eyes as he violently spins out of control. His car almost clips Aiden's, who expertly avoids Ryan's unmanageable rotations. If they weren't driving on open country roads with nothing but empty fields surrounding them, Ryan definitely would have flipped after hitting something.

I jump up and down, my excitement threatening to burst as Aiden speeds toward the finish line. He zooms past the finish line as Ryan finally gets his car under control, and the crowd goes absolutely *insane*.

Again, I jump off of Julian's pickup truck, but this time my emotions are completely different.

High off of the energy and excitement in the air, I don't even think about it when I sprint to Aiden, who's getting out of his car, and launch myself at him. He's caught slightly off guard but catches me with ease, and I wrap my legs around his waist and hug him to me, my elated excitement blocking all other rational parts of my brain.

"You won!" I cheer as he hugs me, my joyous attitude contagious as I hear him chuckle at me.

"I told you I would," he brags.

I pull back to look at him but stay suspended in his arms. "And that drift! That was *amazing*! How'd you learn to do that?"

"Ahem, should we come back or something?" Noah coughs.

I was so caught up in the excitement and Aiden and his dreamy amazingness that I barely noticed our friends staring openly at us.

My head snaps toward them and my face heats up. Like last time, I awkwardly and reluctantly untangle myself from Aiden, trying to remember to breathe so that I don't literally die of embarrassment.

Aiden looks at our friends, then looks back at me before breaking into a gorgeous smile and doing the unthinkable: he opens his arms and engulfs me in a tight hug, making me oblivious to everything but his warm and comforting embrace.

Then—as if he wants to see how long he can make me stop breathing for—he lowers his head and places a kiss on top of my head. On the outside, I'm sure I look just as shocked as I feel, but on the inside, my inner fangirl is squealing and jumping around like a kid on a sugar high.

Annalisa recovers faster than all of us. "Congratulations, Aiden!" she cheers, referring to the race.

Annalisa's praise breaks the shocked and awkward spell, and everyone else congratulates him and cheers, talking about how awesome he was. He releases me from his hug but keeps one arm around me and pulls me into his side, and I bite my lip, trying to (unsuccessfully) hide my overjoyed smile.

Jonesy comes up to us and hands Aiden the two envelopes of four thousand dollars each. "Good job out there, man."

"Thanks." Aiden takes the envelopes and shoves them in the inside pocket of his leather jacket.

In the distance, I notice Ryan throwing a complete bitch fit, yelling at his friends before shouting at Kaitlyn and Makayla to "Get the hell in," and they drive off. The other Silvers send us death glares, but I'm so hopped up on excitement and Aiden that their threats don't even reach me.

Plus, how can you feel threatened when *Aiden* has his arm around you? You can't, that's how; it's scientifically impossible. Other people come up to Aiden to talk to him or congratulate him on winning, and the whole time he keeps his arm around me, holding me to his side as if proudly showing me off.

17

After Aiden finishes talking to some people about some boring car stuff, he leads me back to the Boys' trucks, where Julian and Noah are talking to some other guys in the near distance.

"Did you have fun?" I ask him randomly.

He looks at me thoughtfully as we get to Julian's truck and pauses. "Yeah, I guess I did." He opens the tailgate of Julian's truck and turns to face me.

"I guess it would be pretty fun to take four grand from Ryan." I laugh.

He smiles at me, an action that I'm quickly becoming addicted to. "That wasn't my favorite part though."

Just when I start to blush, he puts his firm hands on my hips and hoists me up to sit on the tailgate with my legs dangling down, and steps closer to me, resting his hands on either side of me on the open tailgate.

I don't know how to breathe. My lungs have forgotten how to work. Clearly, I can't be too close to Aiden; he affects my respiratory system. That would be such an awkward cause of death on my death certificate. Cause of death? Aiden Parker's charm.

"Honestly, you were amazing," I admit, trying to distract him from my evidently racing pulse. "But why did it seem like you were holding back in the first race compared to the second one?"

He holds me hostage with his intense and unwavering gaze. "Because I was."

"Why?"

"He makes my life hell, he harasses you, and, most importantly, he threatened my little brothers. In my mind, two grand isn't a big enough loss for him to suffer."

"I get it. Once the bet for two grand was made, you couldn't raise it, so you needed a rematch for more money. But why didn't you just beat him the first time and then offer him a rematch instead of going through all the effort of losing then provoking him?"

"See that bitchfit he threw when he lost? And how he stormed off after? He would've done that if he lost the first time, too, and I wouldn't have had the opportunity to challenge him for more money than he would've offered the first time."

I nod, understanding and agreeing with what he's saying, even if it is a bit hard to focus with our current intimate position, and how he's so close to me.

"It was either that or take Anna up on her offer to break his kneecaps with a tire iron," he chuckles.

"*Shit*. Where's Anna?" I ask, looking around frantically.

"What's wrong?"

"I ran into this guy when I went to the bathroom—"

"You went to the bathroom alone?" he interrupts harshly, looking at how far the bathroom is from where we currently are, and how many people are between the two.

"No, Mason took me," I add quickly. "Anyway, he told me his name was Luke and he wanted to know about Anna. I don't know, I just thought she should know someone was looking for her. I didn't get a bad vibe from him, but I didn't get the best vibe either."

His eyes narrow in thought. "That's not good."

"Why? Who is he?" I panic.

He looks around, as if searching for Luke. "No one she wants to see."

"Where is she? Why isn't she with Julian?"

Aiden looks over at where Noah and Julian are talking with some guys. "Hey, Julian!" he calls. "Where's Annalisa?"

Julian looks at us and catches himself from doing a double-take at our intimate position; meanwhile, Noah very blatantly waggles his eyebrows suggestively at us. If I wasn't so worried about Annalisa, I would've been more embarrassed.

"Mason and Chase took her and Charlotte to the bathroom. They drove to the nearest coffee shop, since Char refused to go in this bathroom," Julian calls back with a chuckle, and they turn back to talking to the other guys.

"Should we go get her?" I ask Aiden nervously.

He shakes his head. "No. When they get back, we'll just leave right away."

I nod, relieved that I finally told somebody, especially Aiden, who always has a plan. "Hey," I start timidly. "How come you didn't tell me that Ryan's your stepbrother that night at my house?"

Aiden sighs and moves from where he was positioned in front of me, immediately making me regret asking him about his personal life, but he leans back on his elbows on the open tailgate to my left, his toned arm resting against my thigh, and looks away from me, out into the distance.

He runs his hand through his hair. "It was a horrible time in my life, and it's not something that I can talk about easily."

"But I'm not just anyone," I say softly.

He looks at me as if he's weighing some major decision in his head, before coming to a conclusion and admitting determinedly. "No, you're not."

This is it. Prepare the awkward death certificate because I think Aiden just stopped my heart.

"It's hard for me to open up to people."

Believe me, I know. I reach out and gently place my hand on the back of his neck, my arm resting on his sculpted back, and gently brush my thumb back and forth in a comforting motion.

"You know you can tell me anything, if you want too."

My touch seems to relax him, and I feel some tension leave his body.

He sighs, still looking out in the distance at nothing in particular. "You remember what I told you about my father?"

"Your real one?" The one who walked out on his nine-year-old son and pregnant wife who had cancer because she refused to abort the soon-to-be-born twins and he refused to deal with the bills.

He nods, and I do, too, before I realize that he can't see me. "Yeah, I remember."

"After he left, my mom was kind of desperate. There's only so much a single mother with a young kid and two newborns can do. You know, what with her cancer coming back and being able to afford her medical bills and all the other ones."

I sit in perfect silence, captivated by Aiden and his words.

"I know that she married Greg more for support than anything else. He was awful, and so was his son."

"Do you blame your mom?" I ask gently.

"No, not really." He looks at me thoughtfully and then back out into the distance. "She did what she had to do for her kids. She knew she was dying, and when she did, we would've gone into the system. I would've been separated from the twins, and that would've been a lot worse than anything Greg's ever done to me."

My crush on Aiden increases tenfold. He loves his little brothers so much that he chose an abusive guardian over never seeing them again. Aiden's probably the closest thing to a father that those boys have ever had.

"Did Greg ever . . . was he—" Abusive? I can't ask him that. "Was he mean to the twins?"

"Never. I'd kill the bastard before I'd let him touch the twins."

I nod and continue the comforting strokes of my thumb on his neck, feeling him calm down slightly. It's obvious that Aiden would do anything to keep his brothers away from Greg.

"He's in jail now, right?"

He nods again. "And in a perfect world, he'd rot in there."

"Why did he go to jail?" I ask, hoping that I'm not pushing anything.

"Of all things, the dumbass was arrested for trying to sell heroin to a police officer."

"I was not expecting that." I raise my eyebrows. "How long did he get for that?"

He shakes his head. "He got the charge reduced to possession, so he's only serving three years with the possibility of parole in two."

"And how long has he been in jail?"

Aiden moves to stand in front of me again, placing his hands on either side of me. My hand is still on his neck, but now it's kind of awkward since it's only one hand. Either I drop it or I bring my other hand around his neck.

Seeing as he doesn't seem to have any objections with me touching him, and how I really don't want to stop, I decide to be daring and bring my other arm around his neck.

"You remember the first day we met?" he asks.

A little off topic, but I answer nonetheless. "How could I not?"

"You ran into me in the hallway—"

"Hey, I think we've established that *you* ran into *me*," I interrupt.

"Never mind that. The point is that I was an extra big asshole to you, when normally I would've just been kind of an asshole."

"Okay, but how does this—"

"That morning I found out that Greg met with the parole board, and that there's a good possibility that he's being let out on good behavior."

Of course it doesn't give Aiden a pass to be an intolerant jerk, but I totally understand now. He couldn't express his anger directly at the source, so he jumped on the first tangible thing that pissed him off. Not that that's the right thing to do, but I don't blame him. It's a perfectly normal thing to do—something I actually did to him the night Kaitlyn and Ryan vandalized my car.

"I'm sorry," I say for lack of anything better to say.

"It's just—"

"Hey, Aiden!"

My head snaps up to look at whoever interrupted my moment with Aiden, and my glare turns into an expression of panic. Walking toward us calmly, with an innocent smile on his face, is Luke. I drop my arms from around Aiden, and gauge his reaction, but he doesn't look threatened or worried. Aiden turns to face him, bringing his back to me, and crosses his arms.

"Congratulations on the win, man," Luke says. "You made me a killing tonight! I knew betting on you was the right move."

"You know she won't want to see you." Aiden cuts through the bullshit with a calm but unfriendly demeanor.

Luke sighs, dropping the friendly preamble. "I need to talk to her. I swear I can explain everything."

"That's not a good idea. You should go before Julian sees you."

"I don't want any trouble with Julian." Luke shakes his head. "Right, Amelia? You know that I don't want any trouble."

Luke looks at me expectantly, probably expecting me to jump to his aid like he did for me, and Aiden looks back at me with his eyebrows drawn together. I suddenly feel very exposed sitting up here on the tailgate, and right when I'm going to spout some bullshit, Julian notices who we're talking to.

"You son of a bitch," he growls at Luke when he's near enough, Noah following behind him.

Luke raises his hands, as if showing he's not a threat. "I only want to talk to her."

"If she wanted to talk to you, she wouldn't have blocked your number or stayed away from you," Julian says.

"I want her to know how I've changed—"

"She doesn't want to fucking hear it! You need to leave before she sees you're here."

"Julian, what's wrong?" A curious voice cuts through the hostile atmosphere.

We all turn to see Annalisa, walking with Charlotte, Mason, and Chase. No one noticed Mason's SUV pull in, returning from their drive to the nearest real bathroom.

"Babe, get in the truck," Julian says simply, trying to block her view from Luke.

Not one to take orders, Annalisa continues to approach us. I know the exact moment she spots Luke because she freezes mid-step, her foot suspended in the air before she recovers and puts it down, staying put.

"Hey, Lise," Luke says cautiously.

"What the fuck are you doing here?" she responds.

"Last I checked, this was a free country, and a guy can go to an illegal racetrack to bet money on the racers if he feels like it," Luke jokes, trying to break the tension.

Annalisa's face is a mix of emotions, like she can't decide if she wants to yell, cry, run away, or kick him in the nuts. Annalisa is clearly uncomfortable with the situation, and she needs to get out of here before something that can't be undone happens. I'll pull Luke out of here and that'll put an end to this—after all, he saved me before, so he wouldn't hurt me now.

Jumping off the tailgate, I step forward, but I'm stopped by a strong hand wrapping around my wrist. Aiden gently pulls me back to his side, shaking his head slightly, as if he already knows what I'm planning and doesn't want me to do it. Julian, having had enough of Annalisa's brother, steps right in front of him with his six foot two, toned body, which is blatantly more muscular than Luke's. But I've seen Luke in action, and I know he's got some strength in him.

"Why don't I walk you to your car?" Julian says in a voice that clearly means this is a command, not an offer.

"I didn't come here to start trouble. I need Anna to understand that I'm different now. I want to be a part of her life," Luke says, more to Annalisa than Julian.

"I don't want you in my life! You fucked that opportunity up when you started all my problems then left when I needed you most!" Annalisa shouts at him from around Julian, the rage in her piercing blue eyes intensified by the black eye shadow and eyeliner.

"Lise, please—" Luke moves from around Julian in a desperate attempt to get closer to Annalisa. Julian sticks his arm out, preventing him from getting any farther.

Annalisa moves to stand in front of Luke, her arms crossed and her hard eyes staring him down. "You don't get to call me Lise anymore. You don't get to be a part of my life anymore."

Luke doesn't bother fighting Julian or trying to shrug his arm off him; he just stands there looking at Annalisa with a heartbroken but determined look. "But I'm your brother."

Looking at Luke and Annalisa, it's hard to spot any family resemblance. He has the same bright-blue eyes as Annalisa, but his hair is a few shades lighter, and his skin is tan where hers is pale. He's tall and lean, and it isn't obvious unless they're standing side-by-side and you already know that they're siblings.

"Anna?" Julian says, asking if she wants him to remove Luke from her presence. She holds up a hand at Julian without breaking eye contact with Luke, telling Julian to wait.

"You're not my brother," she says in a dead, malice-filled tone.

"We may not have the same dad, but we're still blood," Luke corrects.

That explains the obvious difference in appearance: Luke is Annalisa's half brother. I actually don't know anything about Annalisa's home life. Finding out that she has a half brother is really the only insight that I have. She doesn't like talking about her life, and I haven't pushed it. The only thing she gave away was that day I ran into her at the gym.

"Blood wouldn't have done that to me."

"Lise, I know I've done some things, but we *are* still blood."

"*You're not my blood*," she snaps, clearly at her breaking point. "Mason is my blood, for letting me crash at his house. Noah is my blood, for helping me laugh and smile and pulling me out of my spiraling sadness. Chase is my blood, for driving me wherever I needed to go and bringing me lunch every day. Aiden is my blood, for organizing the funeral plans and giving me money to pay the bills."

"*Julian* is my blood," she continues, "for doing all of the above, for picking up the pieces and for being the only stable person in my life. And what did you do? You *killed* our mother. You *deserted* me. I was sixteen with no parents and nowhere to go, and what did you do? You deserted me to find your next high! You're nothing but a twenty-year-old *selfish junkie*, and I don't ever want to see your face again, because I swear to God I'm trying really hard not to bash it in right now."

"Lise—" Luke's voice cracks.

"We're done here," she says, reassuming her calm composure.

She marches over to the passenger side of Julian's pickup truck and gets in, violently slamming the door.

"You heard her. Get out of here before she changes her mind and decides she wants to bash your face in," Julian tells Luke when he makes no move to leave.

Luke looks longingly at Julian's pickup truck before slowly backing up and walking away dejectedly.

That was clearly not the family reunion he was hoping for.

✖

With Luke gone and a very pissed off Annalisa fuming in the front seat of Julian's pickup, the rest of us are left awkwardly digesting what just happened. We're dumbfounded, looking at one another, not knowing what to do after that very tense and emotional situation—even Noah doesn't have anything to say for once. Julian looks torn, like he can't decide if he should go comfort Annalisa or give her some space.

"I'm just gonna—yeah." He starts toward his truck, ultimately making up his mind.

He gets in the driver's side of his truck but doesn't start it, just using the privacy of the vehicle to talk to his girlfriend.

"So, that happened," Noah starts.

"This is all your fault, Noah," accuses Mason.

"*What?* How is this my fault?"

"Ever since you complained you were missing out on the drama, we've had drama coming out of our asses!" Mason smirks, his comment cutting through the tension.

"Sure, I guess you're right. At least I'm not missing out on anything anymore." And with that wisecrack, the uneasy atmosphere is broken.

"Hey, Amelia! Maybe drama can be our thing? We still haven't found one, and it sure seems to love you," Noah suggests.

"Maybe we should keep looking, Noah. I don't want to openly invite drama into my life."

"Fine. But I will find something!" Noah trails off, and we fall into an awkward silence again.

"So . . . that was Anna's half brother," Charlotte states.

Noah nods, answering Charlotte. "That's the first time she's seen him in a while."

"I don't think she's seen him clean in a very long time," Mason adds quietly.

"What did she mean? When she said he killed their mother?" I ask quietly, hesitantly.

Aiden sighs beside me. "It's a long and complicated story."

"But what does—"

I stop talking when I feel a palpable shift in the air, not only within our group, but at the Tracks as a whole. Something is wrong; we can all feel it. Aiden's on high alert, his astute and intuitive eyes scanning the Tracks for the potential threat we all feel. He suddenly tenses with realization, his head whips toward me and he meets my eyes with his now widened ones.

"Leave. *Now*," he commands as he closes the distance between us and puts his hands on my shoulders, roughly shoving me toward Mason's SUV, the closest vehicle.

Sirens.

"*Cops!*" a random person in the crowd yells, sending everyone else in a frenzy.

They aren't far away either—the police probably didn't turn their sirens on until they were practically on top of us, and there's clearly more than just a few cars. There are *a lot* of sirens. The flashing blue and red lights of the police descend upon the Tracks all at once, blocking in many of the frantic people trying to flee.

My heart beats erratically inside my chest. We can't get arrested. *I can't get arrested!* The local cops don't know about me—no one knows about me. Only the specialized team assigned to my case has any idea who I really am. Getting arrested is not an option. I can't compromise this identity, and never see the Boys, Charlotte, Annalisa, or Aiden ever again.

"*Go!*" Aiden shouts, and we scatter into action.

Julian's truck door opens. "*Guys!*" he shouts.

Everything is in chaos. I don't know who gets into which car.

The sirens wail in the distance, growing closer with each second. Cars are taking off in all directions as the entire population at the Tracks registers what's going down. I don't know how we're going to get out of here, and I don't know what will happen when we get arrested. All I know is that Aiden opens the nearest door of Mason's SUV and practically throws me in. He's about to close the door on me when I realize that his car is parked some distance out.

"What about you?" I ask frantically.

He looks from me to his car in the distance. "I'll be fine." He looks at Mason, who's starting the engine. "Get them out, take the back roads and take lots of turns. I'll meet you at Amelia's."

With that he slams my door closed, leaving no room for objection, and Mason takes off without a second thought.

He speeds through the frantic crowd, dodging cars and people and cop cars alike.

A hand grips mine, and only then do I realize that Charlotte is sitting beside me in the back, but the front seat beside Mason is empty. Noah and Chase had better have jumped in Julian's truck and managed to get out of here. My pulse is racing; my adrenaline pumping. There are cops everywhere, cars driving around in every direction trying to escape, and those left behind getting arrested.

"*Mason!*" I yell as a cop car skids to a horizontal stop directly in the path where he's driving.

He swears and swerves, my body jerking to the left onto Charlotte, the SUV narrowly missing the cop car as Mason drives through the fields at top speed. His Range Rover is built for this terrain; we're luckier than most, and Charlotte and I turn around to look out the back window, watching the scene unfold as we speed away.

"Do you see Julian's truck or Aiden's car anywhere?" I ask.

"I can't see anything!" Charlotte admits, trying hard to see through the chaos.

Mason suddenly turns, sending Charlotte and I toppling over with a swear.

"Sorry," Mason throws over his shoulder at us, taking another sharp turn, and I feel the familiar smoothness of asphalt instead of bumpy grass beneath the tires.

Looking back out the window, there are only trees. The only evidence of what just occurred are the loud sounds and flashing lights in the distance. Mason turns again and speeds down the road, quickly putting as much space as he can between us and the shit show back at the Tracks. We're on a dark road, illuminated only by Mason's headlights. No one else is on this road. No one follows us.

We made it.

18

The hour-long drive back to my house is a long and stressful one. I try calling Aiden's phone every five minutes, and worry every time it flips right to voice mail. About twenty minutes after we make it away from the Tracks, Annalisa answers her phone. She confirms that Noah and Chase are with them and that they got out okay. She also says that Aiden isn't answering her calls either.

Now, it's about two thirty in the morning, and we're all huddled on my porch, worried out of our minds about Aiden. Clearly none of us are comfortable enough to call it a night and go home until we know if he got arrested or not.

I thought my mom would be back from work around three or four, but the car in the garage tells me she's already home. At least she's asleep, so I don't have to explain why we're having a slumber party out on the porch in the cold. Let's be real, she probably wouldn't care anyway. She hasn't in a long time. She sent me a don't-stay-out-too-late text around midnight, and I haven't heard from her since.

A car turns onto my street, the bright headlights illuminating the dark houses.

"Is that . . . ?"

The blue jeep passes my house and continues down the street, answering Charlotte's question.

"Should we call him again?" Noah asks. "Maybe he'll answer the twentieth call in the last hour?"

"He's driving, that's probably why he isn't answering his phone," Mason reasons, but we can all tell it's not with much conviction.

"Maybe I should take a drive to his house, just in case he decided to go home instead," Julian suggests.

"If he shows up anywhere, it'll be here. He said he would meet us here, he'll be here," I say with as much confidence as I can.

"It's been an hour and a half since the cops showed up, maybe we should think about bail money—" Mason starts.

"He didn't get caught!" I insist.

"Maybe we should turn on the news and check if there were any high-speed police chases," Chase says, only half-joking.

"He couldn't have gotten arrested, guys. We have an unspoken blood pact that one of us can't get arrested unless another one of us is there beside him. That's brotherhood right there," Noah explains in his backward logic.

"That's only true when you do something stupid, Noah. The saying is that you get arrested with your best friend for doing something stupid, not illegal street racing and gambling," Chase corrects.

"Being a street racer who couldn't outrace cops would be stupid!" Noah explains. "Therefore, he can't get arrested because one of us isn't sitting in that jail cell with him."

We roll our eyes, secretly glad about Noah's natural ability to cut some tension.

"Noah, no one knows about this stupid blood pa—" Julian is cut off when we hear the beautiful sound of Aiden's Challenger coming down the street.

A chorus of relieved sighs are heard as the black Challenger stops in front of my house, and Aiden emerges from it. Learning my lesson from the last time I made a complete fool of myself in front of everyone, I resist the urge to throw myself into Aiden's arms. He walks up to the porch and we all break into relieved smiles.

"See! I told you all! Tell them about the blood pact, Aiden! Tell 'em!" Noah exclaims.

Aiden looks at him, confused. "What?"

"He knows," Noah says to Charlotte, who's standing on his left.

Aiden comes up to me and wraps his arms around me, and I instinctively pull him closer and rest my head on his chest, relieved that he's okay.

"You okay?" he whispers to me while everyone laughs at the ridiculous idea that he was arrested.

"Yeah. You?"

He tucks a piece of my hair behind my ear. "Better now."

I silently thank God that my head is buried in his chest, or else he'd see the bright blush and lunatic smile I'm sporting.

"Why didn't you answer your phone you asshole?" Annalisa scolds. "You had us worried sick!"

Aiden releases his hold on me but keeps one arm wrapped around my shoulders, and I snuggle into him, relishing his closeness and warmth.

I don't know what we are. It's not like we went out on a date, or have even kissed. But being with Aiden feels natural—it's comforting and warm and exciting, and makes me feel safe.

"I dropped it somewhere," he admits.

"Dude, that sucks," Noah says. "Some hobo is gonna hear all my voice mails and instantly fall in love with me. I'm gonna have to change my number so that I don't get hobo stalked."

"You're not going to get hobo stalked, Noah." Annalisa rolls her eyes.

"My phone is password protected anyway," Aiden states.

Mine is now, too. After I dropped it at the Halloween party and Aiden returned it after going through it all, I learned my lesson. Except, that is how I got Aiden's number, so not having a password wasn't all bad.

"Why did it take you an hour and a half to get here? It didn't take us that long," I ask, wondering if he did actually get caught up in a high-speed police chase.

"They blocked the main roads in and out of the Tracks. I had to go the long way around," he explains.

"The *real* question we should be asking is 'What the fuck?'" Noah exclaims.

"Noah's right," Julian says. "The cops have never shown up in all of the Tracks' history."

"And with that many, it's obvious they were called. They didn't just stumble on it," Mason adds.

"Funny how they showed up *after* Ryan's ass was whipped and he and his friends had cleared off the Tracks. . ." Annalisa trails off, leaving us to pick up her thoughts.

"You don't think—"

"I do," Annalisa answers Charlotte.

"But if he called the cops, he can never go back to the Tracks again. They can never use that spot because now the cops know about it. Don't he and his friends make their money from there?" I muse.

"I think in the moment, he was more pissed at Aiden and at losing, and like everything else he does, he let his hot-headedness and anger fuel him," Julian reasons.

"Calling the cops is definitely the type of bitch move Ryan would pull," Mason agrees.

I shift my head on Aiden's chest to look up at him. "Would he do that?"

Aiden's mouth is set in a hard line as he thinks over the possibilities. "He probably did."

A chorus of swears passes around the circle we're standing in.

"What are we gonna do about it? We have to get that asshole back!" Annalisa presses for revenge, probably glad that she has somewhere to direct her anger after the confrontation with Luke earlier.

Everyone else approves and starts thinking of ways to get Ryan back, but I tense, an action that doesn't go unnoticed by Aiden since my side is pressed against him. This is just like my vandalized car all over again; everyone thinking of ways to get Ryan back and me not wanting them to do anything about it.

Aiden uses the hand that's around my shoulder to rub my arm. "What's wrong?" he asks gently.

"We shouldn't retaliate."

"What? Why the hell not?" Annalisa asks.

"They almost got us all arrested, Amelia. *Arrested!*" Noah emphasizes.

"Not to mention that was how we made our money! Aiden has kids to take care of! What's he going to do now? He can't even make a quarter of that much by working part time for minimum wage!" Mason counters, growing more enraged with the situation as he lists the damage.

"Getting him back won't make me money," Aiden reasons calmly.

"What? Aiden, this affects you more than any of us. You should be the most pissed. You can't tell me you don't want to get him back," Julian says.

Aiden looks down at me, briefly making eye contact and seeing the desperation in my eyes, then he looks at everyone. "We don't know it was him for sure."

My heart swells, knowing that Aiden's containing his anger for me. His unfaltering ability to perceive the truth in situations is allowing him to see that I'm uncomfortable. His calculating and intuitive nature is telling him that I don't want revenge, and he's putting my concerns before any of his own needs for revenge.

"Whether he did it or not, we can't do anything to him," I explain, trying to convince them to see my point of view. "I said it before, but if we get him back, he'll get us back, and it'll keep going until we get hurt. It's already serious. He broke the law to vandalize my car, and now he *called the law* and tried to get us arrested. Seriously, the next step is stabbing us or something. Can we *please* be the bigger people and let it go?"

Annalisa snaps, "I'll file his shinbone into a shiv with his teeth and cut off his man bun if he tries anything."

"I agree with Amelia, this is getting out of hand," Charlotte says quietly.

"What is wrong with you guys? We need to hit back harder!" Annalisa states, growing more visibly angry and frustrated.

She clearly hasn't calmed down from her confrontation with her brother. Sure, she's aggressive, and I know that she's not all talk—she actually would fight Ryan—but this anger is probably rooted deeper than just Aiden's asshole ex-stepbrother.

Julian seems to pick up on it as well. "It's late. We're all tired. Why don't we get some sleep and talk about it later."

A chorus of approval is heard through the group. Tonight has been long and stressful as it is without having a debate. I hope I can convince them that revenge isn't a good idea. Not only for my sake, but for all of theirs.

19

After saying good-bye, my friends head to their cars to go home. Aiden hangs back, not making a move to go to his car. Mason stalls for a moment, too, but when he notices that Aiden isn't making any move to leave, he slowly turns and heads to his SUV.

"I'm just gonna—um. I'll meet you upstairs. Good night," Charlotte says, quietly slipping inside.

I sit on the porch steps, and Aiden follows my lead. With everyone gone and Charlotte inside, I'm suddenly hit by the serenity and calmness of the cold winter night, so different from the night's actual events.

"You really don't want to get them back?"

"Don't you think this has gone far enough? I know that you'll never get along with Ryan, and I'd never ask you to," I say. "I just don't think that doing something to get back at him will get us anywhere. We all got out safely, and you still got four grand out of him. I think we came out on top in this situation."

He nods, looking out at the quiet suburban street at nothing in particular. I know that he's pissed at Ryan. Aiden already has his own reasons to hate Ryan, but now he directly attacked Aiden and his friends.

"We'll give everyone time to calm down," he says after several quiet minutes. "They'll change their minds."

I nod again, relieved that Aiden is willing to put his anger aside. Putting this behind us isn't just about me and Tony, it's about everyone. Ryan will end up escalating this situation until it gets even worse, and it'll turn into a full-blown war instead of a stupid high school rivalry.

"What happened with Jonesy and all the others from the Tracks?" I ask randomly.

"I didn't see who got arrested, but if Jonesy or the other guys figure out Ryan called the cops, he'll have bigger things to worry about than just us anyway."

I nod. Despite Jonesy's short height, he has some massive muscle—definitely not someone I'd want to piss off.

"What are you going to do about money now?" I ask quietly.

He looks back out at the street thoughtfully. "I'll figure it out."

"That was how Jonesy made his money, no? He'll find another location for the track and it'll be like nothing happened," I say, trying to stay optimistic. "At least you got four thousand dollars to hold you over until then."

He looks back at me, his expression thoughtful and serious. "No, I don't."

"Did you lose the money with your phone? Oh shit, Aiden. Please don't tell me you lost the four grand you won from Ryan *and* the four grand you used to bet him. Maybe the cops left and we can go—"

"Amelia," he cuts me off from my escalating rant. "I didn't lose the money. It's right here." He pulls out two envelopes—one with his own four grand and one with Ryan's.

"Then what did you mean that you don't have his money?"

He puts his original envelope back in his pocket and hands the other one to me.

"It's your money," he tells me, urging me to take the envelope.

I reach out tentatively and take the envelope, holding it up, confused. "What are you talking about?"

"The only reason I raced Ryan was to get money out of him for vandalizing your car. It's yours," he says, his gaze intense and voice honest.

Aiden's giving me four thousand dollars? That *he* won? That *he* risked his own money for?

"I can't take this," I promptly stick my hand out, waiting for him to take the envelope from me.

He looks at the envelope then back at me. "Yes, you can."

"No, I really can't." I throw the envelope into his lap since he makes no move to take it. "Think of it as paying you back for the new tires and paint job. And the stress of getting a tow truck and mechanic so late and dealing with everything so quickly."

He picks up the envelope and stubbornly throws it back into my lap. "I told you already, they owed me favors. It didn't cost me anything."

My chest aches. My heart squeezes with guilt and regret. Aiden's so honest and genuine with me, and I've done nothing to deserve it.

I throw the envelope back in his lap. "It cost you a favor. Aiden, I don't deserve this; it's yours. You raced for it, you risked your own money for it, and Ryan's more your pain in the ass than mine. Just keep it."

He picks up the envelope and throws it back at me. "I told you—"

"I don't want it." I throw it back quickly.

"But I want you to—" He throws it back.

"I'm not taking it." I throw it back.

Getting tired of the back and forth, Aiden gently but firmly grabs my right wrist and brings it close to him, puts the envelope in my hand, and closes my fingers around it.

"It's yours," he says, voice low, leaving no room for arguing.

We're so close to each other, I can see the dark lashes framing his gray eyes and I can smell how good he smells.

Why can't I just be a regular girl and not one who has to hide who she really is, run for her life, and lie to the people she cares about most? Why can't I just enjoy being with Aiden and not have my conscience make my heart jump up into my throat every time I have to lie to him? Why does it break a piece of my heart every time Aiden calls me Amelia instead of Thea? I wish I could hear him say my real name, just to relish the way it would sound coming from his perfect lips.

God. Get a grip, Amelia. You're sounding like some lov—

No.

Nope. Nope. Nope.

Stay *away* from that word.

I suddenly realize the intimate position we're in—how close we are. During the argument, my right leg ended up sprawled over his left. His warm hand is firmly around my wrist, holding my arm close to his chest. My face is only a few inches away from his.

His eyes flicker to my lips, then back up to hold my eyes hostage. I feel my pulse pick up and my breathing turn irregular. And then suddenly I can't think, and I can't breathe, and my heart has never pounded so fast in my life; all because Aiden is kissing me.

Aiden is kissing me, and all is right in the world.

All my stress, problems, and worries melt away with the softness and intensity of his lips on mine. Everything around us ceases to exist as I focus on the warm, tingling fire stemming from wherever he's touching me and spreading throughout my entire body.

I feel his strong hands on my waist, pulling me closer as his tongue slides over my bottom lip, and I practically melt into him. Never has anything been this perfect. Never have I wanted something so badly. Never has someone kissed me in such a way—my heart can't decide if it wants to stop or speed up.

There's an annoying nudging at the back of my mind, reminding me that I'm not allowed to feel like this; that I'm not allowed to be happy with Aiden. Reluctantly, I pull away to look at him.

"Fine. Since that was such a great argument, I'll keep the money. But I'm not spending any of it on me," I joke to break the intense, intimate silence that follows.

Aiden laughs, releasing me, and I regrettably remove my leg from where it was over his.

"It's your money, you can spend it however you want," he tells me.

"I'll find a way to spend it on all of us. Like a treat for having to deal with all this drama."

As much as I'd love to stay here and make out with Aiden all night, it's getting late, and I'm getting tired. We say good night, and he reminds me that my car will be ready by Monday morning.

"Thanks again for everything, Aiden."

He walks down the porch steps and takes slow steps backward toward his car. "I'll see you later."

I stay where I am, standing on the porch with the envelope still in my hand, and wrap my arms around myself, suddenly feeling very cold.

"Are you sure about the money?" I ask one more time, just to be sure.

"Keep it." He turns around and walks the rest of the distance to his car, and I stand there watching him.

He gets to his car door and opens it, pausing to turn back to me. "Don't forget to study for the calculus test on Monday," he says with an adorable smirk.

I smile back at him. "How could I possibly forget?"

20

All night and all morning I feel like I'm floating on cloud nine. Aiden just has a way of making me feel giddy and nervous all at once. He won four thousand dollars for me for goodness' sake. Still high off of the different emotions Aiden causes, I walk through the house after seeing Charlotte off this morning.

"Amelia," my mother calls from the kitchen, not sounding too thrilled.

I freeze and roll my eyes at her disapproving tone.

"Come in here," she says impatiently.

I sigh and walk into the kitchen where she's standing with her arms crossed, a stern look on her face.

"You got in late. Where were you all night?"

"Out," I say nonchalantly.

She exhales loudly, clearly frustrated. "Well, what time did you get home?"

"Not sure."

"Why are you being so difficult? You need to be more responsible," she lectures unnecessarily.

My hands curl into fists, my nails biting into my palms. "This is the first time you've actually been home in who knows how long," I snap, tired of her "caring parent" act. "You spend more time at work and in different countries than with your own daughter. You normally wouldn't even know if I was home or not, you just happen to be home today. So spare me the concerned mom act."

"This isn't just about me being concerned about your whereabouts. You need to be responsible. We can't have you slipping up! I may not be around a lot, but I notice things. Things like you kissing that boy last night—"

"Were you *spying* on me?!" I can't believe she'd do that! That's an invasion of privacy!

"I'm your *mother*. It's not spying if you're my child—especially if said child has a lot at stake. You've been screwing up. Don't think I haven't noticed that your car isn't here. Where is it? And did you even sleep here Thursday night?"

I stare at her, my face blank. I slept at Charlotte's, but my mom wasn't even home. I didn't think she'd notice.

I'm spared having to answer when she continues. "Look, I've met someone, and I don't want to have to move again. You know that Tony's looking for you, and here you are going around doing whatever you want, with whoever you want, whenever you want!"

My face heats. "Well, that's hypocritical! You can have a boyfriend but I can't?"

"No, you most definitely *cannot*. What do you even know about this boy? He's not the one you can trust with your *life*, Amelia. I am. You shouldn't be getting close to people."

"But you—"

"Who's the adult here? I can do whatever I want because I know how to prioritize our needs."

My world is shattering. "Well, maybe you should move in with your new boyfriend and forget about me altogether! Out of sight, out of mind right?"

She takes a calming breath, her face sobering. "I've called Agent Dylan."

The agent assigned to my case. The one who handles our questions and IDs and moves.

"Okay? And?"

"I've told him that I want to be relocated."

I freeze. Everything freezes. My heart stops beating and all the blood drains from my face.

"But—but you can't just do that!" They can't relocate us! Not now! "You just said you had a boyfriend! You're willing to just leave him?"

"Keeping us safe is more important. Plus, I can just take jobs on flights to the Northeast to see him."

She's cold and detached from this whole conversion, like she's not just dropping a bomb on my life.

"Mom, I'll be more careful. We don't need to leave," I plead in a last-ditch effort.

"Agent Dylan thinks it's for the best too. We need to keep you safe from Tony."

"Then they should just catch Tony instead of moving us around all the time!" I snap.

She sighs. "You know it's not that simple. We need to move before people get hurt, or worse. It's only a matter of time before he shows up. We can stay ahead of him this time. They said it'll take a couple of weeks, maybe after New Year's—"

I can't deal with this anymore. Her, this conversation, the finality in her tone. Not giving her a chance to say anything else, I turn on my heel and stomp up the stairs.

Great. Leave it to my mom to ruin my happy Aiden high. I slam my bedroom door as if that will make me feel better, but her words are eating at me. Is she right? Am I slipping up in my responsibilities? Will I hurt my friends if we don't leave?

I have a major crush on Aiden, no use in denying it. He's starting to mean so much to me, more than anyone ever has, making things so complicated. Even last night, I was thinking about the L word. I've never thought about that word in relation to any boy before. Of course I know I don't L word Aiden, but it's scary to think how easily and quickly I could. Aiden deserves better than me.

Opening my closet door, I pull out the shoebox again and look through all the stories and articles, from my dad's accident to Sabrina's death. I read through all the articles about my kidnapping and about "Isabella" and "Hailey." I look at all the death threats and evidence showing that Tony has always found a way to find me and torment me before trying to kill me. I look at my past fake IDs—all from different states—and the real one, and think about how I've had to keep moving and separating myself from the people I've met in each place. I secretly photocopied my ID before we left the first time, and have done so every move since because it's hard letting go of a piece of me every time Tony comes after us.

That's why I keep this shoebox—as a reminder. To remind me that Tony will never give up hunting me down. That I can't slip up or get too close to other people because I'll eventually have to leave them.

My friends, everyone, even Aiden. They've all found a way to sneak up on me and find a permanent place in my heart. I've never had friends who mean as much to me as they do, not even from before the accident. They've been there for me; they've supported me and defended me. They make me laugh and smile and just generally make me a happier person. They shouldn't be so open and honest with someone who's done nothing but lie and be deceitful to them. I wipe away some tears that managed to escape.

My heart breaks all over again. Is my mom right? Is staying selfish? Should I do the responsible thing and get out before Tony finds me? Before my friends inevitably get hurt? I can leave before I get even more attached than I already am. The truth is as plain as the words on those newspaper clippings: I can't stay here. But I can't leave either.

But what I want doesn't matter; it's already been done. I'm leaving, probably after the New Year if that's what my mom was saying before I stormed out. That gives me a month or less with my friends.

21

Monday, December the first. Today is an important day for many reasons.

First: I had a stupid calculus test (which I actually sort of understood). Second: I finally got my car back (the new tires and paint job look spectacular). And third: it marks a month until I leave this town and my friends forever.

There are also many reasons why today is an awful day.

First: because of Dave punching me in the stomach last Friday, my stomach has a giant, ugly bruise on it (which is only sore when I walk, move, or breathe). Second: Aiden isn't in school to give me the keys to my recently fixed car. And third: it marks a month until I leave this town and my friends forever.

Since Aiden's not in school, I don't tell everyone about my idea of how to spend the money—I don't even tell them that Aiden gave me the money. Of course I will, but I want to do it with everyone here, and the group doesn't feel complete with Aiden missing.

No one else knows where he is, either, but the guys just assume he's pissed about Ryan calling the cops on Friday. I don't think that's the case though. I talked to him on Friday, and he seemed okay with it. It was Aiden who said that the guys would calm down with some time, and they did. They're (thankfully) no longer fixated on revenge, but they do shoot glares whenever Kaitlyn and friends walk past us.

By the end of the day, I'm still thinking about Aiden and why he isn't here. I sent him a few texts throughout the day, but he hasn't replied. Come to think of it, I haven't talked to him since Friday night.

I'm searching my locker, in case Aiden slipped the keys to my car in here. Finding nothing, I sigh, slam my locker shut, and turn, only to jump when I find Mason standing right where my locker door used to be.

"What the hell, Mason?!" I hold my hand to my frantically beating heart.

He chuckles and offers me an unapologetic smile. "Sorry, but you looked so preoccupied with finding your keys I couldn't resist."

I shoot him a glare but can't keep the straight face. "Did Aiden text you where my keys are?"

"Nope. Haven't heard from him."

"Urg! I just want to get out of this hellhole!"

Mason offers me a million dollar smile. "That's why your best friend is here to drive you home."

I look around, then back at him with a straight face. "I don't see Noah anywhere."

Mason scowls. "I meant me."

"I know—that was for scaring me." I laugh. "Thanks for the offer."

Mason's eyes soften as he looks at me. "Anytime, k-bear."

We walk side-by-side in comfortable silence through the halls, but I can tell that Mason wants to tell me something by the way he keeps shooting me glances when he thinks I won't notice.

Having enough of his "stealthy" glances, I sigh and stop walking. "What is it, Mason?"

He looks away from me and fidgets, which is so unlike him. Mason's always confident and a bit egotistical, so it's weird to see him uncomfortable like this.

"Mason?"

"How are you?" he blurts, taking me off guard.

"Good?"

He shakes his head, clearly not satisfied with my answer. "No, I mean, like, how *are you*?"

"I'm *good*?" I imitate his emphasis.

He huffs in frustration. "Look, I know I promised to forget it so that we could be friends again, but I just wanted to apologize again for leaving you alone at the Tracks, which caused you to get jumped. I need you to know that."

"I know, Mason. We're over this. I forgave you, remember?"

"No, I know," he adds quickly, his brown eyes still filled with guilt. "But I want to make sure we are good."

"Of course we're good."

"Wait." He stops walking again and turns to face me, causing me to stop and roll my eyes in annoyance.

"When you slipped and said that Luke saved you, did you mean . . . ?"

"Yes, it was *that* Luke," I reply, referring to Annalisa's brother Luke. "Mason. It's not important. Let's just go, I'm starving."

"Does Anna know?" he asks, clearly not done with the twenty-one questions.

"No one knows. And we're going to keep it that way."

"Not even Aid—"

"*Especially* not Aiden. We're keeping the same deal as before, Mason. I forgive you, and in return, you drop it and don't tell anyone. I meant it when I said I don't want any fights breaking out over me. Aiden knows that I met Luke at the Tracks, but not the circumstances of our meeting."

"If Aiden finds out about it, and I didn't tell him, he'll be furious."

"He won't find out," I promise.

Since it's been a while since school let out, there are not a lot of people left in the parking lot. This makes it really easy to spot the black Challenger parked beside my car, with Aiden himself patiently leaning against it.

"Guess you don't need a ride home. I'll see you later?" Mason says.

"For sure. Thanks anyway, Mason."

He and Aiden exchange that bro head-nod thing across the parking lot, and Mason heads the opposite way to his SUV.

As I head over to Aiden, a mixture of emotions swirl inside me. I haven't seen or talked to him since Friday night, and I can't believe how much I've missed him.

"Hey, I can't believe you skipped the calculus test," I joke to break the ice once I reach him.

Aiden doesn't react, doesn't even look amused, he just straightens up from where he's leaning on his car. "Here are your keys."

He holds out his arm, and I look at my keys, dangling from his hand.

"Sure, thanks," I say, confused by his hostility as he drops the keys into my hand.

He nods and turns around to go, but I quickly grab his arm to stop him.

"Hey, are you okay?" I drop my arm and look at him, concerned.

"Peachy," he says, voice laced with sarcasm and annoyance.

My eyebrows draw together. "Aiden, what's wrong?"

"Nothing, Amelia." But his tone leads me to believe that something is, in fact, wrong.

"Aid—"

"I've got to go," he interrupts me, and this time I don't stop him as he turns, jumps in his car, and takes off.

Aiden's never like that, especially not toward me. Something has to be wrong. Maybe he's stressed about the whole no more Tracks thing? Maybe he's worried about where to find money? No, he was fine with it when I asked him about it. He was fine when we talked at my house on the porch that night. It was after—oh my God. I knew it. He totally hates me.

I ruined everything. He regrets kissing me. My heart tightens, like someone has plunged their hands into my chest and is slowly squeezing.

I can't have him hate me. I know when I leave he probably will, but that day is not today. Stubbornness and impulsiveness driving my actions, I hop in my car and drive in the direction of Aiden's house. He's going to talk to me whether he likes it or not.

Even though I spend the whole drive to Aiden's house running through a mental checklist of all the possible things I could say to him, when I walk up to his front door and ring the bell with a determination I didn't know I had, my mind suddenly blanks.

Of everything. Why am I even here again? Maybe I should just leave before I make things worse.

No.

Deal with it, Amelia. Aiden is practically the best thing in your life right now and you are not going to let your stupidity ruin it. But what could I even say to him?

I stopped kissing you because I'm not really Amelia Collins, and I've been lying to you and everyone else since day one. Oh, and I'm going to relocate to a different state in less than a month and never have any contact with you again. So, like, friends?

Yeah, let's not do that.

Before I can gather my thoughts, Aiden's sturdy oak door opens. My breath catches, my body's automatic response to Aiden, but it quickly realizes something's off. I look down from where Aiden's head should have been and see the face of a curious nine-year-old boy staring up at me.

Caught off guard, I stutter, "Um . . . hi."

The blond-haired, blue-eyed boy tilts his head to the side, analyzing me. "You're pretty."

My mouth opens in a surprised smile, taken aback by his unfiltered, blunt words. "Oh, thank you!"

I can't tell if it's Jason or Jackson since they're identical, and I've never met either of them before, but I can tell I already love them.

"Are you friends with Aiden? You're way too pretty to be his friend. You're definitely a new babysitter! Will you let me eat cake before dinner? Aiden never lets me eat cake before dinner, it's so annoying," Jason or Jackson muses.

This is why I love kids. They speak their minds and don't worry about anything. This kid just called me pretty twice within the first three seconds of meeting me, and is now sharing his opinion about the age-old debate about dessert before dinner.

"Well, actually—"

The door's pulled open wider, and I'm suddenly seeing double. "Jason! Aiden told us we're not allowed to open the door when he's in the shower!" Jackson scolds his twin.

Jason scoffs at his brother and says in a hushed tone, "There's a pretty girl standing at our front door. What idiot *wouldn't* open the door?"

I'm trying my best to contain my laughter. Clearly being a ladies man runs in the Parkers' DNA. Jackson looks at me for the first time, his face turning red in the most adorable way.

"I'm sorry," Jackson says, "but you'll have to come back another time when our brother is around."

"Why can't she just wait inside?" Jason asks his brother.

"*Because*," Jackson emphasizes in a low, annoyed tone to his brother, "Aiden said not to open the door! I'm pretty sure that means not letting strangers in our house either."

I can tell Jason is about to start arguing with his more responsible brother, and I don't want to start any more trouble.

"Listen, guys, it's okay, I'll just come back—"

"Didn't I tell you not to open the door!"

There it is. The reason I'm here. The reason my pulse quickens and slows at the same time. The reason my lungs forget to work and my heart decides to work double time.

The boys look at each other with expressions that can best be described as "Oh shit," when they hear their older brother's booming voice. Come to think of it, I'm probably sharing the same expression, still having no idea what to say to him. Heavy footsteps quickly come to the door and Aiden comes into view, his tense face visibly relaxing when he notices it's just me, before it morphs into an angry expression aimed at his brothers.

"You guys know the rules! This door stays locked if I'm not around!" he scolds, looking more tense than usual.

His hair is still wet and disheveled, and he's clearly just stepped out of his shower. He looks like he realized the boys were talking to strangers, so he frantically threw pants on and ran downstairs, forgetting his shirt. My God. This boy is the perfect specimen of a physically fit man if I've ever seen one.

I force my eyes up from his perfect abs and chest, focusing instead on his face. At least now I know for sure that all that time he spends at the gym and eating clean is paying off. Maybe once we're friends again he could train me. Maybe he could be topless while doing it too . . .

Focus, Amelia.

Not wanting to get either of the boys in trouble, I'm about to say something when Jackson beats me to it.

"I'm sorry. I heard the doorbell and was curious."

Wait. Jason was the one who opened the door. Jackson was the one who told his brother it was wrong. Jason studies his feet and holds one arm, clearly feeling guilty but still letting his brother take the fall for him.

Aiden shuts his eyes and gives a defeated sigh, pinching the bridge of his nose. "Just go upstairs. We'll talk about it later. You, too, Jason."

The boys give me a last glance, which I return with a small smile, and I hear them make their way up the stairs.

Aiden takes a calming breath and turns to fully face me. "What are you doing here?"

Still focusing on keeping my gaze above his bare, sculpted shoulders, I try to organize my thoughts.

"I know why you're mad at me, and I wanted to say I can totally understand. I mean, I'd be pissed at me, too, if I did that, but I know that I can explain everything to you, but I just don't know how, and I really don't want this to ruin our friendship and this thing that we have going here but—"

"What the fuck are you talking about?" Aiden asks, cutting off my incoherent rambling.

"Um, about, you know—you're mad because of me?"

Aiden suddenly snaps. "Not everything's about you all the time, Amelia!"

His outburst takes me completely off guard. "Oh. Okay."

Aiden genuinely looks annoyed and tense. He hasn't talked to me like that since the first time I bumped into him on my first day at school. Taking the hint that he really doesn't want me here, I take a step backward to escape before I make things worse like I always do.

"Sorry, then, I'll just . . . yeah."

I turn around to make my escape, and hear the door slam behind me. Not even two seconds after the door closes, I hear it open again, and Aiden shouts my name. Freezing in place, I don't turn around to face him, refusing to let him see how much he affects me. I can feel him behind me, but I won't look at him, I just can't.

"I'm sorry," he says, sounding sincere and defeated. He turns me around to face him, leaving his hands on my arms. He looks tired. He looks defeated. He looks frustrated. He looks . . . lost.

"I'm not mad at you," he begins. "I'm just taking out my anger on you. You don't deserve that."

"It's okay, Aiden. You know I'm here if you need anything."

"Can you come back inside?"

Aiden steps back on the porch, gesturing for me to follow him. I walk into his house and he closes the door behind me. I take off my shoes as he tells me he'll be back in a second, and he disappears up the stairs.

I can't help but simultaneously pray that he did and didn't go get a shirt to put on. I mean, it'd be a lot easier to think, but *damn* that boy rivals even the hottest Armani model.

Aiden comes down a few seconds later—sadly, with a shirt on—and we head into the kitchen.

I sit on the stool at the kitchen counter and Aiden remains standing on the other side of the counter in front of me. It's quiet for a moment, each of us just looking at the other, not knowing where to start.

"So—"

"I just—" We speak at the same time.

"You go first," I encourage him.

Aiden takes a calming breath. "Remember how I told you that the first day I met you I took my aggression out on you because I just learned Greg could be released on parole?"

I nod.

"I guess I'm doing the same thing now."

"You mean—"

"Yeah. I found out Saturday morning he's being released in two weeks."

That's why he cut everyone out this weekend and skipped school today—he has much bigger things to worry about.

"Shit. I'm so sorry, Aiden."

"It's just, we have a bad history." He comes around the counter and sits on the stool beside me.

"I know, Aiden." Even though he's never directly told me that he was abused, it's been implied.

"I know he's going to come for the twins."

"What? Why?"

He runs his hands through his hair, clearly stressed beyond belief. "He already hates me for being me. Now everything with Ryan, plus he knows I petitioned against having him released on parole. He's going to come purely because he can, and I can't do anything to protect them."

"That's why you were so mad when the twins opened the door."

He nods, resting his elbows on the counter and putting his head in his hands.

"Aiden!" I'm interrupted when the twins run into the kitchen, and he sits up straight.

"Tyler just got a new dog! Can we go over and play with it?" Jason asks, holding a phone in his hand, Jackson nodding enthusiastically.

"No," Aiden replies without giving a reason. "Go play in the backyard. Tell Tyler to bring it here if he wants, but you boys stay here."

"But Aid—"

"No. Outside. Go." Aiden cuts Jason off with a tone implying that there's no room for arguing.

The twins' excitement visibly deflates, and they saunter toward the glass double-sliding door in the kitchen that leads out to the backyard, phone still in hand.

Jason resumes his conversation with Tyler as they walk through the door leading outside. "No, I know you can't come over but—"

"And make sure the gates are closed!" Aiden calls after them as Jackson closes the door.

He's stressed, tired, and probably feels like he's going through this alone. He has no one to help him look after the twins, and now he's being protective because he refuses to let the twins have the same abusive childhood that he lived through.

"We're here for you, Aiden. Not just me, but Noah, Mason, Julian, and everyone else. You're not alone. We'll make sure he doesn't hurt them—"

"You don't understand!" he says louder than he should have, making me automatically flinch, and his expression turns guilty upon seeing this.

"Help me," I reply calmly.

Aiden sighs, rubbing the back of his neck with one hand. "Greg has legal custody."

"What? I thought . . ." I trail off, not even knowing what to say to Aiden.

"My mom listed Greg as their guardian until I turn eighteen. If Greg just stayed in jail a couple of weeks longer, I'd have full custody."

My eyebrows draw together, trying to figure out all the facts before we attempt to come up with solutions. "Who technically has custody of them now, since Greg's in jail?"

"Since I'm not eighteen, Greg still has legal custody. He can give physical custody to a third party, which he gave to his ex-wife. Clearly, since the boys are living with me, it wasn't enforced, and Paula has no desire to support two boys who have nothing to do with her."

So the twins are supposed to be living with Ryan's mom since Aiden isn't eighteen yet. Technically, Greg has custody of Aiden, too, since he's still seventeen and a minor in the eyes of the state.

"Okay, you turn eighteen in January. We can just keep the

twins away from him for those couple of weeks. I doubt he'll try to go the legal route, and even if he did, it takes a while for those requests to process. There would be no point. We can work through this, Aiden. He's not going anywhere near the boys."

As much as I'm concerned about Aiden, the bigger part of me just feels guilty. A huge, urgent, burning sense of guilt is eating me from the inside out. Here I am saying we're here for him, while simultaneously knowing I'm never going to see him again in a few weeks.

"It's just—" he starts, and I give him an encouraging look to continue. "Nothing's really stopping him from getting back on drugs. I wouldn't put it past him to use junkie logic and convince himself that the twins are rightfully his and to take them."

"He will have just gotten out of jail. Do you really think his main priority will be to come for two boys who aren't even blood related to him?"

"I don't know, Amelia! He's a drugged-up sociopath. I wouldn't put it past him to want the twins, since he could have complete control over them, to hurt them any way he wants—" His piercing gray eyes look straight through me with a look that promises to cause someone pain. "All I know is that I'll kill him before I let him hurt the twins like he did me."

In that moment, I believe him. I know Aiden will do anything before he lets someone hurt his brothers.

Unable to resist, I wrap my arms around him in an awkward yet still comfortable side hug, and rest my head on his shoulder. "It'll be okay, Aiden."

"How do you know?" he says quietly.

"I just do."

I don't know. But I believe in Aiden, and I know that of everyone

I've ever met, he's one of the very few people I can completely depend on.

I lift my head off of his shoulder and let my arms drop. I reluctantly pull away and look at him again. "Just loosen up on the boys a bit; Greg's not here."

"I know, I'm just—I'm not taking any chances. The second you let your guard down is the second shit hits the fan."

Don't I know it. Every time I let my guard down and get comfortable in a new town, Tony shows up. That's why this time my mom's forcing us to leave before he has a chance to hurt anyone here.

"I know, but you can't cover them in bubble wrap and force them to stop living life. Why don't we all go out for ice cream tonight? You need to take your mind off of everything; relax a bit—stop being so strict and overbearing and let the twins have some fun!"

"They're still having fun!" Aiden defends his protectiveness.

I raise a skeptical eyebrow and pointedly look through sliding glass doors to the backyard, where the twins are sitting on the ground, picking at the grass and occasionally throwing it at each other.

"Okay, okay. You made your point. I guess letting them see the puppy won't kill them."

"Good." I stand up and tuck the stool back under the counter. "Now, I'm going to go home and text everyone and tell them to meet us at Sweetie's Ice Cream Parlor at seven. You're going to make the twins dinner, then drive them to Tyler's house and come meet us at Sweetie's."

He rolls his eyes at me but smiles at my authoritative tone. "Of course, Your Majesty."

His mood seems to have lightened a bit. He still looks stressed, but he doesn't look as hopelessly lost as he did before.

"I'll text you if the time or location changes."

He looks at me like he can't decide if I'm joking or the biggest idiot he's ever met.

"What?" I ask.

"Amelia, I lost my phone at the track. Remember?"

I literally facepalm myself. How stupid am I? That's why he didn't answer when I called him earlier.

✘

Later that night, all my friends and I are sitting in a big comfy booth in the corner of Sweetie's Ice Cream Parlor.

"Do you have a charger in that huge purse of yours, Amelia? My phone is dying," Mason asks as he finishes off his chocolate cone.

"You know I do."

I twist and kneel on the booth to grab my purse, sitting on top of it, and plop back down in my seat. Readjusting my shirt, I rummage through my bag for the charger.

"You guys make fun of me for carrying a big purse, but you all love to use the stuff inside it," I say, noticing only a beat too late that all conversation around me has completely halted.

The air suddenly feels tense, and my hand freezes where it is in my bag. I slowly look up to find everyone staring at me in either confusion, shock, or horror.

"What?"

Chase starts, "Amelia—"

"What the fuck happened to your stomach?" Aiden interrupts, his gaze burning a hole right through my shirt.

"Um, nothing?"

Smooth, Amelia. Real freaking smooth. Everyone saw the giant fist-shaped bruise on your abdomen that Dave gave you as a "fuck you" gift to Aiden, and the only thing you can think to say is "Um, nothing."?

"It looks like someone punched you," Charlotte whispers in confusion.

"Don't be ridiculous," I reply in a tone I hope comes across as convincingly unfazed.

For some reason, I glance over at Mason, the only other person who has some kind of idea about what happened that night, but he's sworn to secrecy. He's staring directly at my covered stomach, a look of guilt clear on his face.

"Bullshit," Annalisa retorts. "Let me see it again."

"No, really, it's fine." I'm praying that my face isn't getting all red from the scrutiny and betraying me.

Before I know it, Annalisa grabs the bottom of my shirt and yanks it up to reveal my sore, multicolored, bruised stomach.

Annalisa's bright-blue eyes cloud with anger. "Was it Kaitlyn? I swear to God I will cut a bitc—"

"No one hit me," I interrupt, forcing my shirt back down and covering my stomach.

"Then what happened?" Aiden asks in a way that makes me feel like he's a professional interrogator and I'm the criminal caught in his web.

"I walked into furniture," I lie lamely.

"Furniture?"

"Yeah, you know me. I'm the biggest klutz." I'm usually really good at lying—I have to be—but I'm finding it really hard to lie straight to Aiden's face.

"You walked into fist-shaped furniture?! *More than once?*"

"It was just the one time," I mumble automatically.

"*What?* Someone hit you hard enough to leave that mark?!" he says.

"Well, to be fair, I'm pretty sure I bit a chunk of his hand out—" I joke for some reason, stupidly thinking that it'll help the situation.

Aiden's eyes light up with fury before he masks it. "Who?" Aiden's jaw is clenched, his tone eerily stoic.

"Aiden, it's—"

"My fault," Mason interrupts, still looking at my now-covered stomach with a guilty expression.

Aiden's head snaps to Mason. "What?" he growls.

"At the track . . ." Mason starts, his eyes filled with despair.

"You hit Amelia?!" Noah exclaims with disgust.

"Of course not, don't be ridiculous." I defend Mason. "And it's not his fault."

"It is! I know you said we were okay, but I still feel awful about it. We knew something bad was probably going to happen to you and I still left you like that—"

"Can someone explain what the hell is going on?" Annalisa interrupts, tired of looking back and forth from me to Mason.

"At the Tracks the other night, I went with Amelia to the bathroom—you know that little one in the middle of the field? While she was in there I saw Amanda, so I went over to talk to her and I didn't see Amelia come out," Mason explains quickly, eager to clear his conscience.

Aiden's cold eyes turn to Mason, his sharp gaze making it seem like he's looking right through Mason's soul. "Then?"

"I don't know. I found her a while later all bloody, and she was going off about how someone jumped her but she wouldn't tell me who! I'm so sorry, Amelia."

"It's not your fault, Mason. And it wasn't my blood! I'm fine, everyone. Seriously, let's just drop it."

Aiden's usually impassive gaze holds a thinly veiled expression of fury. "Like hell we'll drop it. Who was it?"

"It doesn't matter—"

"*Who?*" Aiden repeats, something in his tone stressing that there's no room for argument.

I sigh in defeat and look down at the table. "Dave."

There are some gasps that go around the table and some muttered curses. I didn't think I wanted to see Aiden's reaction, but suddenly it's the only thing I can think about. I look up expecting him to be looking at me, but instead he's studying something in the distance out the window, his brooding face seeming to be calculating something.

"Tell us exactly what happened," Noah commands, staring at me intensely.

I resist the urge to sigh again. I might as well just tell them now.

"After I used the bathroom, I was looking for Mason when Dave grabbed me and dragged me behind the building. His friend held me while he drove his fist into my stomach."

"That fucking coward," Annalisa proclaims.

"Did Ryan send Dave to hurt you?" Julian asks.

"No, it was all Dave. He was mad at Aiden—"

At the mention of his name Aiden turns his gaze back to me, but it doesn't look like he's actually seeing me. His mind is somewhere miles away.

"Mad at Aiden?" Noah tries to connect the dots.

Charlotte gasps, realization dawning on her. "At the Halloween party. Dave was all over Amelia and Aiden basically knocked him out."

"But what does hitting you have to do with Aiden?" Chase asks, and Charlotte and Annalisa exchange a glance like they already know the answer.

"He said something along the lines of 'Aiden almost dislocated my jaw, so let's break something he's fond of,' or something like that."

"He hurt you to get to me," Aiden whispers.

"I'm fine, really. It's no one's fault. Let's not do anything stupid and start more fights and kick the drama up all over again, please."

My words fall on deaf ears as Aiden slides out of the booth without a word and storms to the door of the ice-cream parlor, not once looking back when we call out to him. He takes off out of the parking lot into the dark night, leaving us all staring after him.

✘

After reassuring everyone I'm okay, I go home and proceed to pace around my room, thinking about Aiden. He doesn't have a phone, so no one can call him, even though he probably would've just ignored our calls anyway.

It's around twelve thirty when I hear a loud engine pull into my driveway. My mom isn't supposed to be home for another couple of hours, so I peek through my blinds and immediately recognize Aiden's black Challenger. Pressing pause on the movie I wasn't watching anyway, I scramble to fix my hair before opening the front door. I catch Aiden walking up the steps and he pauses when he sees me, his face giving nothing away.

"Hey," I say timidly, opening the door for him.

He doesn't say anything as he brushes past me, but waits until I've closed the door. "Why didn't you tell me?" he asks, cutting through all the niceties.

We head into the family room, where we sit on the couch.

"I didn't want you to know," I tell him straight out.

He looks hurt, and this time doesn't bother concealing it from me. "Why? Do you not trust me?"

"Of course I trust you! To tell you the truth, I trust you more than anyone I've ever trusted in my entire life."

And it's true. Besides my mother, I really don't have anyone, and sometimes I feel so far away from her. Aiden's the only one who, for some reason, I know will always be here for me.

My admission seems to warm him up to me, and his face softens as he looks at me. "Then why didn't you tell me?"

"Because I want it all to end. You'd get mad and do something to get back at them. I need everyone to stop getting hurt because of me. Plus, it happened before the race and you needed to focus on that and not me. Of course I trust you, Aiden. I just didn't want you to go and—"

I stop talking when I notice the knuckles on Aiden's right hand. They're busted up and look like they've recently been split open. He follows my gaze and moves his hand so that it's out of my view.

"What happened to your hand?" I ask, even though I already have a feeling I know what happened.

"Nothing."

"Aiden."

"Nothing, Amelia."

"You picked a fight with Dave, didn't you?"

"No," he replies, his expression and tone neutral, as if we're discussing the weather. "I picked a fight with Dave, Rob, Ian, and whoever else could've been that other guy who held you back while Dave . . ." He trails off, as if he can't bear the thought of Dave hitting me.

"Shit, Aiden. Are you okay?" I bring a hand to his face and turn it to better inspect him for injuries. "This is exactly why I didn't tell you! I didn't want you to get hurt over me."

He gently grabs my hand and moves it away from his face, but doesn't let go. "I'm fine, Amelia. They only got a couple of hits in."

"Aiden!"

"It was worth it. Believe me." The way he says it with such conviction and determination makes my pulse race and my heart swell.

I don't know what to say. My thoughts are just so consumed with Aiden I don't even know how to process how amazing he is and how much I like him.

I look into his piercing gray eyes, which always seem to soften when they're focused on me. I notice a small cut on his nose, and briefly wonder which guy was fast enough to get a hit on Aiden's face, before my eyes flicker to his lips.

And then he's there. His hands are on my waist and his lips are on mine, and like last time I'm transported to my own personal heaven.

My mind, body, and soul are consumed with the fire that is Aiden, and I can't think of anything except the burning need to be closer. He must be feeling the same way because his grip on my waist tightens, and he easily lifts me onto his lap, my knees placed on either side of him so that I'm straddling him, and I pull myself closer, my arms wrapping around his neck. No amount of butterflies or fireworks could compare to the feeling I'm experiencing as Aiden's lips move in sync with mine.

It's like all I've ever needed in this world is to be held and kissed this passionately by the amazingly powerful and intense man that is Aiden, and it's like there's nowhere else I've ever wanted or needed to be than right here.

22

I wish I could say that after Aiden and I kissed we became all lovey-dovey and had a perfect happily ever after, but we don't.

Why? Because I'm me.

I'm stupid, stupid Amelia Collins, who technically doesn't even exist, and won't even exist in a few weeks.

I gave in to my feelings and kissed Aiden when I knew I shouldn't have, even though it felt really—and I mean *really*—good. But guilt keeps coming back to haunt me. Whenever I think about Aiden and how he makes me feel, it creeps up my throat and squeezes until I can barely breathe, wrapping itself around my heart and slowly constricting until I'm sure it's going to stop beating.

The way Aiden makes me feel is incomparable to anything I've ever felt, but that's because I *know* him. I know who he is. I know that he's responsible and loyal and smart. I know when he's trying to hide a smile or when he's annoyed or when he's deep in thought about something important.

But most of all, I know his name. Can he even say the same for me?

He doesn't deserve someone who is lying to him all the time and pretending to be someone she isn't. Especially not someone who will skip town without a moment's notice, never to be heard from again. *Definitely* not someone who puts his life in danger just by being near him.

Because the reality is, I'm Thea Kennedy, and Thea Kennedy has been chased down and had multiple attempts made on her life by a madman. Thea Kennedy has caused multiple people to be injured and killed just by being around her, and has a little shoebox in her closet as a reminder. I don't deserve Aiden, and he definitely should be with someone better than me. It's not like I cut him off after that night at my house, but I've been distancing myself, and I've made it my mission to avoid spending any one-on-one time with him.

Sometimes I see him in the hallway and we make eye contact, and he'll start walking over to me, but I'll sprint in the opposite direction as quickly as possible, cursing myself in my head the entire time. I barely say more than a full sentence to him when I see him in class, and I busy myself with studying for exams at lunch. I've even started parking as far away from his spot as I can, just so we won't bump into each other in the parking lot. I wish I could say it was easy, but it hurts almost as much as the guilt does. Every time I see him I remember how it feels to be held by him, to kiss him—but then my head starts to swim and I know I can't keep up the charade.

He's been pretty distracted lately, since his stepfather Greg was released from prison on Monday—not that he's tried contacting Aiden and the twins since his release. Plus, we had exams this week, so it's been pretty hectic and hasn't been too obvious that I'm trying to avoid him.

But Aiden's not stupid. In fact, he's probably one of the smartest people I've ever met (he did manage to get my calculus mark up), not just in school but also street-wise. I know he knows something is up, especially every time I feel him studying me with his piercing gray eyes, but with everything else going on, he hasn't said anything.

Before I know it, two weeks have gone by and I'm clearing out my locker at the end of the day on Friday, the last day of school before the winter break.

"Am I still coming over to raid your wardrobe? I'm sure you'll have a dress I can borrow for my cousin's wedding this weekend," Charlotte asks from where she's leaning on the locker beside mine. "I can't believe my cousin Grace bought the exact same dress I was planning on wearing after I got it, but *I'm* the one who has to change."

"Of course you're still coming over," I reply to Charlotte. "Anna found out and wanted to come too."

"Party at Amelia's?" Noah asks as he, Mason, and Aiden appear beside Charlotte.

For the first couple of days after it was revealed that Dave roughed me up at the track when Mason left me to flirt with Amanda, the relationship between Aiden and Mason was a bit strained.

Aiden was pissed at Mason, since he'd blatantly told Mason to look out for me while he was occupied because we knew that the Silvers had it out specifically for me. After a couple of days, it started getting awkward and making the group as a whole feel strained as well. Then one day they came to school sporting some fresh bruises, and it stopped being strained. They went back to normal, like nothing ever happened, and no one has mentioned anything about it since.

Julian told Annalisa (who then told me and Charlotte) that Mason couldn't take the guilt anymore and went to Aiden's house while he and Julian were studying. Apparently, Mason was yelling at Aiden to "Get it out of your system and just fucking hit me already," to which Aiden replied, "You should feel guilty because Amelia didn't deserve that shit."

Then some more words were exchanged, which Julian didn't care to share, and things got heated. Apparently, Mason just lunged at Aiden and they started hitting each other. After a couple of minutes they hugged it out, and all three boys went inside and ordered pizza, acting like nothing ever happened. Boys are so *weird*.

"Absolutely not," I answer Noah while trying to ignore Aiden's unwavering gaze on me. "Last time I went to a party with you, Noah, you were sent to the hospital with a concussion."

"Can't make the same mistake twice, right?" Noah laughs, subconsciously rubbing the spot on his head where he received stitches that night.

Aiden's gaze burns a hole into my soul, so I pretend to be immensely preoccupied with some loose papers at the back of the top shelf.

I assume Charlotte rolls her eyes at Noah. "No party. It's girls' night."

"Awesome," Mason smiles. "We were planning on inviting you all out tonight, but since you're already at Amelia's, looks like we're all coming there."

"Wait, what?" I automatically turn to look at them, accidentally making eye contact with Aiden, whose expression is one of his normal stoic, impassiveness. But his eyes—the expression in his eyes make me feel like throwing up and digging a hole to crawl into and hide for the next fifty years.

"Coming where?" Annalisa arrives at my locker, ready to drive with me and Charlotte back to my house.

"Movie night at Amelia's. Pizza's on me," Mason announces, not bothering to confirm with me.

"I'm so picking the movie," Noah chimes in, a calculating smile forming on his lips.

I quickly glance at Aiden. What if everyone leaves and he wants to stay later to talk to me privately? Last time we were alone together at my house we made out, and that *cannot* happen again, no matter how much I wish it would.

"Are you purposely pretending you don't know what a girls' night is?" Charlotte laughs as she, Annalisa, Mason, and Noah start walking toward the parking lot, completely ignoring my attempt to protest.

My eyes widen slightly when I realize that it's just me and Aiden at my locker, and he's studying me with those intuitive, captivating gray eyes.

I quickly turn back to my locker and shove random books into my bag as quickly as possible.

"Amelia," Aiden's strong hand on my shoulder makes me freeze.

I quickly slam my locker door shut and turn to look at him, making his hand drop from my shoulder.

"Is everything okay?" he asks me, making my pulse simultaneously speed up and slow down.

His psychopathic, junkie stepfather is out of jail and possibly out to get him and his brothers, and he's asking about me.

"Of course it is. What about you? Is everything okay with Greg?" I ask, unable to stop myself.

I should've escaped, but I can't stop caring about him no matter how much I wish I could.

"I haven't heard anything yet. But I can't stop worrying about him hurting the twins."

"He won't hurt the twins." I hope my tone is comforting. "I know you won't let anything happen to them."

"Damn straight," he responds without a second of denial or hesitation.

When we get to the parking lot, Noah and Mason have left Annalisa and Charlotte by my car, and are heading toward theirs. Aiden and I stop at the top of the stairs and turn to look at each other.

"I'll see you tonight?" I ask Aiden, a small part of me hoping he'll say no, while the bigger, stupider part of me is screaming *Please come!*

"Of course. For you, anything," he responds, the intense look in his eyes making it clear that he's not just talking about tonight, but about life in general.

Feeling the onset of tears, I suddenly can't help but throw my arms around his waist and draw myself into him, burying my head in his strong chest. I can feel that he's taken off guard, but he recovers quickly and puts his muscular arms around me, pulling me in closer. Realizing my mistake, I quickly draw away from him and take a few steps away.

"Well . . . see you tonight." I don't even wait to see his confused expression or hear his reply before I turn around and jet down the stairs toward the two girls waggling their eyebrows at me from beside my car.

I hate myself.

✗

All of my drawers are open and practically empty, and my closet's in the same condition. Almost every single piece of clothing I've ever owned is littered somewhere on my bed or floor. Charlotte has tried on every nice outfit I have at least twice, unable to decide on the one she likes best.

"Julian says they're all almost here,"—Annalisa looks up from her phone—"with the pizza."

"I'll go start setting up the kitchen," I reply as I throw some clothes into a drawer and close it.

"Wait, do you have silver heels that match this dress?" Charlotte turns and gives me a view of the navy dress she's wearing.

"I think I have a couple of options. Help yourself."

I head out of my room and Annalisa follows me to help set up, leaving Charlotte to pick whatever shoes her heart desires. We're just grabbing all of the plates and drinks when we hear the door-bell ring. I let Chase, Noah, and Julian in, followed by Mason and Aiden a few minutes later.

"Thank God!" shouts Noah when Mason and Aiden carry in some pizza boxes. "I'm starving!"

Approximately four seconds later, a couple of the boxes are almost empty courtesy of the five ravenous teenage boys.

"*Char!*" Annalisa yells up to Charlotte, who's still in my room. "Come get some pizza before these pigs destroy the boxes."

"But I'm not done yet!" she yells back.

Annalisa slaps away Noah's hand, which is going in for a fifth slice while his fourth is still hanging from his mouth.

"Save some for us," she scolds.

"Finish later!" I yell back at Charlotte. "Come eat!"

She comes down the stairs in her own clothes and we grab a couple of slices before the boys finish them all, moving into the living room to watch whatever movie they all agreed on.

I notice Aiden glancing at me more than a few times, but I make it a point to avoid making eye contact, sitting on the opposite side of the room between Charlotte and Noah. Everyone gives me perplexed looks, and Aiden definitely looks at me longer than necessary, but I pointedly look straight at the TV and eat my pizza.

About halfway into the action-comedy movie the Boys settled on, Charlotte asks if I have any extra blankets. I jump up to go get some, grateful to be away from the room and Aiden's eyes.

I run upstairs to my room, not even bothering to close the door behind me. My room still has some clothes strewn about, and Charlotte threw a bunch of shoeboxes from my closet onto my bed, half of them not even opened. But I can't focus on the mess. All I can think about is the way Aiden keeps looking at me, and how I much I want him to see the real me. I want to be with him, but I have to put him first.

"Amelia."

I jump and turn around when I hear Aiden's deep, honey-laced voice from my doorway.

"Hey," I reply, trying to calm my raised heartbeat, which of course won't work because Aiden is standing in my room looking all Armani modelesque.

"We need to talk about whatever the fuck is going on with us," he says, cutting straight through the bullshit.

We do. As much as it sucks, I owe it to him to give him some closure. I can't be with him, and I need to stop giving him mixed signals. If I tell him we can never be together, at least it will hold some accountability for me to stay away from him.

"Yeah, I guess we do," I answer solemnly, my heart breaking with what has to be done.

"I just—I don't know what I did to cause you to be so distant lately," he starts.

"No, Aiden, it's not—"

A loud crash from downstairs saves me from finishing the lame "it's not you, it's me" speech. Everyone's talking over each other, and Aiden and I move out of my room and into the hallway.

"Is everything okay?" Aiden yells down.

"Chase dropped his glass and it shattered!" Julian yells back up at us. "Where are your paper towels, Amelia?"

"I'll be right there!" I yell back down.

"Wait," Aiden says. "We're not done here."

"Okay—wait here, I'll be right back," I say before running down the stairs.

I'm going to tell him I don't like him in a romantic way tonight if it kills me. Just do it quick—like ripping off a bandage. Except this pain will probably last much longer and be more intense than some pulled skin and hair, but it has to be done. My life requires sacrifice; this just happens to be one of the biggest ones yet.

We get all the glass and juice cleaned up in under five minutes, all while I'm mentally preparing the speech I have to give to Aiden and reminding myself that under no circumstances am I allowed to cry.

When I get back up to my room, I start talking before I even look at Aiden. "Sorry, Aiden, I just don't know how I can say this but—"

I immediately stop talking when I look up and see Aiden's face. It's a mixture of anger, confusion, disbelief, and betrayal. It's then that I realize what's wrong.

My heart stops and my stomach drops. My lungs stop drawing air. The shoebox. *My shoebox.* It was disguised among the others in my closet, and was one of the ones Charlotte pulled out but didn't have the time to go through. It's open on my bed. And Aiden is holding my three previous IDs in his hand: Thea, Isabella, Hailey. All variations of me with slight changes; all with the same age, so it's not like I can claim they're fake ones to get me into a club.

He holds up various newspaper articles from the shoebox in one hand, my IDs in the other. "What the fuck, Amelia? Or Hailey or Thea or whatever the fuck your actual name is."

It's then that I break my vow not to cry tonight. Tears stream down my face, prompted by the look of betrayal on Aiden's face. He opened up to me. He told me all of the most personal, deepest secrets that he never tells anyone—never *has* told anyone. But me.

He trusted me.

And this is him discovering that he placed all of his trust in a person who's been lying to him the entire time, right to his face, and is the biggest fucking hypocrite to walk the earth.

I can't think of anything to say to him, not one way of explaining myself—except the only thing that's running through my head, the one thing I've always wanted to hear him say. "Thea," I say quietly, and he looks at me in disbelief. "My name is Thea."

He looks back at one of the IDs, presumably my real one, then back at me. He drops everything he's holding in his hands back into the box and looks at me, with what I can only describe as the visual representation of heartbreak. My entire body hurts, physically and mentally. I hate that this is how Aiden has to find out how fucked up I am—through a fucking shoebox.

"Explain," he breathes, his eyes narrowed and distrusting, his low voice turning the blood in my veins to ice.

"I—Aiden, I'm so sorry." I wipe the tears staining my cheek with my hand. "I didn't mean to—"

I don't know what to say to make this better, to make this go away, to erase the look of betrayal written all over Aiden's face. He's the one person who ever really mattered to me, and now he hates me. I can't have that. I need him to understand, to be okay with it, to forgive me. I need him to understand more than I need to breathe.

"It's a long story."

Our friends yell from downstairs for us to come back and finish the movie, and we glance into the hallway.

"Shorten it."

Here it is. The thing I've never said out loud before. I take a steadying breath and refuse to meet his eyes. "I'm in witness protection. My name is Thea Kennedy. In order to keep myself and the people around me alive and safe from the man hunting me, I have to keep this secret. I couldn't tell anyone—I *can't* tell anyone—because then I'd have to relocate or risk him coming here to hurt me, to hurt the people around me."

Aiden sinks down on my bed in defeat. He looks at the articles with a newfound understanding.

"I swear, Aiden, everything was still *me*. I haven't lied to you about anything except my name." I move closer to him, unable to stop myself. I *need* him to believe me, not to hate my guts. "I never meant to hurt you. I never meant to hurt anyone. It was just safer this way."

He looks at me, his eyes unreadable, then back at the newspaper articles.

I feel the compulsory need to fill the silence. "I know it's a lot to take in. I know I'm a terrible person, and I know you don't deserve to be lied to. It's why I've been pulling back the past couple of weeks. You're amazing, Aiden. More than amazing, and you deserve better than me. You deserve more than someone who can't even tell you their real name."

Aiden holds up a newspaper article, the one of me holding my ribs after being attacked in the mall, where three other people died that day. There's an intensity and a sadness in his gray eyes.

"You went through all of this? For a year? Alone?"

I bite my lip, unsure where this is going, but I nod at him. There's a loud pounding at the front door, and we both glance into the hallway. We ignore it as he drops the newspaper article and suddenly I'm wrapped in his arms. I feel like laughing and crying all at once. I expected him to hate me, to yell at me, to call me names, anything other than this.

I wrap my arms around him, holding him to me like he'll disappear, vaguely aware of the incessant heavy pounding at the front door.

"It's okay. I'm here," he soothes in my ear, his voice thick with emotion. "You are the strongest person I know."

My heart skips. "No, I'm not."

He pulls back to look at me. "Yes, you are. You've been through so much—things that would've and should've broken you. But you're here, and you're still so full of life and energy and a fiery attitude."

"You don't hate me?" I ask, needing to know the answer.

A small smile tugs on Aiden's lips. "I think I need the full story one day, but I don't hate you. I could never."

"Are you sure you don't want to run while you can?" I breathe. My heart picks up and he leans his head closer to mine. Aiden's lips are mere inches away from mine.

"I'm all in, Thea Kennedy," he whispers, finally bringing his lips to mine and my heart erupts from pure happiness.

He's here. He doesn't hate me. I'm not alone. And he used my real name.

"Um, Amelia?" Someone calls me from downstairs as the heavy knocking continues.

I reluctantly pull away from him even though everything inside of me is screaming to close my bedroom door and ignore the world.

"Let's just—let's see what they want," I tell him, wiping the tears from my face.

Aiden's intense gaze never leaves my face as he gently wipes the tears still running down my cheeks. "Let's go, then we'll talk."

He grabs my hand and follows me out of the room, my heart ten times lighter. He wants to talk. He's holding my hand. He doesn't hate me. Everyone has left the living room and is looking at the front door, then all look at me once I'm in sight.

"We didn't know if we should answer it . . ." Mason trails off when he notices my tearstained face, and my hand, which is held tightly in Aiden's.

I ignore them and head straight to the door, not even bothering to check who it is first. Swinging the door open, I pause when I see four police officers.

"Is that Aiden Parker's Challenger in the driveway?" the biggest one asks.

"Um." I don't know if I should answer. What if it's related to the street racing and gets Aiden in trouble?

"Yes, it is," Aiden answers, moving in front of me.

"Aiden Parker?" a second officer asks.

"Yes?" Aiden replies.

Before I can even draw a breath, the four police officers storm into the house, pushing me back, and grab Aiden, roughly pushing him up against the wall. An officer violently yanks Aiden's arms behind him and handcuffs him, even though Aiden is in no way protesting. They kick his feet apart and roughly pat him down for weapons, and all I can do is stand there, completely stunned.

"What's this about?" Julian angrily goes right up to one of the officers.

"He didn't do anything! Stop being so rough!" Mason comes up beside him, Noah and Chase right behind them while Annalisa stands back with a panicky Charlotte.

One of the officers turns to face the four concerned boys and he puffs up his chest, making a show of placing his hand on the gun that's in the holster on his hip. "Stay back. Let's not make this more difficult than it has to be."

The biggest officer pulls Aiden off the wall with more force than necessary. Aiden does not resist in any way, his face giving nothing away.

"Aiden Parker, you are under arrest for the suspected murder of Greg Simms. You have the right—"

My ears tune out after that, white static replacing what should have been Aiden being read his Miranda warning. We all move onto the porch and watch helplessly as Aiden is dragged down the driveway.

"Pick up the twins from Tyler's house, Julian! Keep them with you," Aiden yells before he's shoved into the back of a police cruiser.

The Boys spring into action, barking orders and making calls, but I can barely hear what they're saying. The room's spinning like it was when Noah's head was cut open, but this time Aiden's in serious trouble. There's no way he could've done this—he wouldn't risk losing the twins, especially so close to his birthday.

The police cars drift off into the distance, lights fading the farther away from my street they go, leaving us all stunned.

Aiden's stepfather, Greg, is dead. And the police think that Aiden killed him?

✗

To be continued . . .

Acknowledgments

This story would not exist if not for my readers, fans, friends, and Violets. You have and will always be my biggest motivator to get me to unlock my potential. So thank you. Truly, from the bottom of my heart, I appreciate all the kind words, support, and encouragement that you've given me throughout the years. Thank you for following me on this journey and allowing me to follow my dreams.

Thank you to my mom, Carmela, who read to me every night before bed, for teaching me the beauty of words, and for showing me the power behind reading a good book. Thank you for being my biggest fan.

Of course, I'd like to thank my dad, Bruno, for supporting me unconditionally, and for always believing in me without even needing to hear details about the project I'm working on. You're the greatest.

Thank you to my brother, Michael. He didn't really do much, but he's my brother and supports me, so into the acknowledgments he goes.

To the Wattpad community, Wattpad Stars, and Wattpad HQ, thank you for always being such a great support network, and always being so quick and willing to help a Wattpad Star in need. It's an honor to be part of this community.

Thank you to Ashleigh Gardner and everyone at Wattpad Books—editors, publicists, marketing—involved in working so hard to make my book ready for publishing.

Also a huge thanks to Crissy Calhoun, Adam Wilson, Rebecca Mills, and Deanna McFadden for being extraordinary editors, helping me transform this story from a draft to an amazing book that I'm so incredibly proud of.

Thank you to my talent manager, I-Yana Tucker, for believing in me in the first place, for answering all my dumb questions immediately, for being my work mom and biggest cheerleader, for fighting for my stories, and for always having my back.

To all the aforementioned people, and especially the ones I probably forgot, I will always be immensely grateful for having been put in your paths.

Stay With Me

Exclusive Excerpt

1

Sometimes life likes to laugh at you.

I guess things get boring to watch every once in a while, so life goes, "Hey, why don't we fuck around with her a bit? Don't you think that'll be funny?"

And then life's friends, drama, pain, uncertainty, and unfortunate events, go: "Hell yeah, dude! We got your back. Watch the shitstorm we can cause."

And then they all get to work, inserting themselves into your life, stirring up the pot, and then they sit around with a cold beer clutched in their hands and some boxes of pizza shared between them and they laugh and laugh and laugh at you.

At least, that's how I think it happens, because sometimes it seems like my life is just one long fucking episode of let's see how we can fuck with Amelia today.

There's a man out there intent on murdering me. This man has hurt and killed other people in the name of getting revenge on me. And I have the world's biggest crush on someone I know

I can never be with, who just discovered that he was being lied to and deceived from the start, and who was just arrested.

Aiden was just arrested.

The police said he murdered his stepfather, Greg.

But Aiden is not a murderer; he's not capable of doing something like that.

Or is he?

He's a fierce protector of those he loves, and he's been worried about Greg harming his brothers ever since he learned Greg was being released from prison. I know he would do anything to protect his brothers . . . but murder?

Aiden hates Greg with a burning passion—I'm pretty sure he did abuse Aiden as a child, after all—but I can't see Aiden taking his life then coming over to my house to watch movies like it was just any other day.

Why would the police think Aiden did it? He was at my house all night, and he was with Mason before that . . . wasn't he? When did Greg die anyway? He's been out of prison for a couple of weeks; wouldn't he want to spend some time with his son, Ryan, and not bother with Aiden?

Ryan.

I wonder if Aiden's stepbrother has heard about the death of his father. I wonder if he's heard Aiden was just arrested for Greg's murder.

Ryan already hates Aiden just for being Aiden; I don't even want to know what he'll do if he thinks Aiden is responsible for the death of his father.

We haven't been told anything, as the only interaction between us and the officers has been them occasionally glaring at us for taking up practically the entire waiting area at the police station.

After Aiden was arrested, Julian, Mason, and Annalisa picked up the twins from their friend's house like Aiden asked, and took them to Julian's house for his mom to watch. Everyone else went to the police station, and Julian showed up a bit later with Annalisa and his father, Vince.

Julian practically grew up with Aiden, so it makes sense that Julian would go to his dad—who's probably known Aiden since he was a kid—for help. Plus, it's not like Aiden really has any other adult to turn to.

Vince is tall like Julian, with broad shoulders and a stern face, and there's a commanding presence about him that gives him an air of authority.

A bit after Vince showed up, Mason arrived with his dad, Brian. The adults went to talk to the police about Aiden while the rest of us sat worriedly in the tiny reception area.

Brian has dark hair and tanned olive skin like his son, but is a bit shorter than Mason. I can tell where Mason gets his looks from, but Brian's dark eyes lack that certain spark of mischief that Mason's often hold—but then again, perhaps this isn't quite the right situation for him to be happy about.

As Brian and Vince talk to the officers, I can tell Brian is getting frustrated by the way he runs his hand through his hair like I've noticed Mason does, the gold wedding band sparkling brightly in comparison to his dark hair. I just hope they can work out whatever's going on and get Aiden out of here as soon as possible.

After a while, Vince is led by some officers to the back, and Brian comes to sit with us.

"Dad, what's going on?" Mason asks impatiently.

"They have Aiden in holding right now. He's still a few weeks shy of eighteen so they can't question him without the presence of an appropriate adult, which I guess would be either Vince or me," Brian explains, pulling out his phone and going through some contacts.

"But they can't question him without a lawyer! Shouldn't we be getting him a lawyer?!" Annalisa exclaims, more agitated than she usually is.

"He doesn't need a lawyer because he didn't do anything!" Noah defends Aiden. "He has, like, seven witnesses! Eight if you count the guy working the counter at the pizza place!"

Brian ignores Noah and stands up. "I'm calling a lawyer now. Hopefully he'll be here soon."

And with that, Brian walks away to find a quiet place to make his phone call, leaving the rest of us to our unproductive worrying.

A half hour later, a professional-looking man in a pressed suit enters the police station, and Brian gets up to shake his hand. They talk to some officers, who hustle the man I'm assuming is Aiden's lawyer into the back room.

Charlotte is sitting beside Chase, and they're talking in hushed tones between themselves. Annalisa is looking around the police station, glaring everyone down and looking like she's trying very hard not to punch anyone who looks at her the wrong way.

Julian's sitting beside her, talking to Mason and Brian about what could possibly happen to Aiden and what's going on back there.

Noah's beside me, his foot rapidly and incessantly tapping the floor in an anxious manner, the sound slowly driving me crazy.

I'm just sitting in the uncomfortable chair, incapable of doing anything except try really hard to ignore the pit of anxiety and worry building up in my stomach.

After a while, my irritability and stress come to a breaking point and I instinctively slap my hand on Noah's thigh, effectively stopping the incessant tapping.

"NOAH," I snap.

Noah glances at my hand still on his thigh, preventing him from continuing the repetitive anxious tapping. "I know I'm irresistible, Amelia, but now is not the time or place to get frisky."

I remove my hand and roll my eyes at him, in no mood for his Noah-ness at this highly stressful moment.

I just don't know what's taking so long. Aiden didn't do anything, so this all should've been sorted out already. Right?

After a while, Charlotte's strict parents start calling, so her older brother comes to pick her and Chase up, who has his own worried parents to get home to. We promise we'll keep them both updated.

It must have been an hour or two later when the lawyer and Vince come back out, unfortunately without Aiden.

Brian goes over to talk to the other men, and we all sit up more attentively, straining to hear what they're saying. They talk for a while with some other officers, and then the lawyer and Brian leave with two other police officers, leaving us all staring after them, confused.

Vince heads over to us, looking tired but less frustrated, which I hope is a good thing. We all stand up as he approaches, ready to question him about what's going on.

2

"They're going to hold Aiden overnight until his alibi clears," Vince informs us before any of us can interrogate him.

"Aren't we his alibi?" Julian replies.

Julian's father motions us over to the side of the tiny room for some privacy from the other random people in the waiting area.

"Greg's body was found beaten up and very much dead in front of Aiden's house. Aiden's cell phone was also found at the crime scene. They put the time of death around 6 p.m., but Aiden had been at Mason's house since four thirty. Aiden and Mason left to pick up the pizza in Aiden's car around ten to seven, and then they went straight to Amelia's house. The cameras in front of Mason's house can prove all the times, and Brian just left to get the police the tapes to clear Aiden."

We all look at each other, stunned.

Greg's body was found in front of Aiden's house? With Aiden's cell phone?

"His cell phone? I know for a fact that his cell phone was with him at Amelia's house," Mason chimes in.

"His old phone. Remember, he lost it a few weeks ago, at the Tr—school." I very awkwardly cut myself off from saying "Tracks," because Julian's dad is there, and I'm not trying to nark on anyone.

"But how did Aiden's phone end up at the crime scene?" Annalisa asks uselessly, since none of us know the answer.

"Never mind that, how did the dead body of Aiden's despised stepfather end up in front of his house? Was it moved there?" Julian ponders.

Vince rubs his eyes, clearly never having thought that he'd ever have to deal with a murder charge. "Forensics determined that it was the primary location, meaning that Greg died in front of Aiden's house."

"That does not look good for our boy." Noah grimaces.

"He didn't do it, Noah!" Annalisa snaps.

"Geez, I know. I'm just saying . . ." he replies, mumbling about how Annalisa gets crankier than usual when she doesn't get any sleep.

"Noah's right though," Vince says. "With the location of the death, Aiden's phone, and the bruising on Greg indicating a recent fight, it doesn't look too good. Plus, Aiden and Greg's past doesn't help—it's on record that Aiden petitioned against Greg's parole. It could be reasoned that he had motive."

I scoff at how ludicrous this whole situation is. "Aiden is one of the smartest people I know, book and street-wise. He has one of the top GPAs not just in the school, but in the entire school district. I think if he were going to kill a guy, he wouldn't leave the dead body in front of his house."

Everyone smiles tiredly and nods at the truth behind my statement. I mean, really. No one can actually be so dumb as to kill someone and just leave their dead body chillin' in front of their house like no big deal while they go eat pizza and watch movies at their friend's house.

But if Aiden didn't kill Greg, who did? Why was the primary crime scene in front of Aiden's house? Is someone trying to frame him? But why?

"Listen, everyone," Vince commands, authority in his voice. "They're going to clear this all up and Aiden should be out of here before you know it. He asked that you all go home instead of sitting here worrying about him. He wanted me to assure you all that he's fine and that it'll all be okay."

Aiden's literally in jail (or in police holding, whatever, there's still bars) and still, his first priority is his friends? That man literally cannot make me like him any more than I already do.

Vince lightly slaps Julian's back. "Come on, Son, let's go home and get some rest. Everything will be sorted out soon. Annalisa, I'm guessing you're staying at our house tonight?"

Annalisa nods and starts putting on her jacket, and Vince looks at the rest of us. "Do you guys need a ride home?"

"Yeah, I do," Noah says, looking up from his phone. "But maybe I should stay at your house too. I have nineteen missed calls from my mother and don't feel like dying tonight."

We smile at Noah despite the tense circumstances and the exhaustion that's beginning to set in.

"Tough break, kid. Judy's one tough woman when she's angry." Vince chuckles before looking at Mason and me. "Do you kids need a ride home?"

I shake my head no. "I drove here," I inform him, leaving out the part that I have absolutely zero intention of leaving.

Mason looks at me suspiciously, as if he can read my mind. "I'll catch a ride with Amelia."

"Okay, then, you guys get home safe. Try not to worry, everything will be taken care of."

We say good-bye to everyone and when they're out of earshot, I turn to Mason.

"You know I'm not leaving any time soon right?"

He rolls his eyes at me and plants his butt firmly in the uncomfortable chair in the waiting area. "Of course I know that. I just messaged my dad and told him that I'm hitching a ride with you once this is all sorted out."

I take a seat beside him and slouch back, tired.

Aiden has always been there for me; he's always helped me out whenever I needed it, even if I didn't ask him; even when I pissed him off or antagonized him.

Like when he got Ethan Moore to take down the video of me that Ethan had posted on the internet. Or when he put up with all my attitude and tutored me in calculus, helping me pull up my failing grade. Or when Kaitlyn and Ryan trashed my car and he brought me to Charlotte's to sleep while he dealt with the tow truck, the mechanic, and all the repairs, refusing to accept any money. Or like how he won four thousand dollars racing Ryan at the Tracks and gave it to me to spend however I wanted. That's only naming a few; he's done so much and cares so deeply for his family and friends.

Aiden's such a good person with such a genuinely kind soul; I can't bear the thought of just leaving him in jail. I know he told us all to go home and stop worrying, but I can't leave comfortably knowing that he's here. I feel like I'd be abandoning him in a way, especially after he just found out the real truth about me, and wasn't scared away.

He opened up to me, something that I know is extremely hard for him to do, and I betrayed him. I was lying to him the entire time while he was always completely honest and transparent with me. He was so incredibly hurt in the moment when he found out that my entire identity is a lie. Just the memory of the look on his face when he found out what a huge hypocrite I am—the look of complete disbelief and betrayal—still breaks my heart.

He knows my name isn't Amelia—he found the shoebox that holds reminders of my past lives; he found out that I am a lying piece of garbage. But he understood. He's not mad at me and he kissed me. He said that he's all in—so I'm not going anywhere until he's released.

"What do you think he's thinking about?" I ask Mason, trying to distract myself.

"Probably his brothers," he answers honestly.

"You're probably right. He loves Jason and Jackson more than anything."

"Do you think Ryan found out about his dad?"

"I don't know. But I'm one hundred percent certain that this is only going to make the hatred Ryan holds for Aiden so much stronger."

"You don't think—" Mason pauses, thinking through his words. "You don't think Ryan had something to do with this?"

Mason and I look at each other intently for a second, letting the suggestion sink in, before shaking our heads to dismiss that notion.

"No way," I tell him. "Why would Ryan kill his own father then bring the body to Aiden's house just to frame him? Even he's not that psychotic."

"You're right. Ryan is crazy, but not murder-my-own-dad-just-to-frame-my-archnemesis crazy."

I laugh half-heartedly with him, glad that Mason decided to wait here with me. There's got to be an explanation for what happened. And none of us will stop until we know who really killed Greg.

Stay With Me coming September 2020 from Wattpad Books.

About the Author

Jessica Cunsolo's young adult series, With Me, has amassed over one hundred million reads on Wattpad since she posted her first story, *She's With Me*, on the platform in 2015. The novel has since won a 2016 Watty Award for Best Teen Fiction, and has been published in French by Hachette Romans and in Spanish by Grupo Planeta. Jessica lives with her dog, Leo, just outside Toronto, where she enjoys the outdoors and transforming her real-life awkward situations into plotlines for her viral stories. You can find her on Twitter @AvaViolet17, on Instagram @jesscunsolo, or on Wattpad @AvaViolet.

Fresh off the heels of an awkward breakup, Samar has to come to terms with unexpected feelings for her sworn enemy, Benjamin.

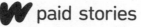

wattpad
Where stories live.

Discover millions of stories created by diverse writers from around the globe.

Download the app or visit www.wattpad.com today.

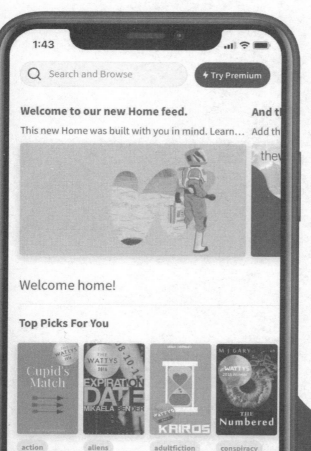